BEST PLACE TO DIE

Charles Atkins

This first world edition published 2012
in Great Britain and the USA by
SEVERN HOUSE PUBLISHERS LTD of
19 Cedar Road, Sutton, Surrey, England, SM2 5DA.

Trade paperback edition first published 2017
In Great Britain and the USA by
SEVERN HOUSE PUBLISHERS LTD

British Library Cataloguing in Publication Data
A CIP catalogue record for this title is available from the British Library.

ISBN-13: 978-0-7278-8208-0 (cased)
ISBN-13: 978-1-84751-799-9 (trade paper)
ISBN-13: 978-1-78010-318-1 (e-book)

Printed digitally.

To Peggy Munro

PROLOG

On Saturday, April 2nd 2011, the last day of his life, Dr Norman Trask, a mostly retired Connecticut surgeon, felt true contentment. The reed-thin and straight-backed octogenarian, with freshly barbered silver hair and clear blue eyes after a double cataract procedure stared at the flat screen monitor and thought, *Norm, life is good.* He smiled at the small webcam eye at the top of the screen and then at his son, Dennis, on the screen. How he loved that kid – *not a kid at all now.* As they did their Saturday Skype check-in Norm took stock of his youngest, his red hair mostly gray, a shiny spot on top, hell of a gut from booze he'd supposedly sworn off thirty years ago – *but settled, thank God. And how did he get so old? But thank God. The kid had been a nightmare . . . and thank God.*

'You sure you don't want us to come over, and cart away some of that stuff? I mean, Dad . . .'

'Don't spoil it. The place is a little messy; it's not a problem,' Norm said, loving Dennis, but not wanting to put either of them, or Dennis's second wife, Britney, through the tired routine of them seeing his collections, insinuating he was a hoarder, and everyone getting upset. The problem was not that he was a hoarder, but that this two-bedroom top-of-the-line 1200 square foot unit in the Nillewaug Village Assisted Living Community was too damn small, even with his double-sized cage in the basement. He'd considered renting a storage unit, maybe two – something he would never tell Dennis.

'Messy?' Dennis shook his head. 'Dad, you can't see the floor for all of your clock magazines. Messy is not the word, and yes I realize your clocks are valuable and you've got a great collection, but how many do you really need? I worry that one of those stacks or those bookcases are going to fall over and you're going to get hurt or . . .'

'Dennis.' Norm felt a twinge of anger. 'Stop it! I've cleaned

out a lot of stuff. I will not have other people going through
my things and throwing out important articles, or moving
things around like Britney did the last time so I can't find
what I need. She's a pretty girl, but she is not to do that again.
As you can see –' indicating the area he'd carefully staged so
that what Dennis saw through the screen was his father dressed
in pressed jeans and a red-plaid shirt backed by a tidy wall
of bookshelves in his favorite leather swivel chair, with the
arms worn bare and the axel squeaking comfortably – 'things
are just fine here.' However, if the camera had a wider focus
the scene would have been quite different. In order to carve
out this area Norm had to shift boxes of clock parts, and
several cubic meters of magazines and journals with titles like
*Clocks, Clock Enthusiast, Clock Connoisseur, The Connecticut
Horological Society Newsletter, Clock Repair Quarterly, The
American Journal of Orthopedics, Journal of the American
Academy of Orthopedic Surgeons.* All his life people had been
on Norm about his stuff, and it was none of anyone's damn
business. It drove him crazy. *All anyone seems to want to do
is throw away my stuff, perfectly good stuff.* Dennis, in particular, after all he'd done for that kid. *Just lay off!*

'Dad . . .' Dennis wasn't letting up. 'I don't mean to get
on your case, but you were at the flea market this morning,
weren't you?'

'So what? I go every week.' And if Dennis had been in a
more understanding frame of mind, Norman would have shared
how this morning had been a corker. He'd scored a huge find
at the Brantsville flea market, which now sat just out of range
of the webcam – an early nineteenth-century wood-movement
pillar-and-scroll mantle clock that he was sure was either Eli
or Samuel Terry. His heart raced at the memory of spotting it
in the early dawn light, the reverse painted glass panel with
its gold eagle clutching a quiver of arrows in perfect condition,
not a scratch, not a chip, just covered in a thick layer of grime.
His hands, still surgeon steady, had shaken as he'd peeled off
crisp hundred-dollar bills. He glanced lovingly at this gem,
now fully dismantled on his much-stained work table. The
clock's finish crackled like alligator skin and was, to an
untrained eye, burnt in appearance, each of the wood gears

cut by hand and worn – literally – by years of ticking time. And the same dealer, a regular who cleaned out basements, attics and barns also had three boxes of clock parts at the can't-resist price of twenty bucks a pop. Just one of those sets of Welch Allyn hands or nineteenth-century German tall-clock weights alone was worth what he'd paid for the three boxes; it would have been foolish to pass them up. 'So what's new with you?' Norman asked, shifting the topic and breathing the heady aroma of his special mix of turpentine and high-grade machinist's oil that would bring this morning's beauty back to life. Not for the first time, he mused how his passion for finding and repairing rare clocks wasn't too different from his decades of replacing and fixing hips, shoulders and knees. Many of his precision German drills, chisels and bits, now flecked with wood shavings and oil, had started in the operating suites of Hartford General, where Norm had been attending and then Chair of the Department of Orthopedics for forty years.

Dennis shook his head and then dutifully gave his dad an overview of the last week of life on Westwood Lane. Starting with his triumphs at his sprawling and hugely successful car dealership on Bedford Turnpike.

As Dennis reported the details of his week and the comings and goings of his two adult sons, Norm thought back to the day he'd purchased the small used-car lot for Dennis after he'd finished his year at Osborn Correctional. Sure, it had just been a Driving Under the Influence (DUI), but it had been Dennis's third, a mandatory sentence, and a felony in the state of Connecticut. Norm hated to dwell on that year of hell, and the realization that as a felon his brilliant and athletically gifted son's options for a future had been radically reduced. Dennis's tears in the holding cell, the fear that in his panic the nineteen year old might harm himself. And the gut-wrenching reality that nothing Norm could do, despite his influence and the best legal defense money could buy, could bail his youngest out. But now, looking through this cyber window of Dennis's stable life in a million-dollar home on three manicured acres . . . *What a handful he'd been and thank God.* So sad that his beloved Kate never got to see the full turn around; she'd died

of a massive coronary a month before Dennis's release. He'd
been their baby, a later-life and totally unexpected pregnancy.
And Kate, always fragile with her porcelain skin and bouts of
depression and paralysing anxiety that would leave her bed
wrecked and too frightened to leave the house, was no match
for their red-headed hellion. His year at Osborn just a stopping
point for a teen who'd put them through hell. *Thank God*, their
tag phrase for all his near misses. The awful middle-of-the-night
calls from the local cops. Parents demanding Norm do something
about his son after he and his two hooligan friends had bullied
some kid on the playground. Parent-teacher conferences, threats
of expulsion after he'd brought the air rifle to school, getting
suspended from the varsity football team after an ounce of pot
was found in his locker, accusations of drug dealing, the slutty
girl who'd accused him of rape; it had been relentless. They
even had to see a shrink. Dr Greene – *what a quack* – Norm
had hated those sessions. '*He's begging for your attention,*' the
shrink once said. '*He desperately wants you to notice him, and
if he can't get it through all the positive things he does at
school and on the field, he'll do whatever it takes.*' It was a
lot of mush-mouthed bullshit. The kid was too smart, too good
looking, star athlete, no sense of consequence and an ability
to talk his way out of just about anything. *But look at him now,
thank God.* And horrible as it was, maybe Osborn was necessary. When Dennis had gotten out, he swore to never drink
again and to pull his life together. *At least he got one out of
two.*

'So, we'll see you Tuesday,' Dennis said, the tone of his
voice indicating their weekly Skype was near its end.

Norm nodded. 'Yup, old man dinner night,' he said, referring
to the Tuesday night special at San Rosa's Restaurant, a town
favorite with your choice of entrée, soup or salad, roll, pasta
and beverage, all for $11.95. They rarely missed a week, not
that they couldn't afford better, but Norm could never pass up
a bargain. Even the cocktails were discounted, though he was
careful to always stop after two Manhattans lest the proximity
of booze have a negative effect on Dennis, who he was pleased
to see only ordered cola. 'Love you, son,' Norm said, knowing
it was true and wondering if he'd said it more often when

Dennis had been young it might have made a difference. As the screen went blank, Norm felt the dull edges of familiar guilt. Truth was, he'd been the big surgeon with a hugely successful practice, on-call for the hospital every fourth or fifth night, twelve-hour stretches in the surgical suites, and dog-dead tired when he'd finally make it home. Then wolf down dinner while throwing back a stiff Manhattan or just straight bourbon, maybe a few – never more – and then grab a journal and read it in bed until he'd passed out. He'd had little time for his youngest, not like his older sons. With them he'd been the father at Little League, had helped them carve their pinewood derby racers as Cub Scouts, and cheered them on when they'd placed their red and blue racers on the rickety track. But in the twelve years that separated Bob, his oldest – now a surgeon like dad – from Dennis, Norm's career had kicked into high gear. Kate had never complained. He glanced at a framed studio still, high on the wall, taken at their wedding and now thick with dust, and one corner seemingly affixed to the ceiling by layers of a spider's web. As his eyes connected with hers guilt stirred, like poking embers. The truth was not kind. Yes, he'd loved Kate and yes his career had consumed his days and many of his nights, but that wasn't the whole truth and nothing but the truth so help him God. Pushing up from his chair, he eased his conscience. 'Done is done, old man.' And another truism picked up from one of the few Al-Anon meetings he and Kate had reluctantly attended at the recommendation of one of Dennis's many drug and alcohol counselors: 'It is what it is.'

Always conscious of potential hazards related to clock repair – the solvents, turps and various oil-based finishes had to be handled and disposed of respectfully – he grabbed his daily rags. It reminded him of counting sharps and sponges before closing a patient. And he was careful not to upset any of the piles of journals, boxes and bags that formed a channel from the tidily staged Skype area to the congested galley kitchen, with counters obscured by stacks of cleaned dishes, overflowing baskets of vitamins and nutritional supplements, mugs with brushes soaking in cleaning solvent, and mounds of unopened mail that spilled from counter to floor. Along one counter was a pyramid of three-pound-size Chock Full o'Nuts coffee cans, their tops tightly sealed. He opened one that was filled with water and oily rags from a previous day and wedged today's deep into the liquid. The skim of blue-black solvent coolly tickled his fingers and left a ring around his wrist. Once a month they'd offer hazardous waste removal, admittedly he'd not taken advantage of one for the past several months . . . maybe a year – *longer than that? Possibly* – but this month for sure; he'd make a note of it.

Then, from next to the double sink – one side not used for over three years on account of needing it for overflow dishes, he selected a medicine bottle, held it up in the filtered light from his second-floor window and checked the label – Sildenafil 10mg. He popped one of the blue blunt-edged diamonds of Viagra into his mouth and swallowed dry. His gaze flicking over the prescriber's name at the bottom – Dr Norman Trask. Cautiously, he opened his fridge just wide enough to reach in, grab a carton of OJ and take a few swigs, but not so wide that the crammed contents would come tumbling out.

His ears perked as a dozen clocks came to life, soft mechanical whirrs presaging the first strike of hammer to brass, bronze and iron bells. An English bracket clock from the second bedroom provided the melody of Westminster as American brass- and wooden-movement clocks, mostly from Connecticut, provided their resonant harmonies. As the last finished striking the hour, his front door buzzed. He grinned in anticipation and felt a giddy rush of relief – with Kate gone this wasn't cheating any more. 'Life really is good,' he said and, passing back through the kitchen and into the long entryway that was lined on both sides with wall clocks that he and Dennis had hung up when he'd first moved to Nillewaug Village, he opened the door.

ONE

Rose Rimmelman's water-blue eyes shot open, her heart raced as she struggled to quell the panic triggered by her dream. *Where are you?* Having to once again remind herself this was no longer the Lower East Side of Manhattan and her familiar-as-the-back-of-her-hand 14th floor rent-stabilized apartment on Rivington. *It's the other place with its silly fake Indian name.* Her nightmare hovered in the dark, bodies falling, waves of dust burying buildings as the towers burned and one by one did the unthinkable – collapsed, and as they did a horrible rain of ash and acid fell to the ground. Her ninety-two – possibly ninety-one, could be ninety-three – year-old body felt heavy and frozen beneath cotton sheets and a down comforter stuffed with even older feathers that her mother had taken in treasured pillows and a now-gutted comforter from her shtetl in the Ukraine. The dream lingered, something too real – *it wasn't raining on 9/11.* Droplets spattered her face, like being caught in the spray of a lawn sprinkler and then her nose caught the smell; *something's burning.* Her heart fluttered, and with it came the pit-of-her-stomach lurch that meant she'd gone back into atrial fibrillation. With each breath her worst fears confirmed; *something's on fire! Just move.*

She eased her thick legs over the side of the bed and tapped the lamp with its clever touch sensor – just one of the many perks her daughter Ada had bribed her with in exchange for Rose finally agreeing to this awful move to Connecticut. Anger surged, mingling with panic as her apartment came into fuzzy view, then on with her thick glasses and the fuzz became a thin and slightly acrid mist. 'Fire.' Feeling for her slippers she gripped the edge of her bed and the adjacent nightstand. A glance at the bright orange numerals on the alarm – 4.12 a.m. *Just get out,* she thought, anger now rolling over her fear as she looked at all her possessions getting ruined by the overhead sprinklers, the family photos neatly hung by Ada, her great-grandson, Aaron, and their Waspy friend, Lil. All of their light-hearted banter, telling her how much happier she'd be here; their non-stop sales pitch about the dining hall with its world-class chef, laundry service, bus trips to Broadway and the casinos. She hurried to the door, grabbing a pink fleece robe. *Serve them right if I die in this hell hole!* And her faithful navy pocketbook with the once brass-colored clasp worn down to the base metal. *Why couldn't they just leave me where I was? Or if she really was that concerned she could have stayed with me. But no! Ada always has to have things her way.* She felt the knob, remembering fire drills past: if it's warm don't open it. Cool to the touch, she twisted. Even without her annoying and too-expensive hearing aids, and no thought of returning for them, she sensed pandemonium in the hall. 'Why isn't an alarm going?' she shouted. 'What's wrong with this place?' *All Ada's fault. Why did I ever agree to this move?*

She took shallow breaths as the smoke tickled her throat. It was impossible to see through the haze and falling water that dribbled down her glasses. Around her, other elderly and semi-infirm tenants emerged from their apartments. Scared faces in cracked doorways. 'What's happening?'

'Is there a fire?'

'I need help! Tell someone I need help!'

Navigating by the red EXIT in the distance and keeping to the side of the wide carpeted hall, Rose held tight to the rail and tried to remember how far it was to the outside. All the while, thinking of Ada – all her fault. *I didn't want to move!* Tears streamed, mingling with the sprinkler water that soaked her hair and dribbled down her back. *I just want my apartment back!* Knowing that could never happen. Not stopping, she shuffled forward on stiff knees and hips, taking careful sips of dirty air, trying not to cough and using her fury to quiet the fear.

'Ma'am,' came a young man's urgent voice, and then a firm hand on her shoulder.

'I'm fine,' she said, not wanting to lose her momentum and only able to glimpse the outline of a dark-haired man in a parka holding the hand of a shorter woman, but something about him familiar.

'Please help her. Just get her out, please; she has dementia.'

There was no arguing, as a woman's shaky fingers were joined to hers. 'Alice, stay with this woman . . . Rose, right?'

'Yes, Johnny,' said the thin woman in a drenched white flannel nightgown dotted with flowers, her dyed hair – impossible to tell what color – plastered to her face. 'I want to go home. Are we going home? I don't like the water.' She looked at Rose. 'I can't swim.'

'Please, help her,' he pleaded.

'Yes,' Rose said. She shifted her pocketbook to her wrist, tried not to think how heavy it was and gripped Alice's hand. 'You're the nurse. But your name's Kyle.'

'It is,' he said quickly. 'She thinks I'm someone else. Please, just help her out. I have to make sure everyone gets out. Just follow the red exits. It's not much further, and please don't let her out of your sight. She wanders.' And then a siren from far off. 'Thank God.'

'You can't go back there,' Rose said, feeling Alice's hand trying to pull free, a part of her wondering . . . hoping, if maybe this were all still part of the dream.

'I have to check on others,' Kyle said, and, squeezing both their hands, he was gone.

'Johnny!' Alice tried to pull free and go after him. 'Johnny! I want to go home! Johnny!'

No dream. 'Come on, Alice, we have to get out of here.'

'I want to go home!'

'Alice.' Rose felt the woman pulling away. The smoke was everywhere and if she let go . . . 'No, You're coming with me!' She clenched the woman's hand with her left, while trying to not lose her grip on the hallway railing with her right. 'I'll take you home. Just come with me, we're going home.' Strangely, just saying those words, gave her hope, even though they contained not an ounce of truth. 'Yes, we're going home.'

'Oh goodie,' Alice said, and like a switch had been thrown, she stopped resisting.

Moments later they'd found their way through the smoke and the frightened cries of the residents of Nillewaug Village

Assisted Care to a still dark and very cold early April morning. The only illumination coming from the burning building's windows, exit signs, and faux gas lanterns that lined the property's drives.

Soaked to the skin, her nostrils thick with smoke, and heart beating out of rhythm, Rose steered them to a wooden bench at the periphery of the sprawling facility. A wave of shivers shook her stocky frame as she sat, pulling Alice down beside her. *We're still too close*, she thought, not more than fifty feet from the side of the four-story structure, where dense smoke billowed through two shattered second-story windows and glimmers of orange flames peeked over the sill. A few other residents trickled through the side exit, one woman with a walker crumpled to the ground, a man with a cane stood behind Rose and Alice, using the bench for support.

'What's happening?' Alice asked, as they stared back at the central building of the assisted care facility, with its ersatz Georgian brick architecture and white shuttered windows. Sirens wailed and the first red engine with its lights flashing roared down the long drive, with its ornamental pond and beautifully tended boxwood hedges.

Clutching her pocketbook Rose had no answers, just a growing ache of loss. She thought of her home on Rivington Street, the three-bedroom apartment in which she'd raised her children and sent them out into the world. The furniture she and Isaac had bought when they'd learned they were going to be able to move out of their cramped tenement quarters on Delancey and into the brand new rent-stabilized towers. *Everything's gone,* she thought, and what little she was able to take from New York, now likely ruined. *What was so wrong?* she fumed. *Why couldn't you have let me be? I didn't want to move. I didn't want this. And now . . .*

'What's that?' Alice asked as her hand patted Rose's. 'Up there, what's that?'

Through smudged glasses Rose tried to see what had Alice so excited. Something sparkly was falling, like glitter coming down. She tried to see what Alice was pointing to, at first she thought it was the windows now spitting flames over thick waves of dark gray smoke, but no, something higher up on the top floor. A blackened window surrounded by jagged shards, bits of glass falling and then something . . . someone . . . at the edge, paused and then dropped to the ground not forty feet from them.

'What's that?' Alice repeated, now pointing at the unmoving shape.

'Oh God, no! Stay here,' Rose said with a sick feeling in her stomach, and, leaving her pocketbook, she stood. Her knees felt like they might buckle, but she had to see, maybe they were OK, just unconscious. But in her gut, she knew it was just like 9/11 – people jumping to their deaths. She edged forward, as flashing lights bounced off the brick. A shiver edged down her spine, and she had to clamp her mouth shut to keep her teeth – mostly still her own – from chattering. As she approached, the crumpled shape didn't move. Through smeared lenses she saw it was a blonde woman with one pump on and one missing. Years of being in retail identified her cherry-red suit as a good Chanel knock-off, probably from Talbot's. Closer still, she recognized her – Delia Preston, the administrative director of Nillewaug Village and the woman who had rolled over her every objection to this ill-fated move. The energetic Delia who had talked, seemingly without need of breath, about the wonders of life in the Connecticut countryside, of clean air and distant mountain views, of picturesque season changes, and activity-filled days. And her obvious pride in Nillewaug: *'Voted four years in a row the best assisted-care facility in Connecticut.'* She was certain the woman was dead, and in this growing nightmare found her voice. 'I need help! Someone help me!'

And from where she'd left her, Alice chimed in, like a parrot with a single phrase: 'Help me! Help me! Help me!'

TWO

Lil Campbell woke to the sound of sirens. She lay still, and wondered if Ada was awake, as she counted at least half a dozen – *that's not good*. Living in a retirement community the occasional ambulance in the night was to be expected, even in the dark of an early Sunday morning . . . Although all the local companies and Pilgrim's Progress's own emergency-response team rarely used sirens out of respect for the sleepy community of well-to-do retirees. What had pulled her from sleep at 4.15 a.m. and had her staring at the drape-hung sliding doors of her bedroom was frightening. She tried to count them, letting the different tones and cadences filter through the night and into her head. She'd get up to six or seven and then lose track – *what's happening?* From the volume, she could tell they were close, not more than a half mile – could be one of the town homes or connected condos in Pilgrim's Progress, the sprawling 'Active Adult' community on the outskirts of her hometown – Grenville, Connecticut. She'd moved here to Pilgrim's Progress nine years ago with her now departed husband, Dr Bradley Campbell, and where she now remained with her best friend and lover, Ada Strauss. That last bit still quite new, and wonderful . . . and strange.

'What's going on, Lil?' Ada asked, pushing back in the bed.

With her eyes adjusted to the dark, Lil turned, catching the outline of Ada's close-cropped silver hair, and glints of moonlight through high transom windows reflected in her blue eyes. Ada's hand reached under the covers and found hers. She squeezed.

'Must be a fire,' Lil said.

'Oh, God,' Ada whispered, clearly frightened.

'I know,' Lil said, the two of them having recently survived a devastating fire. 'It's close, but not that close.' She let go Ada's hand, and got out of bed. Her heart pounded as she went to the sliding glass doors, and drew back the green silk drapes that Ada had just sewn. The moon was near full and dawn – because of the recent shift forward to daylight savings – was still a good hour away. The backs of their adjoined condos in this carefully planned retirement community in the rolling hills of Litchfield County Connecticut faced east and had tremendous privacy on account of acres of protected wetlands.

'Can you see anything?' Ada asked.

'No.' Lil pulled up the latch on the sliders, and bent down to pull out the safety bar. Stepping into the cool and dewy dark morning she caught glimmers of flashing red lights over the condos and sloping hills to her right, and the sounds of sirens wailing from the north. *Something big.* She shuddered, while from behind her Ada had turned on the TV and was flipping through the channels.

A light went on in Ada's condo, her nearly seventeen-year-old grandson, Aaron, was up. He opened the bathroom window and yelled out, 'Lil, what's going on?'

'Has to be a fire; I'm trying to figure where it's coming from.' She stood still, imagining a map of Grenville and the surrounding towns. This is where she'd lived her entire life – all sixty-one years – with the exception of four at Smith College in North Hampton, Massachusetts where she'd gotten an English degree with a focus on journalism. 'It's coming from the north.' *Not Grenville proper* she thought, *but heading out on Old Farm Road.* Her mind ran scenes of the *old* Old Farm Road of her childhood. Harrington's idyllic orchards with apple picking in the fall, berries in late spring and summer and a corn-stalk maze for Halloween. Theirs had been the only pies her mother would buy, and then the Harringtons died and their fourteen hundred acres of mature orchards had been sold. As she mentally traveled down Old Farm, trying to pinpoint the sirens, she realized there wasn't a single patch of farmland left. Instead, it was strip malls, with jumbo-chain drug stores that had killed the two local pharmacies. There was an office-supply megastore, a cluster of old brick municipal buildings that housed the police and fire departments, the spanking-new library whose board she sat on, more strip

malls, the supermarket that had recently changed owners
again, and many empty stores, some quite massive, victims
of the recent recession, which was supposedly over. And
finally, with her gaze focused over a copse of white pine and
budding hickory and maple she saw what could have been a
blossoming cloud, and it wasn't coming from the sky but
from the ground. *Dear Lord,* she prayed, *let it be one of the
empty stores and not . . .*

'Lil,' Ada called from inside the condo, backlit by the flickering
screen, her voice cracked . . . 'It's on Channel Eight. What have
I done? Oh, God!'

'What? Where's it coming from?' But she already knew,
and it filled her with dread.

'It's Nillewaug. My mother. We have to go. Oh Lil, what
if?' And Ada's short, spry frame dressed in blue silk pajamas
bolted from bed and vanished into the walk-in closet.

'Don't even think it,' Lil said as she ran back in and stared
at the flat screen, where a news crew was filming a nightmarish
scene. The central building of Nillewaug Village – the one
where Ada's mother, Rose Rimmelman, had recently moved
to a first floor apartment – was on fire. Bright orange flames
shot over the roof and smoke obscured the upper floors, while
on the ground frail residents in nightclothes and underwear
were being herded by EMTs and firefighters, their glimpsed
expressions confused and frightened. Lil stared at the screen,
searching for Rose Rimmelman's short, stocky frame.

A knock at their bedroom door. 'Grandma, Lil, you guys
decent?' Aaron had let himself in with his key.

'Give us a second,' Lil shouted back, and heading toward
the closet pulled off the thin nightdress, one of several Ada
had made out of a bolt of unbleached Egyptian linen she'd
found at the flea market. In the closet – the right side being
mostly Ada's, as was readily apparent from the lush and vibrant
colors, and the left being mostly Lil's, a symphony of conservative grays, blues, dark greens and browns – the two women
dressed hurriedly.

Ada turned, her expression wide eyed and scared. 'Oh, Lil.'

Without pause, they hugged. Ada's heart beat too fast and
she was fighting back tears.

'Lil, what have I done? Oh, God . . .'

'We don't know what's going on. We have to find out,' Lil said, holding her tight, wanting her to know that everything would be OK.

They threw on whatever seemed quick and right. For Lil it was a pair of flannel-lined LL Bean jeans and a dark gray pullover. And with no time to braid her long, still mostly blonde, hair, she grabbed a seldom-used scrunchy and yanked it back into a messy pony tail. Ada grabbed her favorite robin's-egg-blue fleece sweat suit and zipped up. With rubber-soled walking shoes in hand they headed back toward the bed.

'OK to come in?' Aaron asked from outside the bedroom.

'Sure,' Lil said.

'Are you going to be warm enough?' Ada asked, as her tall and handsome hazel-eyed grandson entered in jeans and a black zip-up hoodie, his sandy hair as badly mussed as hers. Aaron's father, Jack, or, as Ada referred to him, 'That right-wing Nazi', had essentially kicked the teenage boy out of the home for being gay. He'd sought shelter with his grandmother who loved him beyond words. And to this point, he was the only one who knew about Ada and Lil, and that they were more than just good friends.

'I'm fine,' he said. 'Who's driving?'

'We'll take my car,' Lil said, and, grabbing her brown leather satchel, made for the front door. On the way she spotted her Canon digital camera/camcorder – the one she used for her weekly columns about antiques in the *Litchfield Sentinel*. She unplugged it from the laptop and dropped it in the bag.

The trio moved fast down the steep walk Ada had dubbed the 'goat path' that separated their adjoined condos from the others in the cul-de-sac. At the bottom of the hill were a few guest parking spots and the garage. Lil hit the button on the side of her bay and waited as the door rose, revealing her new pearl-white Lincoln Town Car – an absurd gas-guzzler, but a brand and make that held too many good memories for her even to consider something different. Plus, as they piled in, the thing was damn comfortable, reliable as a Swiss watch and if some crazed psycho decided they wanted to ram you – repeatedly – as had happened to her last fall, it was built like a tank.

As she drove, taking the right out of the Pilgrim's Progress gate, she sensed Ada's panic, her gaze fixed out the side window. As the crow flies, Nillewaug Village is less than a mile from their condos, but the drive is more than twice that on account of the swamp that separates the properties. From Pilgrim's Progress a couple of rights brought them to the four-way intersection with Old Farm. But as soon as she'd made that final turn she had to pull to the curb as a caravan of screaming emergency vehicles barreled past – a hook and ladder from two towns away, the Grenville Fire Marshall in a bright red blazer, two ambulances, and a Grenville police cruiser. Behind them other sirens were rapidly approaching, and, rather than lose more time, Lil got back on the road, and sped the rest of the way.

As the widow of Dr Bradley Campbell, Lil was far from squeamish. At least she didn't used to think so. She'd helped deliver babies, applied pressure to gaping wounds that should have gone to the emergency room, but because everyone trusted Bradley – and his discretion – they'd come to their front door, typically in the dead of night. She'd calmed grieving parents, and distracted children as Bradley had set bones or popped dislocated shoulders back into place. But as they drove to Nillewaug Village, the largest assisted-care facility in Western Connecticut, she knew that she'd never encountered anything so horrifying.

Still dark, the morning pulsed with hundreds of flashing lights, but it was the flames – bright orange and clearly not under control, shooting stories high into the sky that made her breath catch and triggered memories of another fire, not so long ago in which Ada and she had nearly died.

'They're not going to let us through,' Aaron fretted, as they approached the drive for Nillewaug. State troopers were setting blue wooden barriers across both lanes of Old Farm. On the wrong side a news crew – likely the one that had filmed the footage they'd seen on the news – had cameras trained on the unfolding tragedy. Behind them, more sirens, and Lil made a quick decision. Pulling into the right lane she headed toward the barriers and lowered her window.

A trooper in gray and blue, who couldn't have been more than twenty-five came over. 'Ma'am, I'm sorry, but you're going to have to turn back this road . . .'

Lil interrupted, and, using the same take-no-prisoners tone that had gotten her entry into countless emergency rooms and operating suites in the past, said, 'I'm Lillian Campbell – Doctor Campbell's wife and assistant.' She didn't want to say more, and hoped this young trooper, whose attention was now being pulled by advancing ambulances and fire trucks, wouldn't ask questions such as, '*Didn't Doctor Campbell die nearly three years ago?*'

'OK, fine,' he said, and pulled back the barrier, as an ambulance laid on the horn wanting to get through.

Without pause, she drove past. Knowing the starfish-shaped layout of Nillewaug, with its wide hedge-lined drive, sprawling central structure and outer buildings, which included an Alzheimer's unit, rehab facility, adult day care, and others whose purpose she didn't know, she steered toward the access road that ran around the periphery.

'Lil, please just park,' Ada said, her hand on the latch. 'I've got to find her.'

'OK.' She edged off the road not fifty yards from the burning building.

Before they'd made a full stop, Ada was out with Aaron jogging behind her. Lil stayed back at a distance, keeping them in view and remembering something Bradley often said: '*The first thing to do at the sight of an accident is check a pulse . . . your own.*' Sound advice, as she surveyed the chaotic scene, more than a dozen fire trucks – Grenville only owned two – ambulances, cruisers, and more arriving. The smell of smoke, but not like a wood fire; this was acrid and laced with burning vinyl siding and something else, like gas or oil. She thought of the hundreds of residents, many of whom she knew. *Please, God, let everyone be OK, let them make it through this night.*

And then she pulled her camera from out of the bag. She looked at it, a part of herself questioning her motives, so much

chaos. *Is this really what you should be doing now?* She started
snapping. Zooming in and watching through the LED screen.
Looking up as Ada and Aaron disappeared down a walking
path dangerously close to the burning structure. 'Wait,' she
shouted, and ran after them. This was crazy, feeling a spike
of terror – Ada wouldn't try to go in . . . would she? The
saga of the past several months of trying to pry Ada's mother,
Rose, out of her rent-controlled apartment in the Lower East
Side, the bitter mother-daughter exchanges. And finally, after
yet another fall where Rose had been left lying on the floor
for more than an hour before emergency personnel were able
to break down her door, she'd finally acquiesced to the move.
Thank God she'd had her call button around her neck, but
even with that . . .

'Ada!' Lil shouted, clearing the edge of the rehab building,
and getting an unobstructed view of the fire. With camera in
hand, she couldn't help herself, the scene both horrifying and spectacular. She framed and captured vivid images
as hoses, braced by pairs of firefighters, shot pressurized
streams of water through shattered windows. She zoomed in
close as a female firefighter, her face blackened, exited the
building, with one arm around the waist of a confused-
looking woman in a filthy pink robe, her other hand pressing
a mask to the woman's face. A pair of paramedics raced
toward them with a stretcher, its green oxygen tank and
bright-red metal kit strapped on top. As the firefighter
released her charge to the medics, the elderly woman looked
back. With a shock, Lil recognized her – Gladys Hendricks,
her face was contorted in anguish, as the medics placed a
new mask over her nose and mouth and strapped her to the
gurney. Lil's thoughts tumbled. *Where's Ada?* Turning in
place. 'Ada!'

'Up there!' a male voice shouted, an arm pointed toward
the roof.

Lil looked up and saw a lump at the roof's edge. Impossible
to make out, and she pressed the telephoto button as far as
it could go. In the screen the lump took on form . . . human
form. As the resolution sharpened she saw it was a woman
– *oh God, no* – with thin gray hair, her scalp visible through

the fine strands. She wasn't moving and, ignoring tears that spilled down her cheek, Lil sidled to the left, not wanting to impede the firefighters and medics ferrying Nillewaug residents to a string of ambulances that had coalesced into a kind of taxi line on the access road. Staring at the camera's LED screen, she kept the focus grid on the woman's head, all the while praying that some movement would show she was alive, that they'd get up to the roof, bring her down and all would be well. Nearly banging her knee on a small bench, she moved a few steps forward, and had a clear shot of the woman's face, as she lay with her eyes closed, her head resting on the brick edging. 'Betty . . .' Lil's breath caught as she recognized Mrs Grasso, a retired first-grade teacher at Pond Elementary. She stared at the screen – *please be alive* – willing her to breathe. Tears spilled as she tried to steady the camera. A ladder with a firefighter in a cherry picker telescoped up the side of the building, and while Lil knew that recording this was ghoulish, she shifted the camera to video mode and followed him.

The rescuer anchored to the roof's edge and ran toward Betty. Lil watched him check for a pulse at her throat. He shook his head, then he scooped her up as though she weighed little more than a child. Lil's hands shook as she held the camera in both, trying to steady it. *She's dead, and what was she doing on the roof?* The answer that came to mind too awful: *she was trying to escape.* As the firefighter ran Betty in his arms to the ambulance at the front of the queue, she shut off the video. Sobbing, she turned slowly, aware of dawn creeping up the eastern sky, the flames through the second-floor windows still visible but no longer so high, as focused jets of water bombarded their target. Smoke billowed thick and black; windows shattered, and, barely audible over the sirens, cries for help.

Ada, where are you? Putting down the camera she started to jog around the building's periphery, trying to gauge where Rose's first-floor apartment was. Her closest exit was toward the back, and, shouldering her bag, Lil broke into a run. As she fled from the heart of the fire, she saw smoke billowing from broken upper-floor windows. Unbidden and unwanted thoughts hounded her, like having recently survived a fire she knew that death from smoke inhalation is not the worst way to go. The smoke was too thick, anyone still inside . . . It could take someone in their sleep. Not slowing her pace, she realized it probably had tonight. *People are dying here . . . people are dead.*

Lil coughed as she rounded the back of the building. 'Ada!' Spotting her silhouette in the bright blue sweats standing by a bench with the much taller Aaron on the other side and two women seated between them.

Now winded, but so relieved. 'Thank God you're OK.' Lil took in Ada's worried expression, and then that of her mother Rose, and a second woman with dyed red hair in a white nightdress with sprays of purple petunias, both of them drenched, the redhead with Aaron's jacket draped on her shoulders. They were strangely silent and focused on something in front of them that Lil couldn't yet see. And then she could.

'It's her,' Ada said, as Lil caught her first glimpse of the blonde woman, in her late thirties – maybe early forties – on the ground not more than forty or fifty feet in front of them. 'Delia Preston.'

'She jumped,' Rose spat out. 'She jumped to her death!'

The redhead looked across at Lil. 'I want to go home. Can you take me home?'

Not often at a loss, Lil again thought of Bradley's truism: *the first person's pulse to check is your own.* 'Are any of you hurt?'

'I don't think so,' Ada said.

'How would you know?' Rose shot back, her rage at the boiling point. 'How could you possibly know what you've just put me through?'

'Is anything hurting, Mother?' Ada asked. 'Have you broken anything?'

'And if I had what would you care? Connecticut's safe, you said. I can go on bus trips and visit all my friends back in the city. Safe? Safe? You call this safe?'

Lil kept quiet and surmised that, based on the volume and pitch of Rose's fury, she was probably OK. But it was Delia

Preston she couldn't take her eyes off. Her neck twisted unnaturally to the side, her skirt hiked up revealing well-toned legs and the tops of her stockings, held in place by a black-lace garter belt – *people still wear those?* She approached the fallen body, her feet crunching in tiny shards. She looked up at a shattered window on the fourth floor, the only broken pane in this portion of the building. There was no smoke coming out, at least nothing like on the other side. Aaron came up beside her. 'I checked for a pulse,' he offered. 'I'm pretty sure she's dead.'

Lil knelt and placed two fingers on Delia's badly twisted neck where the carotid pulse should have been; she felt nothing. 'What now?' she said to herself, as she looked up at Aaron and then at Ada, her mother and the other woman on the bench. She needed to get everyone out of here, but you don't exactly walk away from a dead body. Fishing through her bag she found her iPhone. She knew that Hank Morgan, Grenville's Chief of Police, had to be here. His line was busy, but he picked up on the second try.

'Lil?' His deep voice was backed by sirens.

'Hank, I know you've got more on your plate right now than you want, but I'm at the back of Nillewaug and there's a dead body just next to the ambulance bays; it looks like she jumped.'

'What are you doing back there? You shouldn't be here, Lil.' Something paternal and a touch patronizing in his voice.

'Ada's mother is a resident. We heard the fire and . . .'

'How'd you get by the road block?'

Not wanting to get that young trooper in trouble she lied, 'We came through before the barricades went up. Something else, the body; I know who she is. It's the administrative director for Nillewaug, her name's Delia Preston.'

'Delia? Shit! You said she jumped?'

'Looks like.'

'Lil, don't touch a thing, I'm on my way.'

'Sure,' she said, and as the phone went dead she dropped it in the bag and retrieved her camera. She took quick stills of Delia, of the window, and zoomed in on clusters of Nillewaug residents, some sobbing, but most eerily quiet around the periphery on benches placed as ornamental stopping points on a carefully measured and maintained walking path. Checking the battery – not much juice left – she shot a video, remembering long-ago lessons from college, when she'd harbored a fantasy of becoming a journalist with a major newspaper or magazine. This of course never happened, her life took a different turn – wife, mother and office manager for her physician spouse. As she panned the horrific scene she thought about the who, what, when, where and why of reporting. With the camera's red light blinking she narrated, keeping her voice soft, 'It's five a.m. on Sunday, April third, two thousand and eleven. I'm on the scene of a multi-alarm fire at the assisted-living complex, Nillewaug Village in Grenville, Connecticut. There is at least one fatality, Delia Preston.' She zoomed in on the dead woman's face. She'd met her twice, last fall and then again this past winter. Both times in Delia's light-filled office, the first time with Ada, who'd grilled the director about the workings of Nillewaug, and then with Ada and Rose. Delia, with her every hair in place, seamless make-up and pressed skirt suits, was one of those people who was always camera ready. Like a pitch woman on the Home Shopping Network, or a beauty queen twenty years after the pageant. Lil filmed her dead face, half pressed flat to the ground the other eye open as though staring off into space. *Who was she?* Lil knew little about her other than she was an outstanding salesperson who met a prospective resident's every objection – and Rose Rimmelman had more than a few – with quick answers, humorous anecdotes and direct eye contact. Whether real or feigned, Delia deftly communicated caring and that hard-to-fake belief in the inherent goodness of what Nillewaug offered. '*We take care of everything,*' she'd said, at the December meeting where over the course of two and a half hours she'd clinched the deal with Ada and Rose. '*It's called the Promise Plan. And we keep the promise. Once signed on, a resident is assured that their every need, whatever it might be, will be seen to for as long as they remain at Nillewaug.*'

Rose, and to a lesser extent Ada, had picked away at Delia's assertions like a pair of crows on a tasty bit of roadkill. *'And if I get sick? Or God forbid,'* Rose had said, *'Alzheimer's?'*

Delia had merely amped up the volume on her warm and pearly smile. *'Excellent questions. Our goal is to keep our residents in their own apartments. Our twice-yearly resident surveys show this to be the strong preference. In rare occasions this is not possible.'*

'And you ship the poor sucker to some hell-hole nursing home,' Rose had shot back.

Delia had laughed as if Rose were a professional comic. *'Brilliant! But no, we are licensed to run both intermediate and fully skilled nursing facilities. If a resident needs a rehab stay, or permanent placement the care and comforts in Nillewaug's extended care units are unparalleled. And this isn't just a sales pitch, but for the past five years we've ranked in the top fifth percentile of nursing homes – and those are national surveys. We have only private rooms and our Alzheimer's and Dementia complex is state of the art. All of which gives us tremendous flexibility. The Promise is truly a promise. We will take care of you.'* And she'd artfully turned to Ada. *'We will take care of your mother, regardless of what the future brings.'*

'What the hell?' A man's booming voice startled her. 'Lil, what are you doing? You shouldn't be here.'

'Hi Hank,' she said, and, with the camera on, she unobtrusively let it pan up the Chief of Police – mid sixties, full head of silver, square jaw and broad shoulders, belly a bit bigger since his wife Joanne died of breast cancer five years back, but all in all still robust and not bad on the eyes in his jeans and navy parka with the Grenville logo on the right breast.

He walked to her side and looked at Delia. 'Shit! I'm assuming you checked a pulse.'

'Yes, she's dead, Hank.'

'You took pictures?' He stared at the camera, which she was holding at her side, the lens trained on his face.

'Yeah.'

'It's still going, isn't it?' He sounded tired.

'Yeah,' she said, knowing what was coming.

'Lil, shut it off. You're going to have to give it to me; it's going to be evidence.'

'Hank, we've been friends forever, but I work for the paper now. You want these images, which I am more than happy to share, but if you want the original you'll need a court order.'

'Jesus! Fine.' He turned around, spotted Ada. 'Mrs Strauss . . . what's she doing here?'

'Her mom's a resident. I don't know who that other woman is. Do you know what started the fire?' *Yes, Lil, good question – who, what, when, where, why.*

'Fire Marshall just got here, too soon to know.'

Lil made a mental memo to put a call in to Sam King – Grenville's Fire Marshall. While not exactly friends with Sam, her prior life as Dr Campbell's wife, office manager and pseudo-nurse had given her an unobstructed view of the layered reality of her hometown and its residents. Sam would take her call, not that she'd ever blackmail a former patient of Bradley's. No, that's something she would never do, but would Sam – married with children and treated, on two occasions, for the clap – know that?

Hank looked down at Delia, pulled out a digital camera from an inside pocket and, circling the body, started to snap photos. 'Shit!' He pressed the button on the camera. A red light blinked. 'I really hate these things.' His forefinger jammed on the button, but nothing.

'Dead battery?' Lil asked.

He nodded and after trying a couple more times jammed the camera back into his pocket.

'It looks like the fire was hottest on the second floor,' she offered, switching from the what to the where.

'Looks like,' he said, being deliberately obtuse.

'I saw them take Betty Grasso off the roof . . .' She felt her throat close off. She didn't want to cry. 'She's not OK, is she?'

He shook his head in the negative. 'No,' he said, and he pulled out his cell. He turned his back to her and stepped away. With sirens in the background, some from miles away, it was near impossible for her to hear him. Her battery was nearly dead as she aimed the camera's microphone toward Hank, figuring she could plug it into the computer and try to up the volume later. A pair of state troopers rounded the corner of the building.

'Over here,' he shouted. 'Lil, you need to take your friends and get out of here.'

'Of course.' As the red light blinked faster signaling the battery's last few seconds she caught his instructions to the troopers. 'Treat it as a crime scene. And for Christ's sake be careful. The state's going to be here in force and let's not look like morons.'

THREE

Not long after, Hank Morgan was staring at another dead body. Dr Norman Trask – *Dennis Trask's dad* – dead in bed. 'Shit!' He wondered how many hours had passed since he'd moved from being more tired than he'd ever been in his life, to this weird state. His thoughts zipped as he and Grenville's Fire Marshall, Sam King, got their first look at the ground zero of what would become the most devastating fire in their town's history. On the barely scratched surface things were shaping up as one God-awful accident. But Hank, who over thirty years ago had been Grenville's first police chief – prior to him it had been all resident troopers – made no assumptions. With a borrowed camera in hand, and Sam doing the same with a state-of-the-art Nikon, they'd pushed their way into Trask's overstuffed rooms.

'What the hell!' Sam had muttered. The balding Fire Marshall had to squeeze to make it through the narrow, ceiling-high paths of charred boxes and magazines bundled in twine. 'Are you kidding me?' A look of abject disgust on his face. 'Why the hell wasn't this reported? It's one thing to have a hoarder in a private residence, but when we're talking shared walls . . . Shit!' And with dirty water swirling around their thick-soled boots they'd trudged through soaked plastic bags, bundled newspapers and stacks of God knows what that had been scorched and then drenched into unrecognizable mounds.

Hank listened to Sam's tirade while he collected first impressions. Including the strange feelings that seeing Lil Campbell had kicked up; she still looked good in that I'm-drawing-no-attention-to-myself sort of way. Of course she shouldn't be here, but that hadn't been it. They were close in age, had been friends for decades – always as one married couple doing stuff with another, or the rare golf foursome when the workaholic Bradley would join in. It was more, and not the kind of thing he'd share with anyone, not even her. *What's the harm?* he'd thought. *You're alone, she's alone . . . albeit always with that cute little friend of hers. And you're thinking about asking her on a date in the midst of this? Get a grip.* And he'd followed Sam in tracking down the fire's point of origin. Little doubt that it had started in this unit where the flames had blazed the hottest. The smell hit them first as they'd made their way into the apartment, the door demolished by axes. Acrid fumes with notes of petrol and burned plastic and rubber. And everywhere he'd looked, clocks and jumbled rubbish in boxes and black plastic bags. Solid walls of pure crap that obscured everything from the floor up to the ceiling in places. The first door off the long narrow hall was a galley kitchen, the hoard reducing the small space to less than a square yard of cluttered floor where someone could stand. The bottom cabinets probably not opened in years because of the mounds in front of them, the top ones unable to close, their contents forming an avalanche that spilled on to the buried counter and from there to the floor. And the stove was dangerously obscured by stacks of forms – this was an accident waiting to happen – but not where the fire had started.

'Solvents, not gas . . .' The experienced Marshall sniffed, like a connoisseur swilling a Pinot Noir. 'Definitely turpentine . . . alcohol, some kind of lacquer, and oil, too. I knew it from the dark gray smoke when I got here. There should be laws against having this kind of stuff in a nursing home . . . there are. This should have been reported. Someone knew about this, and if word gets out . . .'

'It's not a nursing home.' Hank corrected him as he examined the forms on the one semi-clear area of counter space – all medical in nature, and neatly stacked; like the guy who'd been living here was using it as a desk. 'These are apartments.' And, careful to leave things as he'd found them, he focused his camera on the top three forms and snapped close ups. At the bottom of each page was a signature line, below which was printed, Norman Trask, MD. From there he systematically took shots of each surface in the kitchen, getting a couple extra of the weird pyramid of jumbo coffee cans in front of the room's only window. As an afterthought he pulled a random envelope from the bottom of a mail stack – it was an advertising package filled with coupons for local businesses; the postmark was June 2001, not long after Nillewaug opened over ten years ago. 'Jesus, why would somebody keep this kind of crap?'

As they'd climbed over tumbled and drenched stacks of boxes, clock gears, and papers they came to what had once been a bright and spacious living and dining area. With the exception of a small cleared area, in front of which sat a melted computer and flat-screen monitor that now looked like odd pieces of modern art, the room was packed. Blackened shelves lined three walls, but only the very tops of those, filled with incinerated old clocks and books, could be glimpsed. The bank of windows on the fourth wall had all been broken, and the floor was a drenched swamp with thick puddles. The only other slightly passable space was in front of a cluttered table to the left of the computer, positioned to catch light through the windows.

'You've got to be kidding.' Sam pulled a partially melted yellow plastic lid off a coffee can, one of several that lined the back of the table and identical to ones in the kitchen. He stuck in a finger, smelled it.

'What is it?' Hank asked.

'Cause of the fire . . . but where . . .' Turning slowly in place, the Fire Marshall scanned the floor and the stacks of charred and drenched clutter. His gaze landed on mounds of garbage behind the workbench so blackened it was impossible to tell what they'd been, other than fuel for a fire.

'Hank, give me a hand. I think we just found ground zero.'

They both took pictures and then gingerly edged the table
back a few inches so Sam could squeeze his ample gut through.

As Hank stood back, he caught himself in a kind of prayer:
*Please God let this be an accident, just one God-awful fucked-
up accident.*

'From the burn,' Sam said, 'I'd say this is it . . . rags in
solvent. We'll get it analyzed but I'm willing to bet it's turpentine and some other crap this geezer was using.' The Marshall
dropped what might have been a clump of rags into a plastic
evidence bag.

Hank, who'd been around at more than his share of Grenville
fires, felt something lighten in his gut, as Sam vented, 'Can't
people read the friggin' labels? They say right on 'em, dispose
of the rags in a sealed container. Danger of spontaneous
combustion.'

Hank caught himself about to defend the resident; if this
was really Norman Trask's place the guy knew the risk. For
God's sakes, he was a doctor. That's why all the sealed coffee
cans were filled with water-soaked rags. *So what happened?*
Knowing their time alone at the scene – *of the accident, not
crime . . . at least not yet* – was limited. 'Sam, I want to check
the bedrooms.'

And that's when they found him. The firefighters – or
evidence eradication unit – as he'd come to think of them,
hadn't made it back here. If they had, they'd have taken
Norman Trask – who was quite obviously dead in bed – hauled
him out, tried to resuscitate and then pack him in an ambulance. At the hospital they'd have pulled him out, all the while
doing CPR, shooting drugs into his veins, and zapping him
with a defibrillator. They'd put him in an emergency-room
cubicle and finally have a nurse and then an ER doctor state
the obvious – DOA. The room had been untouched, the door
shut. The densely packed clutter, long hall and closed door
had deprived the fire of oxygen. Cause of death was going
to be smoke inhalation, which from all reports wasn't the
worst way to go. The guy looked peaceful, eyes closed, head
neatly centered on his pillow, covered in a sheet up to his
bare shoulders, glass of something evaporated by the heat,
by the bedside. Went to bed, forgot about an oily rag, few

hours later . . . nothing, just one hell of a nightmare for the living.

'Hey, Hank.'

He grunted at the sound of a deep female voice. 'Was wondering when you guys would get here,' he said. 'So Grenville's yours now?' He turned and nodded, noting Detective Mattie Perez in black pants, turtle neck and state-issue blazer. Her dark curly hair shot through with strands of silver, her deep brown eyes, on him and then back to the body in bed. Beside her was a tall young woman in navy slacks, dark shirt and a vest covered with pockets. Her face eager and intent, her glossy auburn hair tied back in a ponytail. Clipped over her right breast was a state police picture ID with large letters at the bottom – DETECTIVE JAMIE PLANK.

'We were working the overnight,' Mattie explained. 'Heard it called in and figured, what the hell? Seems I've got a soft spot for this town.'

'Yeah, right . . . murder capital of Connecticut.'

'Getting there,' she said. 'But your Fire Marshall says it's an accident.'

'If there's a God it is . . .'

'So how'd it get so big?' she asked. 'You'd think in a place like this at the first whiff of smoke there'd have been a response.'

Hank felt a wave of déjà vu as Mattie, a seasoned detective with the state's major crime squad, quickly honed in on uncomfortable details, the kind of things that could quickly turn this from a tragic accident to arson, and from there, with three dead that he knew about, to homicide.

'Alarms never went off,' Sam said, having followed Mattie from the living room to the bedroom. 'It got called in a little after three a.m. by a guy delivering papers. I picked it up on the scanner, and got here pretty much with the first truck.'

'I don't get it,' Mattie said. 'The sprinklers went off but the alarms didn't? Aren't they connected?'

Sam looked troubled. 'Yeah, when water flows through the pipes it triggers the audible alarm . . . except.'

'Except?'

'If someone put it in test mode, or the wire to the flow alarm got disconnected or, God forbid, someone cut it.'

'All things to check. How long ago do you think it started?' she asked, carefully stepping over the mounds of debris around the dead man's bed.

'Well, figure for those rags to combust you're talking four hours from whenever they fell. Lord knows there was ample fuel, so once they sparked, lots of dry paper, plenty of oxygen. It spread quick.' He paused. 'It was big when we got here, had to have been going at least a couple hours.'

She put on light blue propylene gloves, and pulled back the soaked sheet, noting that Dr Trask was naked, and trim, from the scars on his knees he'd had the joints replaced, but other than that . . . healthy-looking old guy. The once white sheets now soaked with ashy water. 'A place like this; there's smoke detectors all over the place. Right? Not just the ones connected to the sprinklers. Why didn't they go off?'

'Just one reason,' Sam offered. 'They weren't on.' He glanced up at the round white sensor outside Norman Trask's bedroom. He watched and waited for the flashing red dot; it never came. 'They still aren't.'

'How can that happen?' the young detective asked. 'Aren't they hard-wired?'

'Sure they are,' Sam said. 'Somebody shut them down. I'd be willing to bet both the smoke detectors and the flow alarm were on the same system and that's why there were no audible alarms.'

'Not good,' Mattie said, lifting the crystal tumbler off a stack of journals that obscured a nightstand. She looked in at a sludge of viscous amber on the bottom. 'Any chance this place is wired into your fire department?'

'Not for years,' Sam said. 'Wish it was, but it's cheaper using central stations – just pay a monthly fee. The calls go to Jersey, Miami, Atlanta, then they call it in to the local police and fire. I think it's just a matter of time before even those get shifted to India.'

She sniffed the glass, the liquid boiled off in the heat of the fire, an oily residue on the bottom, she detected bourbon, the hint of something else – *vermouth?* – and a desiccated maraschino cherry on the bottom. *Drinking alone in bed . . . and cocktails?* 'Hank, do me a favor and find out when the alarms went down.' Her gaze raked over the jumbled room, her focus wide, taking in random bits of information, and landing on a bit of unmistakable green sticking out of a shoebox wedged between a black plastic bag, and a dangerously canted yard-high wall of yellowed newspapers. She pried the box out, careful to not start an avalanche. The lid slid back. 'Wow!'

'Holy shit!' Hank muttered as he stared in at the packed contents, all hundred-dollar bills in small folded clumps, one jammed on top of the next.

Mattie grabbed a smallish wad. 'All new bills,' she said, and she counted the stack and then a couple more. 'Six hundred, one thousand, four hundred, one thousand three hundred . . .' She looked up at Hank. 'You knew him?' she asked, while quickly guessing the box's contents as upwards of forty grand. Her gloved fingers dug down to the bottom and retrieved a small stack of old folded documents. She opened them out and examined the one on top. It was beautifully engraved with the image of Lady Liberty in ink the color of mulberry wine and '$5,000' written in the four corners and spelled out across the bottom.

'What are those?' Detective Jamie Plank asked, her height giving her an unobstructed view over Mattie's shoulder.

'Some kind of bond,' Hank said, 'and old.' He found the date. 'Forty-nine. Just after World War Two. How many are there?'

Mattie pried the notes apart. 'Ten. So face value of fifty grand.'

'Bearer bonds,' Sam offered. 'I don't think they make those any more. But if that's what they are, they're still good. Don't need any proof of ownership to cash them, just walk into a bank, turn 'em over, and get your cash.'

'Who was this guy?' Mattie asked. 'Who keeps this kind of money in a shoebox? And are there more of them?'

Hank gave her the rough outline of Dr Norman Trask, retired surgeon, father of three boys. The oldest had played on the Grenville Ravens during their brief glory years in the 1970s.

As he spoke, he watched Mattie carefully examine the piles of stuff packed in the surgeon's bedroom. He remembered her first outing in Grenville last fall when she'd been the lead detective in a string of murders that had created a panic in Grenville. This brief trip down memory lane was like a drill ripping through his gut. *If this turns into a homicide . . . shit!*

With her gloved hands deep inside a garbage bag filled with sweaters, she turned back to him. 'Can you think of any reason someone would want this guy dead?'

'No,' he said, but his thoughts spun fast. *Could this have something to do with Dennis?* And, wishing he could keep his mouth shut, but knowing she'd find out anyway, 'His youngest son, Dennis. Got in a lot of trouble when he was young, occasionally still gets up to something . . . but nothing big. At least nothing that sticks.'

'What kind of stuff?'

'Kid's got a temper, and used to drink. Did some time for a DUI. Sold pot when he was in high school and had a couple short stints in detention.'

'Fights with his dad?'

Hank's thoughts skittered back thirty-odd years. 'Not recent, not as far as I know. But when he was in high school. He was your typical rich kid in and out of trouble. Had his parents wrapped around his finger. Middle of the night, kid would get picked up drunk at a party or behind the wheel, and dad always showed. A couple times I told him it would be good to leave Dennis in lock-up for the night, maybe scare some sense into him. He wouldn't go for it.'

'Spare the rod,' Mattie commented, staring at the naked dead guy, running likely scenarios. On one end, guy gets buzzed on bourbon, goes to bed, forgets some oily rags and presto. On the other, homicide, but with a box full of cash and God knows what else of value. If this was murder a simple robbery seems out. The guy was a doctor . . . 'Hank, how old was Dr Trask?'

'I'll find out, but at least in his eighties.'

'So retired, right? Has to be.'

'You'd think, but . . .' He told her about the forms he'd found in the kitchen.

Mattie listened, taking in Hank's information, the scene in front of her, and the doings of the local Fire Marshall – Sam something – on his cell in the background. She'd been pulling an extra overnight shift when the call had come in – five-alarm blaze in Grenville. Just the mention of the town perked her interest and when she'd heard it was Nillewaug Village, well, something about this place had stunk the last time she was here. It had been a no-brainer, at least go and make sure this wasn't a crime. It had been a good call, with three dead – at least that they knew of – crime scene or not this was big. At the very least there'd be civil suits, and one hell of a mess for the insurance companies. She retraced her steps from the bedroom, pulled out her cell, and called for the crime-scene team. Her young colleague trailed behind – *me and my shadow*, she mused, a part of her glad to have someone so obviously interested in learning, while another part wondered how she'd gotten to this point where she'd become the mentor.

'Around ten last night,' the Fire Marshall said, as he answered her earlier question about the alarms, his phone in hand.

'Really? Who turned them off?' she asked.

'Someone with the access code.'

She paused, standing in the center of the living room that reeked of smoke and mingled solvents. Her feet sloshing through blackened water. The windows shattered, charred crap that created a casing around mostly unscathed stacks of stuffed garbage bags and cardboard boxes so tightly crammed the fire hadn't gotten to them. 'Why would someone turn off the fire alarm in a place like this?'

'Few reasons,' the Fire Marshall offered. 'System gets brought down for servicing or testing . . . but you sure wouldn't do that on a Saturday night. Maybe there was a false alarm or a faulty sensor and they needed to check it out, and figured it's just easier to shut it down and then fix it during the work week. Or . . . you know it's probably not just the fire that got shut down. All the systems go through the same line.'

'Right,' she said, following his train. 'It'll be security too.'

She turned to her partner. 'Jamie, call the security company, have them fax us a list of everyone who could disarm the system. And see if there's any way of telling who shut it down.'

'You got it.'

'Good.' Mattie slowly turned in place, her thoughts clicking. 'I want you to stay here and don't let anyone else in until the CSI team gets here. I'm going to check out the office of the jumper . . . if she really was a jumper.'

Jamie Plank struggled to contain her excitement. This was the biggest case she'd ever been a part of. As a new detective she'd been exiled to third shift – the land that time forgot. Having someone like Mattie as her partner was an unexpected bonus and this . . . 'Anything else?' she asked. 'You think this was arson?'

'We'll find out,' Mattie said, 'but I've got a bad feeling.'

FOUR

'**Y**ou should have just let me burn to death in that hell hole!' Rose spat at Ada from the back of Lil's Lincoln Town Car, as she pulled past the roadblock outside Nillewaug. It was just after seven a.m., the last hour and a half a confused blur. Retrieving the car, trying to get it around to the back of the burning building. Various emergency personnel and cops asking what Lil was doing there, lies tumbling from her lips, as she'd maneuvered her way back to Ada, now next to her, and Aaron, Alice and Rose now in the back. Along the way, she'd spotted familiar faces, old patients of Bradley's who'd moved to Nillewaug for its promise of safety and comfort. And one face that made her wonder if maybe there'd be more to this story than just a fire – Detective Mattie Perez.

'Mother . . .' Ada's jaw was clenched. 'Are you sure you won't let us take you to the hospital?'

'Why? So you can kill me there?' Rose turned to her new, albeit confused, BFF, Alice in her soaked nightdress, the two of them huddled under a red wool horse blanket that

Lil kept in the trunk for emergencies. 'Do you have children, Alice?'

'Vicky. But she's no use,' the redhead offered, shaking her head. 'I want to go home. Please take me home?'

'Where do you live?' Aaron asked.

His question worried her. 'I don't know.'

He switched tactics. 'Do you know where your daughter Vicky lives?'

'Who?'

'Your daughter.'

'She's no good. Can you take me home?'

Lil glanced in the rear-view mirror at the two older women under the blanket, with Aaron on the far side in a smudged white tee shirt, having given his leather jacket to Alice. She cranked the heat, and the car filled with the mixed smells of wet wool and char. She tried to figure what made the most sense. A pair of medics had tried to talk Rose into getting into an ambulance so she could get checked out at Brattlebury Hospital. Not only had Rose adamantly refused, but had insisted that Alice didn't need it either. All of Lil's years with Bradley, and a decent amount of common sense, told her that neither of the women was in medical peril. They had the occasional cough, but Rose was right. Hospitals were places of last resort, and best avoided. Which meant they were headed back to Pilgrim's Progress. Lil threw Ada a glance, and, with her voice low, said, 'You doing OK?'

She shook her head, and cracked the tiniest smile. She leaned toward Lil and whispered, 'She thinks I set the fire.'

'And this is what I get,' Rose declared, ostensibly to Alice, but clearly meant for Ada. 'I wish I were dead!'

'Mom,' Ada said, 'you don't mean that.'

'I most certainly do! What do I have? Everything is gone. Everything! I didn't want to come to this place. But no, I'm not safe in my own home where I've been living for fifty years. I've got to move to Connecticut, and that pushy Delia woman.'

'She's dead.' Ada was struggling to keep her temper in check. 'And you're safe. That's what matters.'

'What do you know?' Rose spat. 'This is your fault.'

Ada's hands balled into tight fists as Lil turned into the gates of Pilgrim's Progress. She longed to reach across the seat and comfort her, but didn't. Instead, she kept silent as they passed one of the two eighteen-hole golf courses, the man-made three-acre lake and finally came to their cul-de-sac.

Ada unbuckled and leaned toward Lil. 'I'll put them in my place.'

Lil nodded, and waited as Aaron helped his great-grandmother and Alice out of the back seat. Unseen by the older women, Lil took Ada's hand and squeezed. 'We'll get through this.'

Ada shook her head, her beautiful sapphire-blue eyes sought out Lil's. 'She hates me.'

'No, she's just scared and angry. She doesn't hate you.'

'Maybe . . . you know I haven't told her about us.'

'I know.'

'She's smart. She'll find out.'

'We'll deal.'

'I love you, Lil.'

'Love you too. And it just amazes me.' And with that she let go her hand, and got out.

Ada jogged up the walk passing Aaron and the two women. Her first impulse was to unlock Lil's condo on the right, but instead opened the door to hers on the left. *One thing at a time*, she told herself, as she waited for the trio to make it up the path. The phone started to ring. Leaving the door ajar, she went in and saw the answering machine on the granite kitchen pass-through blinking with recent calls.

She picked up. 'Hello?'

'Mom, where were you?' Her daughter, Susan – Aaron's mother – sounded frantic. 'I've been trying to get you all morning . . . Where's Aaron?'

'He's with me . . . I'm assuming you've seen the news.'

'Is Grandma OK, what's going on?'

'Everyone's fine,' Ada said, looking down the hall as Aaron held the screen door for Alice and Rose.

'Did you see Jack?'

The question stopped Ada. 'Jack?' The mere mention of her son-in-law blackening her mood further. 'Why the hell would he be here?'

'The fire,' Susan said. 'He got paged a little after five. I've been trying to reach you ever since.'

'Susan, it's been one hell of a morning, and maybe I'm losing it, but what would Jack be doing here?'

'The Clarion underwrites that place. He got paged and was out of here like his job depended on it. You know him, he thinks he's always one paycheck from getting his pink slip.'

'I didn't see him,' she said, 'and your grandmother is fine. Just furious with me, but that's nothing new. Aaron's with her now; she'll be staying for a while. Maybe later you'd come down for a visit.'

Ada felt her daughter's hesitation. 'I'll have to check with Jack.'

'For the love of God, Susan, your son and your grandmother are both down here, and would love to see you. Not to mention your mother could use a little help right now.'

'I know, Mom, it's just . . .'

'Forget it!' Ada snapped, wondering what had happened that had so entirely robbed her daughter of every ounce of courage and self esteem. The answer flew back with a single syllable – Jack. A man she'd disliked from the very first, who over the years had bullied and belittled her once brilliant and enthusiastic daughter into a scared mouse. 'If you can make it great. But don't worry, everyone's fine. I've got to go.'

'Mom, it's just . . .'

'Goodbye, Susan.' She ended the call, as Aaron thoughtfully spread an old quilt over her sofa and settled Rose and Alice in their drenched and filthy nightdresses.

She overheard him talking to the women, his voice calm.

'I'll make tea,' he said. 'Then we'll hunt down some warm clothes, Nana Rose. It's going to be OK, you'll see.'

Ada watched from the kitchen, her chest filled with pride and wonder.

'You're a good boy,' Rose said, and she looked toward the kitchen pass-through and Ada. 'Unlike some others who boss people into things they don't want to do.'

Ada's cheeks flushed – *this is not my fault* – and was

about to remind her mother of all the falls, the middle-of-the-night distress calls and how she'd been going back and forth to New York for years trying to keep her mother in that damn Rivington Street apartment, when the phone rang again.

'Hello?'

'Mrs Strauss?' A man's anxious voice.

'Yes.'

'Hi, my name is Kyle Sullivan, I'm a nurse at Nillewaug. You're listed as the emergency contact for Rose Rimmelman. Do you know where she is?'

'With me.'

'Oh, thank God,' he said. 'Has she been checked out at a hospital?'

'No, she refused to go, and at this point I'm not going to argue. She seems fine though, and we have another of your residents with us.'

'Alice?' His voice caught. 'Please tell me you have Alice Sullivan.'

'I didn't know that was her last name, but yes, I think so. Red hair, probably in her seventies, has some kind of Alzheimer's.'

A pause on the line. 'Thank God. Thank God.'

Ada could swear the man was crying. 'Are you OK?'

'Not really,' he offered, 'but a little better now. Alice is my grandmother. Her apartment is next to Rose's. I got her out of her apartment and asked your mother to stay with her and get her outside, but I haven't seen her since, and she gets so confused; she wanders, too. I didn't know where she was, or if . . . thank God. Things are so crazy here. I know we don't know each other, but I can't leave here right now, is there any way you could keep an eye on her for the next few hours? I'll try to get there as soon as I can.'

'Stop right there,' Ada said. 'She's safe, we can keep an eye on her for as long as you need. Let me have your numbers, and I'll give you mine. Do what you need to do. Your grandmother is fine. Does she have any special needs? Medications? Foods she can't eat?'

'Not really, just some pills for the dementia that don't really

work. If she misses a dose or two it doesn't matter. I'll call
you as soon as I can. And, Mrs Strauss—'

'Ada,' she interrupted firmly.

'Ada . . . thank you so much. I can't tell you what a load
you've just taken off my mind.'

As Ada hung up, she spotted Lil coming up the walk, and
glancing behind at Aaron in the living room tending to her
mother and Alice, she went out. Across the walk she spotted
Clayton Spratt in the window of the unit directly across
from hers, holding back the curtain and staring. *Bastard*,
she thought, glaring back, and wondering when the other
shoe would drop on his threats about reporting Aaron living
with her to the homeowner's board. She kept her voice low.
'What a mess.'

'At least she's OK, and that Alice woman . . .'

'Her last name's Sullivan. A nurse at Nillewaug called
checking on Rose. Apparently he's her grandson. I told him
not to worry. It seems like he's trying to track down all the
residents.' Ada's gaze met Lil's. 'What am I going to do? I
feel sick, all my mother's things; she could have died in that
place . . . What have I done?'

Standing there, feeling exposed as their across-the-walk
neighbors stared. 'We'll figure this out,' Lil said, desperately
wanting to hold Ada, to tell her that everything would be
OK, but she didn't. And something about that felt
dead wrong. If Ada had been Bradley, he'd be holding her,
and no one would have blinked an eye. Lil turned her
head and spotted Clayton in the window with his pinched
lemon-sucking expression, and then in the kitchen window
of Bernice Framm's directly across from her unit, movement
in the corner of her cutesy cat curtains. 'Life in a fishbowl,'
she whispered.

'She's going to have to stay with me.' Ada stated the
obvious.

'I know.'

'Lil, I can't believe I'm going to say this, but . . . I don't
know how long I'll be able to take it. You heard her. As far
as she's concerned I lit that place on fire.'

'She's scared, and you're the only safe person around.

And she's still angry about leaving New York. But what were you supposed to do? Her visiting nurse had said they couldn't keep her on as a patient because of the liability of her living alone, and she absolutely refused a live in. She left you with no choice.'

Ada stared down the walk, which was lined with daffodil shoots, about a week from blooming. In the distance they heard a lone siren as it made its way from Nillewaug to Brattlebury Hospital. 'You know what she wanted . . .'

'But that wasn't going to happen,' Lil said, mentally tracing Ada's profile, her firm jaw and high cheekbones. 'Yes, she's your mother, but you were supposed to just give up your life here, and be at her beck and call? I wouldn't have let you.'

'And now . . .'

They turned at the sound of a phone. 'It's coming from mine,' Lil said. She paused, not wanting to leave Ada when she was so clearly distraught.

'Get it,' she said. 'I'll be fine. Just need a few minutes to collect myself.'

And Lil left her alone in the crisp spring air. Although, as she sniffed, and maybe it was on her, she still smelled smoke and burn. By the time she reached the phone the machine had picked up. It was barely eight. *Who would call this early on a Sunday morning?* She stood and waited as the outgoing message played and then a woman's voice. It took her a couple of seconds to realize who it was; she picked up. 'Mattie?'

'Lil, glad you're home. I've been trying to get you for the last hour and was starting to worry.'

'I'm fine,' she said, trying to figure out why Detective Mattie Perez would call her at the crack of dawn.

'Hank Morgan said you were at Nillewaug this morning. He said you were taking pictures.'

'Yes . . . are you there?'

'I am. He said you got shots of the fire and of Delia Preston.'

'I did,' Lil said. 'I haven't had a chance to look at any of it yet. We just got back. He practically confiscated my camera.'

'It's all digital, right?' she asked.

'Yeah, I think I got both stills and some video.'

'Do me a favor, Lil, and I'm dead serious.'

'Of course.' She could feel Mattie carefully choosing her words, this woman who'd only months earlier had saved her life. 'Mattie, whatever it is you need, just ask.'

'Lil, and please don't repeat this. Or at least not to anyone other than Ada. Things are shaping up in a bad way. I'm treating this as a crime scene.'

'Arson?'

'Too soon to know for sure, but here's a piece of the nightmare. You're the only one to get shots of Preston's body before it was moved.'

'I heard Hank tell his officers to treat it like a crime scene,' Lil said, feeling the need to defend the local Police Chief.

'Yeah, well . . . apparently a pair of paramedics scooped her up and brought her to the ED. Hank said you got bent out of shape when he asked for the film . . . something about needing a court order. Really, Lil?'

For the first time that morning she laughed. 'He didn't say please.'

'And if I say please?' Her tone shifted. 'This is serious, Lil, even if this all turns out to be just some tragic accident, that film – depending on what you got – could wind up in dozens of civil suits, with everyone and their son and daughter suing Nillewaug and anyone else who might have contributed. I need you to not touch that camera, or connect it to anything until I get someone from the crime unit to do it. I swear you'll get copies of everything. But with digital recording the whole chain of custody thing gets dicey. It's already bad, where you've left the scene.'

'Mattie,' she said, trying to figure what a real reporter would do in this situation. Then again – *just do the right thing, Lil.* 'If it's that important, just come by and get it.'

'Lil, much as I'd love to see you and Ada, I've got too much to do here. I'll send another detective to pick it up.'

Lil's heart sank. Not only was she about to give up those pictures and video, but her shot at an exclusive with the lead detective on the biggest story in Grenville was flying out the window. It's strange how snippets from journalism classes

she'd taken over thirty years ago came back – being a reporter
has everything to do with being in the right or wrong place
at the right or wrong time. 'I'd love to have seen you too,'
she added, figuring at least that wasn't disingenuous. 'But
more importantly I'd have thought you'd want to get a
statement from Ada's mother, Rose Rimmelman.'

'Her and seven hundred other residents of Nillewaug, not
to mention the staff.'

'Yes, but Rose saw Delia jump,' she added, dropping the
carrot in front of the detective.

Mattie paused. Lil could hear someone ask her a question,
and the funny echo of a siren over the phone and then over
the crow-fly path from Nillewaug to where she stood. 'Huh,'
she practically grunted. 'I don't remember you being quite
this devious, Lil.'

'I don't know what you're talking about.'

'I'm sure you don't and I'll be there in twenty.'

The call ended and Lil was moving fast – twenty minutes
is not much time. She clicked the computer on her dining
room table out of sleep mode. The hook-up cable for the
camera was already plugged in and, without pause, she
attached it to the nifty little Canon. The screen flickered
with images and a message screen appeared asking her if
she wanted to delete the files once they'd been uploaded to
the hard drive. Figuring that might be tantamount to obstruc-
tion of justice, or some other term that tumbled to mind
from watching crime shows, she pressed *no*. The first shots
were from yesterday's opening of the Saturday flea market
in Brantsville. It now being Sunday, she somehow needed
to find the time to whip up seven hundred and fifty words,
with two to four pictures, for her *Cash or Trash* column
about antiques and collectibles in the *Grenville Sentinel*.
She'd figured on the large open-air market as a likely subject.
She and Ada went most Saturdays from spring through fall.
Fire or not, she'd need a solid two hours to hammer this
out. A few dozen pictures of the market, interesting dealer
stalls, and colorful vendors flickered on the monitor. There
were a couple of disquieting moments as she stared at those
seemingly benign images. It had to do with one stall, a not

especially likeable dealer whom she and Ada mostly avoided – they called him Grumpy. Ada had spotted the stuff first, stacks of pictures and knick-knacks that had once belonged to Gwen Carrington, a friend of theirs, who had died in her sleep of a massive coronary last winter. The creep factor, in an otherwise fun early spring morning at the flea market, had been fast and big. Gwen had a thing for dachshunds, and Grumpy's forty-by-twenty double-sized booth had hundreds of her little figurines, pictures cut from calendars that she'd framed, tops of cardboard boxes filled with little dog-shaped brooches and earrings, mugs with dachshunds. With a pit in her gut, she'd asked the dealer how he'd come by them. He'd told her that he'd done the clean out on Gwen's condo. 'Not the good stuff,' he'd said with regret, 'the leftovers. In exchange for getting the place emptied out, I keep and sell whatever I find.' Clearly, this was the story she was supposed to write, how all this stuff people collect is just on loan. But how to do that without turning into Dolly Downer, something her young and ambitious editor, Corey Bingham, did not want. She stared transfixed at close ups of Gwen's ceramic dachshunds piled in mounds being pawed over by prospective buyers, who, continuing with her ebb-and-flow theory of tchotchkes, would one day have their finds returned to a different stall in the future. The first images of the fire flew past, and she thought about Mattie's instruction not to download or copy them. This was followed by a surge of pride; these were good, really good, in focus, clearly framed. Firefighters in motion, a pair of medics wheeling a resident toward the queue of waiting ambulances, flames shooting from the second-floor windows. As they sped past, she'd realized that they'd arrived not much after the first responders. She had clear images of the first ladder being raised, and of firefighters hooking up hoses and running in heavy boots and yellow coats into the burning building. If they'd gotten there even a couple minutes later they'd never have been allowed through.

She startled at the sound of the screen door opening and then closing. She glanced through the kitchen opening at the clock on the stove. *That was no twenty minutes,* she thought, feeling her heart in her throat, and then Ada appeared.

'What's the matter?' she asked, her gaze riveted to the first image of Delia.

'You don't see me doing this,' Lil told her.

'What are you talking about?' Ada stood beside her, and they watched Lil's handiwork as she'd circled that poor, dead woman with her neck twisted too far to the side, her face mashed into the asphalt, her skirt raised over splayed stocking-clad legs. 'I didn't feel right leaving her like that,' Lil said, unable to tear her gaze from the images. 'I should have at least pulled her skirt down.'

'No, I'm pretty sure the cops wouldn't want that . . . These are really good, Lil. But who wears garters?'

'I know.' The resolution was sharp, the camera automatically adjusting to the low light, occasionally filling in with a flash. And then the screen went dark and a message box informed them that the computer was now uploading the video files, as a barber-pole-like bar appeared and under it an estimate of how long it would take – eight minutes.

'Mattie's on her way,' Lil said, and walked quickly back to the rear bedroom, with Ada trailing. She stared out the window at the parking lot. 'She wants that film and told me not to copy it.'

'I see.'

'Crap!' a boxy black Tahoe with dark tinted windows was pulling in. *'That was no twenty minutes.'*

Mattie emerged with a phone to her ear. She looked up, and, realizing they'd been spotted, Ada waved.

'I'll intercept her,' Ada said. 'Try to slow her down.'

'She wants to talk to Rose, I told her she saw Delia jump. Take her into your place, and I'll come over as soon as the download finishes.'

'Got it.' And she scurried back through Lil's condo, locking the door behind.

FIVE

Attorney Jim Warren sat rigid in front of the computer screen in his richly appointed home office. Ignoring the phone ringing on his mahogany desk and his cell, which he'd silenced soon after the first call came at four a.m., his thoughts raced – *Delia, you bitch! You fucking bitch! Why?* At fifty-two with a net worth in the tens of millions, he was master of the life he'd wanted. Hair, a shock of pure silver, and his body trim from daily runs on the treadmill and circuits with free weights in his state-of-the-art home gym, where Gaia, his twenty-five-year-old Norwegian personal trainer and masseuse came three days a week. His body-fat content was under ten percent and he could annihilate men twenty years his junior in tennis and racquetball. A perfect life, a perfect home, a lovely wife, Joanie, who long ago stopped asking questions about late-night meetings and weekend business trips, and two kids in high school – a boy and a girl. Jim Junior was the quarterback for the Grenville Ravens – *just like dear old Dad, although they'd never win a championship, not even close* – and Kayla, who even as a freshman was the even-on favorite for class valedictorian.

Aside from the hum of his computer and the phone, the house in Eagle's Cairn – a high-end development with multimillion-dollar mansions on multi-acre parcels perched on Grassy Mountain Road with the best views in the Nillewaug River Valley – was quiet. The computer streamed images of Nillewaug from one of the local stations, and if he strained he could hear the sirens in the valley below. His baby was going up in flames, and that, he mused, was a good thing. *Let it burn to the ground, and her with it.* A tight-lipped smile crossed his face as he pictured Delia. *I should never have hired the bitch . . . or slept with her. Don't shit where you eat. I should never have promoted her, or . . .* But then other thoughts, the feel of her hair in his hands, the way she'd look at him, the rasp of her voice as she gave him permission . . . encouraged him to realize his every sexual fantasy. '*Use me, Jim,*' she'd said, her words more potent than Viagra. And her ambition, her eagerness, her intelligence and, of course, her greed. *How could you do this to me? What were you thinking?* And most importantly: *how far did she go?*

The desk phone began to ring again. He read the lit caller ID. 'Idiot . . . moron.' He didn't answer. Nine, ten, eleven . . . Twenty-one, twenty-two, twenty-three . . . 'What?' He angrily picked up the handset.

'Jimbo!'

'Yes, Wally.'

'I'm at the Village. You got to get your ass down here. It's a fucking nightmare!'

'I'm aware,' he said. 'And what am I supposed to do about it? I'm not a fucking fire fighter and neither are you.'

'But Jim . . . people are hurt . . .' Fat Wally Doyle's voice cracked. 'There are dead. Jim, you need to be here.'

Jim Warren couldn't remember when exactly he'd started loathing his once good friend and teammate. But the man was an idiot, which at times served him well, but now could be catastrophic. 'Go home, Wally. There's nothing you can do there.'

'Jim, we need you here. There's no one in charge . . . Delia's dead. Did you know that?'

'What are you talking about?' Wondering if not only was Wally a fool, but trying to do something else.

'I feel like I'm in hell.'

Jim felt something catch in his throat and a twist in his gut – *watch what you say, something's going on here.* 'Dead! That's terrible. What happened to her?' He felt panic take hold. He hadn't touched her . . . not in that way. He pictured their last meeting. '*It wasn't me, Jim, I swear.*' He didn't believe her, Delia was one hell of an actress – both in bed and out.

'I don't know, they say she jumped, must have been trying to escape the fire.'

The frantic knot in his belly eased. 'That's horrible. Poor
Delia,' he said, his mind zipping, now back in her office,
thinking through each step. *Fuck!* Did he get all the back ups,
was there more of a paper trail? *You bitch! You greedy, stupid
bitch!* '*Where are they?*' he'd screamed at her, and her tears,
her protestations that she was just as surprised as he at the
empty shelves in the wall safe. '*Where the fuck are they,
Delia?*' Staring at the TV, and the chaos of dozens of emergency vehicles and cop cars, he could go back. *But how stupid
would that be?*

'We need you, Jim.'

'So Dennis is there?'

'Yeah, I called him, he's been here since just after five. I've
been trying to get you for hours . . . Dennis's dad is dead.
He's all broken up. Jim, we need you.'

You little pussy, can't you do anything for yourself?
Knowing exactly how he'd come to despise Wally. The grossly
obese and intellectually stunted linebacker could steam roll
over anyone in high school, protecting him or keeping the
field clear for Dennis sprinting down the field. They'd been
high school royalty and then town superstars when the
Grenville Ravens, always a second- or third-tier football team
did the unthinkable and won the state championship . . . two
years in a row. Like having the fucking world on a silver
platter, and the three of them – Ravens of the Apocalypse –
front and center at the banquet. Dennis out of control, his
dad forever bailing him out, only to end up drinking himself
into a year in jail. Fat Wally needing to be told how to wipe
his butt, which girls to date, which one to marry. Which free
ride at which college to take, even his career in finance – and
God help his poor clients – was Jim's suggestion. And him,
quarterback Jim, taking all the best morsels, the full scholar-
ship to Dartmouth and then law school at Yale, the prettiest
girl in Grenville from the richest family, and business offers
from men who wanted to bask in his reflected glow. Old-money
men who knew that whatever golden-boy Jim invested in
would sprout returns beyond their wildest hopes, like
Nillewaug Village and Eagle's Cairn.

'Jim?'

'Yeah, Wally, give me half an hour.'

'So you're coming?'

'Yeah, just stay cool. If anyone asks, tell them everything's going to be OK.'

'Is it, Jim? I mean, this is bad.'

'Don't sweat it, Wally. Things will be fine,' he said, picturing the relief on Wally's corpulent face. He remembered something Dennis's father, Dr Trask, once said about Wally: *'Strong as an ox and just as smart.' Poor Dennis,* he thought, wondering what he'd do without his dad. Who'd pull him out of scrapes, now? *Not your problem . . . not any more.* 'I'll be there soon.' And he hung up.

Getting up from his leather chair he headed toward his home office's marble bath. He stripped out of his dark gray Dockers and black sweatshirt. As the room steamed up he caught his wonderfully toned reflection in the mirrors. His belly flat and ripped, his arms and chest defined. If it weren't for the silver hair he could easily pass for a man in his thirties. *Maybe I should dye it,* he thought, stepping under the brushed nickel rainforest shower heads.

Toweling off he picked up his fallen clothes, and put them to his face. He inhaled and smelled traces of Delia's Chanel. 'Shit!' Wondering what other unseen evidence of their frantic tumble might be hidden in the folds. He stuffed it along with the running shoes he'd been wearing into a gym bag, all indecision gone. Jim Warren believed in contingency plans; they were a part of his nature and had always served him well. If plan A doesn't go well, then he could easily shift to plan B, C or D. Decisions were made in the flash of an eye, or the snap of a wrist and forearm sending the pigskin hurtling long or in shorter stabs cross field to Dennis's waiting hands.

'Honey?' Joanie's voice from the distant kitchen.

'Up here, sweetie.'

'There's something happening at Nillewaug. A big fire.'

'I know,' he shouted back, as he pulled on clean underwear, jeans and a baggy sweatshirt from the office's walk-in closet where he kept an entire wardrobe. Over that he grabbed his leather bomber jacket. 'I'm heading there now.' And he pulled down a wheeled carry-on suitcase, and stuffed it with shorts, tee shirts, a pair of sandals and a couple of favorite Tommy Bahama short-sleeved silk shirts.

'You want some coffee?' Her voice rose up the steps.

'Don't bother, I'll get some at the Donut House,' he said, picturing his still pretty wife, ten years younger than himself.

'Call me, if there's anything I can do,' she offered. 'Those poor people.'

'You got it.' And with the gym bag in one hand, and his carry-on in the other, he opened the outer door to his home-office suite and took the back stairs to the garage. Glancing across the high-vaulted structure with its polished cement floor he pressed the button for the bay door behind his BMW. *Time to go long, Jim*, he thought, feeling almost giddy as he tossed the bag and suitcase into the trunk. Joanie was a good kid, maybe getting a little long in the tooth and the house was great and he couldn't have asked for a better pair of children. But would he miss any of it? *Not so much*, he told himself, pulling out of the garage, and down the winding drive that gave stunning views of the Nillewaug River Valley.

Focused on the road, he turned right off Grassy Mountain on to River Road and then left on Main. He was completely unaware of two dark-suited men in a black Ford sedan, who'd been waiting behind his neighbor's dense hedge. Heading down Main, he did glance to the right at Old Farm Road, where he'd normally turn to go to Nillewaug Village. 'Let's go long.' He drove straight and then left toward I-84. Before merging on to the ramp he detoured at the drop off for 'We Care', a local church-run charity that ships clothes to third-world countries, and tossed his gym bag into the bin. He never once spotted the Ford, which kept pace three cars back as he sped toward Bradley Airport. Nor did he notice the two dark-suited men as they trailed him from the parking garage to the ticket counter, and then through security.

It wasn't until he stood in line for first-class boarding that he noticed the men as they too headed toward the roped-off gate, where a smiling blonde flight attendant was checking tickets and running them through a machine.

'Jim Warren?' one spoke.

He turned, his mind going fast, assuming some colleague or neighbor had just recognized him. *Not a problem, going for a little trip, a mini vacation.* His eyes flitted from the first man, mid thirties, conservative haircut – *not familiar* – to the other, African-American, dark gray off-the-rack suit – *never seen him before in my life.* 'Yes?'

'Jim Warren.'

And his eyes flashed on the black man's hands as he reached back for something and the other continued to speak.

'Jim Warren,' the black guy said as he reached out and grabbed his wrist.

'What's going on?' Adrenalin surged, as his hand was firmly twisted behind his back, and he felt something wrap around his wrist. 'What the . . .!'

'Jim Warren, you're under arrest for conspiracy to commit fraud against the federal government. You have the right . . .'

SIX

As Detective Mattie Perez climbed the walk to Lil and Ada's adjoined condos – cell phone to ear – her thoughts raced. She ended the call with young Jamie, again trying to instil in the newbie detective the vital importance of crime-scene integrity. A tall order in the best of circumstances, and beyond impossible with fires. *And no,* she thought, *still not officially a crime scene,* but little doubt before this messed-up morning was over it would be. Maybe murder, maybe arson, maybe something she hadn't yet considered. And then there was Hank Morgan tromping through the scene with his buddy the Fire Marshall, who kept insisting it was an accident caused by spontaneous combustion. Sure, she liked Hank, had since they'd first met, but trust him . . . not so much. Something about him, and not the usual differences between local and state cops, where the former is more about keeping the peace and the latter about solving crimes and catching perps. Since first coming to Grenville last fall, Mattie had developed a series of partially tested hypotheses about the place. Postcard pretty on the outside, but something rank festered below the surface. And Nillewaug, with its pricey apartments and polished administrator with her French-tipped nails and perfect blonde coif were emblematic of a town that thrived off the fleecing of old people as they downsized, got ill and eventually passed. The series of murders last fall, the killing of high-end antique dealers who'd gotten fat off of Grenville's wealthy old folk, had seemed a fitting, albeit gruesome, crime spree.

Even here, in the vast retirement community of Pilgrim's Progress she sensed something corrupt. Yes, pretty to look at with pruned crab apples and weeping cherries starting to bud, beautifully maintained stone walls, and walkways with sturdy iron rails to help support wobbly residents. *Thousand of these condos*, she mused, having forgotten the exact number. *Each worth a few-hundred grand, maybe a little less in the down market, but still, someone's making a killing.*

She spotted Ada Strauss coming out of Lil's condo. Despite her funk, she smiled and waved, taking stock of the spry woman in her robin's-egg-blue tracksuit, that made her silver hair sparkle in the morning sun, and set off her amazing sapphire eyes. If it weren't for the hair, Mattie mused, Ada could pass for forty.

'Mattie,' Ada called out and came down to meet her. 'We've been dying to have you come and visit, but I swear, this was not our doing.'

Mattie smiled, taking note of Ada's choice of pronouns: 'we' and 'our'. *Interesting.*

'You look tired.'

'It's been a long morning, and fires make the worst crime scenes.'

'Why's that?' Ada asked.

'Too many people, with too many agendas,' Mattie shared, her anxiety close to the surface, and wondering if maybe leaving Nillewaug so soon wasn't a mistake. But glad to be away from the noxious smells and the devastation.

'I'd never really considered that,' Ada said, leading Mattie

up the path to her condo. 'But yes, they do have to put out
the fire and make sure everyone's OK, don't they? I can't
imagine there's a lot of concern for leaving things alone. Has
to wreak hell on collecting evidence, and trying to reconstruct
what happened.'

'Exactly,' Mattie said, immediately reminded of Ada's keen
intelligence, as she followed her into her elegant home, with
its polished Chippendale, and lit glass shelves filled with a
stunning collection of iridescent Tiffany, Steuben and Loetz
art glass. She looked around. 'Hi Aaron,' she said, taking note
of Ada's tall grandson and two older women huddled in quilts
on the living-room sofa, their faces smudged with soot. *At
least this feels and smells like a real home*, she thought.
'Where's Lil?' she asked.

'She'll be right over,' Ada said. 'Aaron, can you pour Mattie
some coffee?'

Mattie couldn't suppress the feeling that she was being
managed, as Ada brought her into the living room and made
introductions.

'Detective Perez, this is my mother, Rose Rimmelman. Lil
said you wanted to get a statement from her.'

Mattie met Rose's angry gaze, noting similarities between
the mother and daughter; similar high cheekbones with more
sag around the jaw and a wattle throat, but Rose's eyes much
paler in color behind thick glasses and bloodshot. Her body
stocky where Ada was thin. And beside her a younger woman,
probably in her seventies with dyed cherry-red hair and large,
dark eyes, who, in her day, had been a knockout of the Rita
Hayworth type. 'And you are?' Mattie asked.

The redhead smiled, a half-eaten granola bar in her hand.
'I'm Alice. Have you seen Johnny?'

Ada tapped Mattie on her shoulder and whispered, 'Alice
Sullivan, I'm thinking Alzheimer's and we're keeping an eye
on her till her family can pick her up.'

'A detective?' Rose looked appraisingly at Mattie. 'So it
was arson!' She glared at her daughter.

'We don't know yet. The Fire Marshall's preliminary report
says accident.' Mattie pulled out a small digital recorder. 'Do
you mind?'

'Of course not,' Rose said, shaking her head. 'And accident my ass! From the beginning I knew there was something bad about that place.'

'That may be,' Mattie said, sitting in a wing chair across from the two women and placing the recorder on the coffee table that separated them. 'If you could start by saying your name, address, and today's date.' Mattie then ran her through a series of questions to establish the sequence of events that led to Rose and Alice being under Delia Preston's office windows at the time she jumped. 'Describe, with as much detail as you can remember, what you saw.'

Rose sat back, her lips pursed. 'We were on the bench and I saw something shiny falling, like a shower of glass sprinkles, and I looked up and saw her go through the window.'

'Was she standing or hanging from the ledge?'

'No, more like a child in a swimming pool, just sort of plopped over the edge, not quite a somersault.'

'Head first?' Delia asked, trying to picture what Rose described.

'Yes, but not fully.' She made a fist of her hand and indicated with a downward motion of her wrist how she'd seen Delia fall.

'And then?'

'I stood up and walked over to her.'

'Was she still alive?'

'I don't think so. She didn't move.' Rose hugged the quilt tighter. 'Her head twisted.' Rose made a face. 'It was wrong . . . broken, like the neck had snapped.'

Mattie looked at Rose and then Alice, who was contentedly sipping some juice Aaron had gotten for her in a large plastic tumbler. She heard the front door, and Lil, her straw-blonde hair in a loose ponytail, came around the kitchen. Her forehead was smudged with ash and she seemed jumpy.

'I brought you the memory card,' she said, holding out a small black plastic case.

'Thanks.' Mattie took the tiny bit of plastic, pulled out a plastic evidence bag from one of her inner jacket pockets and dropped it in. Using an indelible Sharpie she wrote across the white strip, noting the date and time, and put down Lil's name and address. 'Before I leave I'll need you to sign a form for this.' *Something's up,* she thought. *Why wasn't she here when I arrived? And where's the camera?* She was about to ask when her cell phone vibrated and then rang. 'Excuse me,' she said, pulling it out and reading the LED, which gave the number and read 'State of CT'. She knew who it was. 'Arvin, what you got for me?'

'It's long and hard and . . .'

'For Christ's sakes Arvin,' she snapped, picturing the rotund and mostly bald medical examiner, who was forever propositioning anything female with a pulse. At least, she hoped it only extended to those with pulses. She bit back a scathing remark. After all, she'd called him at home on a Sunday when she'd discovered Delia's body had been whisked off to Brattlebury Hospital. She was deep in favor territory. 'Anything?' she asked.

And like a switch being thrown, Dr Arvin Storrs dropped the creepy flirtation. 'Her neck was snapped at C-3, pelvis shattered in four places . . . but all post-mortem.'

Mattie's breath caught. 'What are you saying?'

'She'd been dead a good four hours before she went out that window, that's what I'm saying. So unless you believe in zombies she didn't jump; she was dropped, pushed, tossed, given the old heave ho . . .'

'And the cause of death?'

'Blunt trauma, to the back of the head, right above the occiput, a single blow from someone who knew what they were doing. You're looking for something smooth, round and heavy. Say between a bowling ball and a baseball. Think grapefruit sized. I'll tell you more when I have it, but thought you'd want to know this was no accident . . . and something else you might want—'

'Yes?'

'She'd had intercourse within an hour of death, two tops.'

'Rape?'

'Nothing to indicate that, absolutely no signs of a struggle, some minor abrasions and a bit of bruising.'

'DNA?'

'Not a hair that wasn't hers, at least not so far. And no

sperm if that's what you're looking for . . .' Unable to stop himself, he added: 'And if that is what you're looking for, I'd be happy to—'

'Not in this lifetime, Arvin.' She cut him off short. A familiar excitement in her belly as the information sank in – homicide. She was about to hang up and then stopped. 'Arvin?'

'What?'

'There were four other dead at the scene. One is an old doctor found in bed. It's probably smoke inhalation, but . . .' She remembered the tumbler of bourbon residue.

'What? The only one they brought here was the Preston woman. Who was the doc?' He sounded annoyed.

'Norman Trask, a surgeon.'

'Where's the body?' he asked.

'I don't know.'

'Crap. If one's a homicide, and it turns out to be arson . . . then they're all homicides. Why the hell aren't they here?'

'If I give you the names, will that help?'

'I hate my job,' he said, at the prospect of multiple labor-intensive autopsies heading his way. 'You know I've been cut back to a single assistant. And they're still looking for another ten-percent cut.'

'It's the same everywhere,' she said, not wanting to get into another discussion on the wretched state economy and the new governor's promise to balance the budget, even if it meant closing prisons and laying off hundreds of state workers. She gave Arvin the names of the dead, and likely locations for their remains. 'With Dr Trask,' she added, knowing from experience that the more information you gave Arvin about the crime and the scene, the more focused his findings would be. 'The fire started in his living room. The state Fire Marshall won't commit to arson, and the local one insists it was an accident caused by oily rags spontaneously combusting in the guy's apartment. Either way, there was definitely accelerant. I'm very interested in the toxicology on him. He was found in bed, likely had been drinking.'

'And you want to know how much?'

'Yeah, and anything else he might have been taking.'

'This day's going to go on forever,' he griped.

'Sorry,' she said and hung up.

'Is everything OK?' Ada asked.

'Yes and no.' Mattie retrieved her recorder, noting how close Ada had moved; she'd obviously been listening. 'Rose, thank you so much. If you remember anything else, anything at all, it could be important.'

'What's happened,' Lil asked.

Mattie looked at Lil, who finally met her gaze. *What's going on here?* Feeling as though she were the one being interviewed. 'What time did the two of you get to Nillewaug?' she asked.

'A little after four,' Lil said. 'What's happened?'

'Looks like it might not have been an accident,' Mattie said, getting up, her thoughts back at the scene. 'I'll need a statement from both of you, you might have seen something . . . or someone.'

'Was that call about Delia?' Lil asked.

'I have to go,' the detective said.

'Just tell me this.' Lil persisted. 'Was Delia Preston murdered?'

And then Mattie understood. The last time she'd been in Grenville Lil and Ada had been valuable resources. Lil especially, with her vast insider's knowledge of the town and its residents. Since then, the two women had kept up a friendly email correspondence, Mattie had even read some of Lil's local columns about antiques. They were good – informative, conversational, even funny – and that's why her antennae were up. 'Are you planning to do a story about this?' she asked point blank.

'Yes,' she said.

Mattie nodded and thought, *what's the harm? In fact . . . if the fire had been deliberate . . . an attempt to conceal a homicide, what would the perp do if he or she knew it hadn't worked?* 'OK,' Mattie said, knowing these things can work for or against an investigation, but it would only be a matter of time before the results of Arvin's findings were known. 'I'll give you a scoop. Delia Preston was dead before she went out that window. She'd been murdered.'

Lil didn't blink. 'How much before?'

'Wow!' Mattie said. 'You've changed.'

Lil nodded, her dark eyes eager.

Like a pair of cops grilling a perp, Ada didn't miss a beat coming at Mattie from the other side. 'Was it hours . . . minutes? And why did you ask if she'd been raped?' she asked, having clearly overheard Mattie's half of the conversation.

'Maybe later,' Mattie said. 'Got to go. Ladies,' she said, nodding to Rose and Alice. And to Lil and Ada: 'I'll call.'

SEVEN

Lil cracked her right eye open, and then shut it fast. *Lil, what did you do?* Her tongue scraped the back of her front teeth, a layer of mucus clung there and to the roof of her mouth. A vein twitched on her forehead and with it the first dull thud behind her eyes. *Not good,* she thought as snippets from last night flooded in. *How much did you drink?* She pictured one . . . no two bottles of top-shelf single malt on Ada's dining room table. *It's Monday!* Hangover or no, her brain went from zero to a thousand with that realization.

Trying to ignore her head, which felt like it had been squeezed into a hat two sizes too small, she swung her legs out of bed, and caught sight of Ada. Like oil on rough seas, she stopped. She was still asleep, her lips gently parted, a look of peace on her lovely pixie face. Just the sight of her sent a flutter. Glancing down, she spotted her fleece lined slip-ons, and reached over for yesterday's sweatshirt that lay crumpled on the oak rocker next to the bed. It was five a.m., and she had work to do – her column should have been finished and emailed to her editor by seven last night; she hadn't started it. Which is different from saying she hadn't gotten something in to the paper. She most certainly had, and as her slipper-clad feet landed on the bedroom Tabriz that was foremost in her thoughts. *Did they run it?*

Trying not to wake Ada she headed to the kitchen, but, ever a creature of habit, flicked on both the coffee maker and the electric kettle. This was an unspoken rule of their still-young relationship: whoever gets up first makes coffee, black and strong, for Lil, and tea, for Ada, with two teaspoons of sugar and a dollop of milk. With the coffee making its first rhythmic chug and the kettle humming to life, she checked the screen door for the morning paper – not yet there. Frustrated, but not defeated, she went to the computer on the dining-room table. Since she'd started the weekly columns this had turned into an accessory office. Wary of being hacked, or of getting a virus, she reserved the HP in the dining room for editing photos, email and the Internet and the Dell in the tiny third bedroom was where she wrote.

She clicked the link for *The Brattlebury Register*, one of the three largest dailies in Connecticut, and the paper that owns the weekly *Grenville Sentinel* that runs her *Cash or Trash* column. She didn't even have to enter her password for full-text access. Her article was on the front page.

Five Dead, dozens missing as Blaze Ravages Grenville's Nillewaug Village Assisted-Care Facility: Murder and Arson suspected
– Lil Campbell, correspondent

The call to 911 came in from paper delivery man Avery Osborn at 4:08 a.m. By the time first responders were on site less than ten minutes later, flames and clouds of dense black smoke were visible for miles. Fire companies from as far off as Hartford, Danbury and New Haven responded to the five-alarm blaze, which swept through the central four-story residential complex of the Nillewaug Village assisted residential facility. As of this morning there are five known dead, including Nillewaug's Administrative Director, Delia Preston, age 42.

It has been determined by the state medical examiner that Preston, who it was initially thought had jumped to her death, was in fact the victim of homicide, the details of which have not yet been released.

In addition to Preston, retired area physician and orthopedic surgeon Norman Trask, MD (82) was found dead on the scene, as were long-time Grenville residents:

*Elizabeth Grasso (85), and Hillary Flanders (90).
Margery Rayburn (94), who had moved to Nillewaug
Village from Salisbury CT, was pronounced dead of smoke
inhalation at Brattlebury Hospital.*

The article stopped there, with a prompt for subscribers to
enter their user ID and password, which she did. Her heart
raced as she read the rest of the one thousand words she'd
agonized over yesterday afternoon. To say she was conflicted
over submitting this would be an understatement. The fact that
the editor and chief, Edward Fleming, had actually run it was
a tribute to the importance of the story, and the fact that she'd
managed to scoop it. Her phone conversation with him had
been strained to say the least. 'I already have a reporter covering
it,' he'd said.

'But I was there from the beginning.'

'He was too.'

With her heart in her throat, she'd laid it all out. Her words
had tumbled fast, she'd been on the good side of the barricades, had pictures . . . 'I know that Delia Preston's death is
a homicide.'

That had gotten him. 'What? How do you know that?'

'I heard it from the lead detective.'

'Will he go on record with it?'

'She, Detective Mattie Perez, and I think so, and even if
she doesn't I promise that it's true. I heard her talking to the
state M.E.'

'She a friend of yours?'

'Yes,' she'd said, matching his no-nonsense tone with
simple answers. 'And I have photos of Preston's body –
close-ups. And if Preston's death was a murder, is the fire
a coincidence or . . .'

She could almost hear his thoughts, as he'd paused. 'Arson,'
he said, completing her sentence. 'I doubt we'll use the pictures
of the dead woman, much as I want to. Maybe post one on the
website if it's not too gory.' And then Edward Fleming, known
for being stingy with compliments had said, 'Well, looks like
you want to be a real reporter. Get me one thousand words by
four p.m. and be damn sure of your facts . . . I'll have someone

check them, but if you're wrong about the homicide angle, you'll not get this chance again. And Lil . . .'

'Yes?'

'Make it good.'

Apparently, it was good enough. Other than changing the headline, the text had been edited with a light hand. While yesterday's horror was still fresh in her mind – the cries, the smells, seeing poor Betty Grasso – she couldn't stop this other feeling. *What's wrong with you?* Wondering at what point she'd turned into a ghoul, but no denying – *you got a front page byline.*

The tea kettle clicked off, and she went back to the kitchen. Her emotions mixed as she poured Ada's tea and deposited it on her bedside table. Her eyelids fluttered at the sound, and she muttered 'Thanks', without waking.

Lil kissed her forehead and returned to the kitchen. She poured a generous mug of coffee and superheated it for sixty seconds in the microwave, and took it back to her office.

'Just write,' she said, staring at the lit screen. Knowing that the subject on her mind was the fire and not some puff piece on the local antiques industry. Then again, she was thrilled to be doing these columns, and, lead story or no, she was behind on the deadline. 'Just write.' Her headache eased as her fingers rested on the keyboard – *nothing's coming.* But then – *he won't want it* – thinking of frightened little Corey Bingham, the editor for the Grenville Sentinel. Corey, in his early thirties with a lovely wife and two sweet babies, was convinced his tenure at the small local paper was contingent on keeping everyone happy, most notably Edward Fleming at the parent paper. 'It's all about the advertisers,' Corey had explained when he'd offered Lil the chance to do the column after the prior antique expert had decided it was too small potatoes for him. 'Keep it light, keep it local and keep it positive, Lil,' had been his words of advice. Followed by his attempt at a stern tone: 'And whatever else, get it in on time . . . please.' Having already missed her Sunday deadline, but thinking if she could get it done before he made it to the office, she'd probably be OK. She started to type. For Lil, writing was a passion, even though this was the first

time she'd been paid for it. She'd always journalled, but
rarely shared the contents. Occasionally, she'd pull one out
to look at her thoughts at age twenty or thirty. Like going
through old photos. But now, as her words flowed about the
opening of the Brantsville flea market on Saturday, she was
simultaneously looking at the turns her life had taken in the
past and now. *Your first lead story, Lil.* Feeling an urge to
get up and check to see if the morning paper was here yet.
From there her thoughts zipped to the local newsstand, and
wondering how many copies of the paper she'd buy – a
dozen, two. And then back to the task at hand. *Keep it light,
keep it local, keep it positive . . .*

Tchotchkes in the Mist
By Lil Campbell

*Like the running of the bulls in Pamplona, Spain, the
first Saturday of April drew an excited crowd of over
5000 eager treasure hunters to the Brantsville Fair
Grounds. The near-freezing temperatures and dense fog
that shrouded the five hundred dealer booths did little
to dampen the mood, as long-time Flea Market manager
Daryl Crane welcomed back the throngs of eager
buyers. At six a.m. sharp he made the announcement,
'Open the gates.'*

As she wrote, trying to stay light, local and fluffy her thoughts
were pulled in darker directions. It wasn't just the fire and
the awful – from certain perspectives wonderful – photos of
Delia Preston that were in the same digital photo album as
the flea market pictures she'd shot the day before, but the flea
market itself. She and Ada adored the Brantsville market, and
mourned its closing each November. But this Saturday, what
started with the usual anticipatory excitement as they waited
for the gate to open, had a number of queer notes. Starting
with the obvious and really irritating, which she didn't think
fit into her fluffy little column. But what had crept into the
Brantsville market over the past few years were a number of
practices that had wrung some of the joy out of the Saturday

morning treasure hunt. Firstly, years back you could go on to
the field as the dealers were setting up. This added an element
of excitement – and risk – as they'd all head out in the dark
with flashlights to look at the merchandise as it came out of
assorted vans and trucks. Clearly, 'buyer beware' took on
added meaning as chips, cracks and outright forgeries were
much harder to spot in low light. That changed when the
owners – three local antique dealers – fenced in the field
about five years ago and began to charge admission. The
stated reason had to do with liability and concern that excited
buyers would trip, fall, and injure themselves in the dark. But
really, it was greed. The market's owners realized that the
thousands of antique and collectible aficionados who showed
up each week would shell out a buck or two. The market was
a cash cow, so in addition to the rent they charged for the
spaces and the cut they got off the food concessions they
were now raking in over ten grand a week from admission
fees. Sure, a couple bucks is no big deal, but it rankled and
the loss of the free-for-all fun of scurrying across the field in
pursuit of bargains at five in the morning was sad to lose.
But this Saturday, and what she'd noticed for the past couple
years, by the time they paid the two bucks and made it through
the gate on to the field, other buyers had been there long
before them. What had apparently happened was dealers, and
some of the locals, were slipping bribes at the gate and getting
on to the field hours before the official start time. The going
rate was around fifty bucks. Which, yes, some antique shows
advertise early buying for which they charge a premium. But
not Brantsville, so essentially it was graft. Low-level, annoying
corruption at Lil's favorite place to spend a Saturday morning.
So while she dutifully typed in all the details about the flea
market for her column – how to get there, the URL for the
website, how much it cost for the dealers to set up, etc., she
ran a parallel piece in her head, and jotted down a few notes
for a future column. *Stay on task.* Easier said than done, as
she remembered something that sent her scurrying back to
the other computer on the dining-room table. She scrolled
through the flea market photos, flagging the ones that would
accompany the article, including a beautiful long shot of the

dense mist hovering over the market, and the long line waiting to go through the admission gate. But that's not what she was looking for. 'Wow!' And there he was. Dr Norman Trask, a man she knew peripherally through Bradley, who'd clearly gotten on to the field well ahead of the rest of them. As they were just clearing the gate, the tall silver-haired surgeon was heading in the opposite direction toward the parking lot pushing a battle-scarred shopping cart laden with bulging cardboard boxes and a large wooden clock, hastily wrapped in a stained blanket and duct tape. The expression on his face a combination of exertion and glee. 'Wow!' she repeated, as Ada emerged from the bedroom. With her tea in hand, she looked at the photo.

'What a difference a day makes,' was her somber comment. 'He seems happy at least.'

'He does, and now he's dead.' Lil looked at Ada, her eyes bright, her spiky silver hair squished down on one side. 'How's your head?' she asked.

'Nothing a lobotomy couldn't fix.'

'Do you mind checking on them?' Lil asked, referring to her mother, Alice and Aaron over in Ada's condo.

'Later,' she said. 'You know, sleeping dogs and all that. Quite a Scrabble game,' she commented.

'I thought it was brilliant,' Lil said, referring to last night's somewhat bizarre events.

'If nothing else, it helped Mom. That woman likes nothing better than trouncing me at Scrabble.'

'I still don't think all those interrogatives count. I mean really? "Er, hm, uh"; I don't think so.'

'Rose Rimmelman knows her two-letter words.'

'I think she cheats. And exactly how much of the Yiddish-English dictionary is acceptable?'

'Apparently a lot,' Ada said, 'at least according to the Oxford Unabridged. What a night . . .'

'It wasn't boring,' Lil said, feeling pulled. It was clear Ada wanted to rehash the events of yesterday, but she had to get back into her cave-like office and finish the column. *Priorities, Lil, it's not like you're either Woodward or Bernstein. And the Grenville Sentinel . . . not quite The Washington Post.*

Sensing something, Ada asked, 'You get your column done?'

'In the middle of doing something on Saturday's flea market.'

'You going to use that one?' Looking at the picture of the ebullient, but now dead, Dr Trask still on the screen.

'Absolutely not, and if that scared-of-his-own-shadow editor of mine found out . . . not worth it. I like doing this too much.' Ada was smiling. 'What?'

'Go get your piece finished,' she said. 'We'll talk later.'

'God, I love you.' They smooched, but while she'd clearly given Lil permission to hole up and get her work done, something gave her pause. 'We never asked: "How long?"'

Ada shook her head. 'What are you talking about?'

'That nurse last night, Kyle.' Her fluffy column seemed increasingly unimportant. 'We never asked him how long until he'd get Alice settled somewhere else.'

'We kind of did,' she said. 'It was early going, but I think you'd already had a good bit of whiskey.'

'I must have,' Lil admitted, realizing portions of last night were wrapped in a boozy haze. 'I'm not an alcoholic . . . I promise.'

'Yes, well . . . Isn't denial the number one symptom?'

'So what did he say?' Lil asked, ignoring her jab and recalling the tall and handsome, albeit exhausted, dark-haired man – Kyle Sullivan – who'd come over, ostensibly to pick up Alice. It had been around eight, he'd called first, thanking them effusively for keeping her safe and getting directions to their place. When he'd shown up, the wild west Scrabble tournament was in full swing, the five of them around Ada's dining room table, swiveling her de luxe edition of the game, while sipping exceedingly good single malt from Bradley's vast collection of Christmas and give-the-doctor-a-thank-you presents they'd amassed over the years. Neither Bradley nor Lil were big Scotch drinkers, but somehow there must be an etiquette book instructing people to bring their local GP a good bottle of single malt at the holidays, or following the birth of a baby or after setting a son's broken arm in the middle of the night, or covering for a drunken night of debauchery where you needed a bit of patching up before facing the wife . . . or husband. Regardless, Lil had a closet filled with cases of the stuff, including some truly stellar bottles of Bowmore, Balmore and the old standby – Glenfiddich.

'You really don't remember?' Ada asked. 'Is this like an alcoholic black out? Do I need to find a program for you?'

'Fine,' Lil said, 'I remember him showing up . . .'

It all came back. Yes, she'd had a couple . . . OK, maybe a few. She was excited about having finished the piece on the fire, and wondered if they'd actually run it. She was also feeling weird about how giddy it had her – people were dead, and she was experiencing a writer's rush. 'He said he was going to take her to his condo.'

'Right, and then you asked how he was going to look after her. Clearly Alice has at least a moderate degree of Alzheimer's.'

Lil remembered Ada putting a mug of tea in Kyle Sullivan's hands, and settling him in a chair next to his grandmother and Rose, who were playing as a team. Admittedly Alice's Alzheimer's restricted her participation to the occasional – 'Can I go home?' and the eerie, 'Where's Johnny?' But she had seemed to enjoy herself. To his right was Aaron and then Ada and she was across the table.

Kyle had smelled of smoke and his blue scrubs were filthy at the bottoms. Rose had told them how he'd gone back into the burning building to check on residents, and how he'd asked her to stay with his grandmother and get her out.

Something about Kyle had pulled at Lil's heart. The way his deeply set brown eyes had looked at Alice, so clearly devoted to her. The caring in his voice, whenever he spoke to her. The fact that he didn't want to talk about his heroics throughout the day, which she'd pulled out of him, as Ada got him to eat a turkey sandwich. 'She'll stay with me,' he'd said, his long fingers blackened with soot as he took hungry bites. 'Before we moved here, she was with me. I'll call an agency in the morning and get a live-in, until I can figure out what makes sense.'

'Don't they need you back at Nillewaug?' Lil had asked.

He'd looked at her, something haunted in his expression.

'You can't imagine what it's like right now. Everyone is so scared, there's no way any of the residents can return to the main building so we're looking at six hundred people, many of them with special needs and complex medical issues who are essentially homeless. The scope is unreal . . . I feel guilty even leaving for a couple hours.' He'd seemed on the verge of tears, his voice choked. 'There are nearly forty residents we've not been able to find.'

When Lil had filed her article late in the afternoon she'd been aware, via Hank Morgan, that a number of residents were unaccounted for. He'd assured her it had to do with the unprecedented scale of the disaster. By late morning, Brantsville Hospital's emergency room had closed and patients had to be diverted to hospitals in the adjoining towns. Hank had been hazy about exact numbers. *'Maybe a couple dozen still unaccounted,'* he'd said. But this . . .

'Forty?'

Kyle had nodded. 'Yes, I'm sure they're mostly fine . . . But no one was keeping track of where people were being sent. I have the list of all the residents and their emergency contacts; I've been trying to account for everyone . . . There's no one really in charge.'

'How can that be?' Ada had asked.

'You know that Delia Preston died in the fire.'

Ada had nodded. 'But there have to be other administrators . . . a second in command?'

'There is – the director of nursing – and she's on two weeks' holiday in Barbados for her honeymoon,' Kyle had said. 'I tried her cell, but either they don't get service there or she turned it off.'

'What about the owners?' Lil had asked, knowing a little about the corporate structure of Nillewaug from when it first had opened and for the very brief time Bradley had been their medical director.

'Good question. I've been trying to reach Jim Warren since five this morning. And not a word. And to be honest, I've been so caught up in just trying to account for people, call in any staff I could . . . I don't have the authority to do any of this stuff. I was the nurse on charge last night . . . I finally

got through to this Wallace Doyle guy – the Chief Financial
Officer – who told me to contact Jim Warren. He started to
give me this whole story about how he just managed the
finances . . . Like I care about that? And I don't get it, because
I know he was there at the fire. The guy must weigh over
three-hundred pounds; he's hard to miss.' He shook his head.
'Everyone keeps looking to me like I know what's going on
. . . I really don't.'

'It's OK, man.' Aaron had placed a hand on Kyle's back,
as the nurse's jaw clenched.

'I should have seen something, smelled smoke, something
. . .' he'd said, struggling to maintain composure. 'And why
didn't the alarms go off?'

Alice, sensing her grandson's distress, kissed him on the
cheek. 'Are we going home, Johnny?'

He'd smiled at her, the bond between them so affectionate.
'Soon,' he'd said, smoothing back her recently shampooed
shoulder-length cherry-red hair.

To which Ada had replied, 'She can stay here. She has to.'

'That's kind, but I'll figure this out.'

'Don't be ridiculous,' Ada had said. 'Look, we've got plenty
of space, she'll stay in my condo with Rose and Aaron. It's safe
here, and during the day Lil and I can keep an eye on her.'

'It makes sense,' Lil had agreed. 'We both know what to
do . . . I cared for my mom for years, and Ada's Harry had
severe dementia by the end.' She'd made eye contact with
Kyle. 'Let us do this.'

Reluctantly, he'd agreed, and then his cell rang. Shaking
his head he'd pulled it out, and, getting up from the table, had
commented, 'It's my sister . . . Hello, Kelly.' He'd stepped
away and the game resumed half-heartedly as Ada had watched
him. Her heart bled for the man who was being tested by
circumstances beyond anyone's control. His conversation on
the phone apparently not helping things. Not quite catching
his words she'd focused on his lips, and could discern phrases
– 'I can't . . . I'm doing my best . . . No, absolutely not.' And
then his voice had raised in anger, and they'd all heard.
'Remember the last time you took Alice. Absolutely not!' His
frustration had been obvious, as he looked back at the Scrabble

game and caught Ada's gaze. Alice had turned at the sound of his voice. 'Are we going home?' she'd asked.

'Fine,' he'd said into the receiver, 'you want to talk to her, you think this is something you can handle?' His tone shifted and, stifling his anger, he'd called to Alice, 'Alice, Kelly wants to talk with you.'

All pretense of playing had dropped as Alice bounded up from the table and let Kyle hold the receiver to her ear. To Ada it looked a bit like a child playing as Alice smiled broadly and yelled into the small cell phone. Curiously, she did remember her granddaughter's name – 'Hi, Kelly, are we going home?' Her smile never dropped as her granddaughter said something back to which Alice had replied, 'Are we going home?' A bit more unheard conversation from Kelly followed by Alice: 'Are we going home?' and Kyle took back the phone and had encouraged his grandmother back to the game table.

He'd turned his back and whatever he'd next said to his sister, none of the others could hear, other than: 'Satisfied?'

After he'd hung up, his jaw was clenched, and he let a slow stream of air through his mouth. 'I love my sister,' he'd said to no one in particular. 'But she just doesn't get it.'

He'd brought Alice's medications in from his car, apologized that she had no clothes, and then left. Ada had made him promise to at least try and get a few hours sleep before returning to Nillewaug. But as he'd pulled away, she'd turned to Lil and said, 'He's going right back there.'

'Of course,' she'd said, 'I'd put money on it.'

It had been a very strange night, and now, as Lil looked at Ada in her Prussian blue robe, her eyes bright in the morning light, she said, 'I don't remember him saying how long he needed us to keep Alice.'

Ada sipped her tea. 'As long as it takes, Lil. You know that. Now get your piece finished.'

EIGHT

Detective Perez needed sleep, and she knew it. Her thoughts raced dangerously fast, and it was all she could do to keep from snapping at the excited and well-intended Jamie who'd earlier delivered the latest salvo of bad news, and what had them now being buzzed through looming outer gates at the low-security Federal Correctional Facility in Danbury. 'He's in federal custody,' Jamie had said an hour and a half earlier after having been given the task of contacting Attorney James Warren, the CEO and president of the for-profit Raven's Flight, LLC that owned Nillewaug.

Jamie, who was driving and apparently needed no sleep, followed the blue-and-white signs toward the weathered brick administration building. During the half hour drive from Nillewaug, Mattie had been furiously trying to figure what Attorney James Warren was doing in federal custody, while fielding Jamie's non-stop questions. 'If the Feds are involved does that mean they take over?' she'd asked.

'It depends, but probably.'

'Why would they be involved?'

'No idea, just drive.' She stared at the on-board computer. Sadly, she had full access to the state databases, but limited ability to anything related to inmates in federal custody. This was exactly the kind of thing that post-9/11 Homeland Security was supposed to address, and never had. Unable to even get the names of the arresting agents, all she had to go on was the limited information on the Internet inmate finder – conspiracy to commit fraud (multiple counts). There was no mention of bond, and it appeared he'd not even gone before a judge yet. What exactly had Mr Warren done? *And does it have anything to do with this? Murder, likely arson and now . . . why is he here?*

The one break she'd caught was knowing the assistant

warden at Danbury, whom she'd called just as he was showing up for work. He'd told her that the prisoner was waiting for his attorney and refusing to say a word. She was welcome to be present for the interrogation, but early indications were not hopeful. She'd asked to speak with the arresting agents, and was told he'd do what he could, but they were holed up trying to prep for what would likely be a lengthy interrogation. Her frustration was palpable, but she knew to tread lightly. What did they suspect James Warren had done, and, if they'd just arrested him, how much of this had to do with the fire, or the murder . . . or murders?

She felt rattled and torn, like shouldn't she still be at Nillewaug? *All being handled,* she thought, picturing the swarms of detectives and crime-scene technicians who'd replaced the earlier ambulances and firefighters. Lots of grunt work, getting statements from residents and employees, then the locals who'd seen the fire, or thought they knew something. Attempting to protect the crime scene and the obvious source of the fire, that horrible apartment. And then Preston's office, any evidence of what had happened badly compromised by the fire, the firefighters and quite possibly whoever had pushed dead Delia out the window. *Let it go,* she told herself, knowing her desire to stay in control was pointless.

'I've never been here before,' Jamie said, as they parked the car in one of the visitor spots. 'I thought it was only for women.'

'Used to be and still is mostly, but for white-collar investigations they keep men here pre-trial. After sentencing it's a different story.'

'The country club,' Jamie said, referring to the prison's long-time reputation of being a nice play to stay if you have to do time.

'Yeah.'

Jim Warren, in an orange jump suit, his face covered with salt-and-pepper stubble, said nothing, his gray eyes fixed on the steel table in front of him. His hands manacled as his attorney – Craig Windham, the best money could buy and sharp as a pin in his five-thousand-dollar charcoal suit, blinding white shirt and Italian silk tie – deflected questions from the two federal agents who sat across from them in the dingy interrogation room.

'So, based on some anonymous tip –' his attorney's tone incredulous – 'you decide that my client, a highly respected attorney, is somehow involved with a plot . . . no, a *conspiracy*, to defraud the Feds. And yet other than badger him with irrelevant questions about paperwork and Medicaid claims you've not brought up a single shred of real evidence. I have to say, gentlemen, no judge is going to buy this.'

'Mr Warren.' Agent Fitzhugh's jaw twitched as he tried to make eye contact. 'Are you aware that over three hundred of the residents at your facility, Nillewaug Village, receive Medicaid long-term-care benefits? Which, considering they're not in long-term care, and judging by the cost of their units – unlikely to be eligible for Medicaid at all – is fraud, thousands of counts of it.'

Jim kept his expression blank, sizing up the two agents, both in their thirties. One white, Agent Fitzhugh; one black, Agent Connor. They reminded him of chess pieces, someone's pawns, nothing higher in value. Not like him. *They think they can capture the king . . . we'll see how long that lasts.* Since his arrest early Sunday his only words: 'I'm not saying anything until my attorney gets here.' What sort of idiots did they take him for, and their feeble attempts to intimidate him into self-incrimination? Yes, of course he knew all about the numbers and it was four hundred and twenty-seven on the Medicaid rolls. And no, he'd not be sharing that with this pair of morons. *Of course the real issue, that bitch; it had to have been her. Fuck you, Delia!* He looked up at his attorney. Windham leaned his head close. Jim whispered. 'They don't have a fucking thing. My name's not on anything. I signed nothing. Get me out of here!'

'Gentlemen, I appreciate the gravity of the situation and what you erroneously believe my client was involved in. But . . . unless you have any real evidence, I insist you release Attorney Warren and we forget this entire unfortunate incident. If there were any billing irregularities at Nillewaug – as you allege – it's not anything my client would have had knowledge of.'

'How is it, Mr Warren,' Fitzhugh persisted, his broad face showing signs of strain, his lips tight, 'that so many wealthy people, people who paid hundreds of thousands of dollars for the amenities at your facility, were on the Medicaid rolls?'

Jim looked up, a half smile on his lips. 'As I said before. I don't know.'

Attorney Windham looked at the digital camera that had been recording the interrogation and sighed. 'Agent Fitzhugh, Agent Connor, with all due respect that is the seventh or eighth time you've asked the same question. My client has answered that he does not know how any of the residents at Nillewaug were on Medicaid, and you have brought forward nothing to refute that. Unless you have any real evidence, you need to release my client, or I will be forced to bring a wrongful imprisonment suit.'

Agent Connor, who'd been silent for the past hour, looked over his shoulder at the dark mirrored surface behind him. He shook his head, and, turning back to Warren and his attorney, began to speak: 'You are aware of the fire at Nillewaug early yesterday morning?'

Jim glanced at his attorney. *But really,* he thought, sensing a shift in the wind, *now they're going fishing.* 'Yes.'

'I believe,' Agent Connor continued, 'there are five confirmed dead, and quite a few more who remain unaccounted for.'

Jim said nothing, his thoughts skittering back to his early morning arrest, clearly they'd been waiting for him . . . had him under surveillance. *How long had they been there? Had they been there Saturday night? Say nothing, let them show their hand. All her fault. You bitch!*

'Your point, Agent Connor?' Windham broke in. 'Yes, we're all aware of the tragedy at Nillewaug. And if you weren't holding my client he'd be able to assist in helping those poor displaced elderly.'

Agent Fitzhugh appeared at his breaking point. 'By flying to Grand Cayman?'

His colleague shot him a warning look, and then added, looking first at Warren and then his attorney, 'I think the judge will be interested in that detail, as well. Might consider Attorney Warren a flight risk.'

'And what possible difference will that make,' Windham replied, 'when it comes on top of your flimsy, unsubstantiated and totally erroneous allegations?'

Agent Connor's dark eyes revealing nothing. He looked straight at Jim Warren. 'When were you last at Nillewaug Village?'

Jim met the agent's gaze, the one question spinning through his mind – *how long had they been following me?* 'I don't remember.'

'I see,' Connor said, his tone free of emotion. 'More than a week ago?'

'Possibly.'

Agent Connor leaned on the table, his eyes fixed on Warren. 'Possibly. Hmmm. Possibly less than a week?'

'Yes.'

'What about Saturday night?' Connor asked.

Jim gave his attorney a worried look. *They know!* And for the first time since his arrest over twenty-four hours ago, Jim Warren felt fear. *You bitch! Delia, you fucking bitch! Was her office bugged? She sure as hell wasn't wearing a wire.*

Agent Connor placed a form sealed inside a plastic evidence bag on the table in front of Warren. 'Do you recognize this?'

'No.'

Connor shook his head slightly. 'Look at it more carefully, Mr Warren. You can pick it up if you'd like.'

'I told you I don't know what it is.'

'Really?' Fitzhugh's tone was skeptical. 'It's a Medicaid treatment plan for Betty Grasso. Please, look at it carefully.'

Warren looked at his attorney, who nodded slightly.

'Fine.' Warren picked up the document. 'So?'

'Look at the signature, and please read the names.'

Attorney Windham interjected. 'What is the point of this?'

'The point,' Agent Connor said, nearing the end of his patience, 'is this is a treatment plan that generated payment for nursing-home services for an individual at Nillewaug, who was not in a nursing-home level of care. And that's just to start. I need your client to read the names of the people who signed this form. After that, there will be a series of questions about those two individuals. Regardless of your objections, the questions will be asked and answered. The amount of time it takes is entirely up to the two of you.'

Mattie and Jamie watched the interrogation of Jim Warren from behind the two-way glass.

'They can't really let him go?' Jamie asked, intent on the scene before them.

'They might have to,' came Mattie's reply. They'd had only a few minutes to speak with the agents prior to the interrogation in the small observation room. Fitzhugh and Connor had admitted they'd not wanted to bring Warren in yet, didn't have enough to make what they believed were millions, possibly tens of millions of dollars worth of fraud allegations stick. But the attorney's run to the airport had forced their hand, and quite possibly blown the case. For the past week he'd been under surveillance. The Nillewaug scheme, which she still didn't fully understand, had been tipped anonymously by a female caller through the Medicare and Medicaid fraud-abuse hotline. What was now abundantly clear, and possibly a motive for murder, was that a very frightened Delia Preston – 'scared shitless' according to Fitzhugh – was in the process of trying to save herself and hand over Jim Warren.

'These investigations usually take months, sometimes more than a year to unravel,' Connor had explained. 'It's all about tracing the money, and figuring out was this the result of stupidity and ignorance – people who just didn't know the rules – or was this a deliberate attempt to bilk the system. But this . . . we've never seen anything quite so calculated. And if the tip hadn't come in, it could have gone on indefinitely.'

'I don't get it,' Mattie had said. 'If so much money is being falsely billed, how could it go unnoticed?'

'Easy.' Fitzhugh had said. 'Whoever's behind this did their homework and knows the system. To start you have to understand that the Medicare and Medicaid programs are massive with hundreds of billions of dollars disbursed annually, most of it for necessary medical services. Most billing irregularities get flagged electronically, whenever something goes above or below a predetermined value.'

'You lost me,' Jamie had said. And Mattie had been grateful as she was on the verge of losing the train herself.

'Cut-off points.' Fitzhugh had explained. 'If you're one of the top billers for a particular service, a cursory review is automatically triggered. If there's even a hint of impropriety, the Office of the Inspector General begins an investigation. If in the course of that investigation it appears that something was being done deliberately it gets shifted to Department of Justice and that's where we come in. The Nillewaug scam is unlike anything we've seen, and certainly never on this scale.'

Connor had then explained: 'From the time this facility was created someone had this in mind. From the three cases we've started in on it boils down to this, although there seem some variations throughout. Essentially someone buys into Nillewaug at considerable cost, and pays a monthly fee. These are people of means – not impoverished Medicaid recipients.'

'I thought all old people get Medicaid,' Jamie interjected.

Mattie shot her a look. 'No, that's Medicare. Medicaid is for the poor.'

'Yes,' Fitzhugh said, and to Jamie: 'Most people don't know the difference, until they actually try to access one of the programs. But with Nillewaug the Medicaid benefit they were billing was for nursing-home care. You can only be eligible for it if you fall below the poverty line for at least three years. Which, considering the buy-in for an apartment at Nillewaug is a quarter million on up, and then you have monthly fees of about three grand . . .'

For Mattie this was familiar territory. Her own mother, with early Alzheimer's and advanced diabetes, had been in a nursing home outside of Bridgeport for the past three years. And yes, Medicaid picked up the tab for her mother whose only remaining material asset was a modest burial plan. 'How could they possibly qualify for Medicaid?' she asked. 'Anybody who can afford a quarter million dollars is way too wealthy.'

'Yes,' Connor said, 'but in the cases we've started to drill down through what appears to happen is at the point someone enters Nillewaug they begin a financial reconfiguring. Essentially, they are stripped of any recordable asset, through a combination of divestment and trusts. And five years after their balance sheet dips below the critical mark, an application is filed with Medicaid. So not only does Nillewaug rake in on the front end, by selling expensive units that aren't really owned by the tenant, they receive their monthly fees through very clever end-of-life estate planning. On paper the resident has nothing, but their families are still paying the monthly fees. And after five years Nillewaug then begins double-billing the government for those same fees.'

'But,' Mattie said, recalling a long-ago conversation with Preston, 'Nillewaug is an assisted-care facility, only a small portion is a nursing home.'

'Yes and no, and that's part of the beauty of this scam,' Connor had said. 'When licenses were filed with the state, the entire facility was given nursing home designation. So while in fact maybe one hundred beds are truly nursing home, all seven hundred residents could theoretically be counted – and billed – as extended care. Now, nationwide the average nursing home will have between seventy-five and ninety percent of their patients on Medicaid. It's by far the number-one payment source for that level of care. Nillewaug, as a licensed nursing home with seven hundred beds is staying way below those percentages.'

'And never triggered an audit,' Mattie had said, following the logic.

'Clever, huh?' Connor had said, just as Jim Warren was being led into the interrogation room.

Now, watching through the glass, pieces of heretofore random information clicked for Mattie. And with it her anxiety ratcheted up. Connor and Fitzhugh had pretty much admitted their hand was too weak to hold Warren on the fraud charges; they needed more time to trace the money. Warren's attorney knew this, and had his client on a tight leash. And now her gaze was riveted on the scene unfolding before her. Agent Connor was holding up a black leather gym bag wrapped in a see-through evidence bag. He raised it and then placed it on the table in front of Warren. He proceeded to put on a pair of disposable gloves. 'Do you recognize this bag, Mr Warren?' he said as he unzipped it, revealing a change of clothing, each piece in its own evidence bag.

Jim Warren seemed frozen in his metal chair. His eyes fixed on the items as they emerged.

'Mr Warren?'

'We observed and filmed you depositing it and its contents early yesterday morning into a donations bin, before proceeding to the airport.'

'So?' Warren said, his eyes darting to his attorney and then back to the agent. 'So what, I'm giving clothes to charity?'

'Yes,' Connor said, 'the very clothes we filmed you in on Saturday night when you "probably" visited Nillewaug Village at eight oh-two p.m. . . . What were you doing there, Mr Warren?'

Jim looked to his attorney, and shook his head.

'My client has answered all he intends to. I suggest we leave things in the judge's hands at his arraignment this afternoon. But, gentlemen, based on what's been presented so far, unless you pull a rabbit, Mr Warren will not be with you much longer.'

Mattie pulled out her cell and punched in the number Fitzhugh had given her. She sensed the two agents' frustration as they glared across at Warren and his slick attorney. Through the speakers she heard the phone ring and Fitzhugh pulled out his cell. 'Yes?'

'The M.E. said Preston had had sex within hours of her murder. Maybe that's why he was there.' And then, thinking it through further: 'And that's why he wanted to ditch the clothes. He knew she was dead. He's scared of what physical evidence we'll find on his clothes.'

Fitzhugh nodded slightly and put his phone away. 'Earlier,' he said to Warren, 'you said that your only knowledge of Delia Preston was as an employee of Nillewaug. Is that accurate?'

'Yes,' Warren answered, his eyes narrowed.

'And you hired her when the facility first opened?'

'Yes.'

'So she'd be your employee.'

'Yes.'

Attorney Windham interjected, 'I don't see the point of this. We've already discussed Mr Warren's employer/employee relationship with Ms Preston.'

Keeping his gaze fixed on Jim Warren, Fitzhugh didn't even acknowledge the attorney. 'Do you sleep with all your subordinates, Mr Warren, or just Ms Preston?'

'Oh my God,' Jamie blurted, her eyes riveted on Warren's face.

Mattie held her breath.

'Don't answer,' Attorney Windham quickly warned.

'Why not?' Fitzhugh's expression blank. 'Here, let me make it simpler. Were you having a sexual relationship with Delia Preston?'

Silence filled the room.

Fitzhugh persisted: 'A yes or no, Mr Warren.'

Jim Warren turned to his attorney.

'Don't answer, Jim.'

'I see,' Fitzhugh said, looking at his partner, and then at Warren. 'Will you answer the question, Mr Warren?'

'No.'

'For the record,' Fitzhugh said, with a slightly theatrical flare, 'Mr Warren has refused to answer the question as to whether or not he was having a sexual relationship with Delia Preston, the administrative director of Nillewaug Village and one of the two signers on Betty Grasso's treatment plan.'

From behind the mirror Jamie turned to Mattie. 'He was sleeping with her?'

'Appears that way,' she said.

'Betty Grasso is the woman who died up on the roof,' Jamie added. 'Don't you think it's strange that it's her treatment plan? Was that deliberate?'

'I don't know. But it's an excellent pick up. What I do know –' watching and listening as Fitzhugh and Connor continued to question the tight-lipped Warren – 'they don't have enough to hold him.' She empathized with the two agents' frustration, a major case being carefully built and now possibly destroyed by prematurely bringing in their major suspect. All hopes of catching Jim Warren with a smoking gun evaporated as the man lawyered up and clammed up.

'They're going to let him walk?' Jamie was incredulous.

'Yes,' Mattie said, realizing several things. 'At least for now. They'll keep a close eye on him. He's obviously guilty of something. But is it just millions of dollars of fraud, or a few homicides as well?'

'And because of the federal fraud piece, this whole thing will be a federal case?'

'Yes, if in fact the murders have any connection to the fraud,' Mattie said. And realizing Fitzhugh and Connor would get nothing further from Warren and that it would be only a matter of hours before Warren was released, she added: 'We need to get back, and we have to work fast.'

'What are you thinking?' Jamie asked.

'I'm thinking maybe we can find something that will make a charge stick. We've got possible motive for murder – Preston implicating him in fraud, maybe blackmailing him. We have him at the scene of the murder, and know he was trying to leave the country. What we don't have is a witness or physical evidence.'

'The clothes in the bag?'

'Possibly, obviously he's worried about them.'

'You think he killed her and set the fire to try and cover up the fraud?'

'I don't know. But if he didn't, I bet he knows who did.'

NINE

Kyle Sullivan stared out the window of the charge nurse's office on the euphemistically named Safe Harbor Pavilion, the fifty-bed Alzheimer's unit where he'd been working when the fire began. His view was of deep woods and a brook swollen with snow melt and spring rains. He sighed and turned back to the computer screen where he'd been flipping between spreadsheets of the facility's residents as he tried to account for everyone.

His cell rang . . . again. He was beyond tired, operating on adrenalin and caffeine. Everything a blur, from the horrors of Sunday morning, to the realization that no one was in charge. *And how did this fall to me?* And that was the story of his life; he was the responsible one. *It's what you do, Kyle, so deal.* But worse than the responsibility was the guilt that twisted inside . . . *Why didn't I smell smoke? How did it get so big?* Realizing it had to do with how the building that housed the fifty dementia patients was sited to take advantage of the beautiful scenery in the wetlands behind Nillewaug. *This wasn't your fault.* And that horrible feeling when he'd heard the first fire truck, gone outside and seen . . . His immediate thought, *Grandma Alice!* He clicked on his cell, noting he'd need to recharge it, while a part of him wondered what would happen if he just let it go dead. He looked at the caller ID. 'Oh crap! . . . Hello?'

'Kyle?'

'Hi, Lil, is something wrong? Is my grandmother OK?'

'She's fine, you asked for us to check in.'

'Right.' Picturing the taller of the two women who'd graciously agreed to look after Grandma Alice. It had been the one blessing in this nightmare.

'Are you at Nillewaug now?' she asked.

'Yes.'

'Have you been home at all? Have you gotten any sleep.'

'I can't.' He glanced at the clock, a little after noon.

'The body has limits,' Lil said, reminding him of Grandma Alice in her younger, clearer days. 'But everything's fine here. And Ada wanted to thank you for helping get her mother out of that place.'

'Rose is a hoot, and I'll get my grandmother settled as soon as I can.'

'Not a problem,' Lil said, 'it really isn't. We have ample space and having someone to look after is good for Rose. So please don't worry about your grandmother, we've got things handled. Kyle?'

'Yes?'

'I'm going to ask you a favor, but you need to know you don't have to do it, and if you say no, it's totally fine.'

'Sure, if I can help.'

'You may not want to . . . I did a piece on the fire for the Brattlebury Register. It's on the front page of the morning paper. Would you mind if I asked you some questions?'

'For the paper?' he said, thinking of just how many reporters had tried to get through to him, and were hounding the other nurses and aides. Still, she was taking care of Grandma Alice . . . 'Shoot, but if I want something off the record . . .'

'Absolutely. Thanks so much. You mentioned last night that a number of the residents still hadn't been accounted for. Do you have a number?'

He stared at the computer in front of him, and toggled to the spread sheet that listed all the Nillewaug residents, their vital information and contacts. 'I've got it down to thirty-eight.'

'Any chance you can get me the names?'

'Sorry, I think that would get me in trouble with the HIPAA police.' Referencing laws around patient confidentiality.

'Right.'

'But you know,' he offered, 'the cops have the names, they could probably release them. It might actually help in tracking folks down. Because I think what happened – at least this is what I'm hoping – is some families came and got people directly off the grounds. Kind of like what you did with Rose and Alice. There was so much confusion. I've been calling hospitals as far off as Hartford and New Haven, and still . . . thirty-eight unaccounted for.'

'That's a lot.'

Over the line he heard the click of a keyboard. *Well*, he thought, *this is news, better she get the story*. A part of him, what his savvy twin sister, Kelly, called the smart part, wondered if getting the story might have been part of the motivator for this total stranger to magnanimously agree to take in Grandma Alice. The thought made him feel ashamed. He loved his sister dearly, but her cynicism . . . It worked for her, he supposed, but to go around constantly thinking the worst of people? Not for him. There was too much good in this world to focus on the negative. 'I'm hoping by the end

of the day everyone is accounted for. I don't know if that's
realistic, but it's what we're shooting for.'

'I hope you're right,' Lil said. 'I can't imagine what those
families must be going through. Hopefully it's what you said,
and relatives took them directly from Nillewaug. Kyle, earlier
you said there was no one in charge. I understand it would
have been Ms Preston, and that the assistant director is out of
town. You said she's on her honeymoon.'

'She's the director of nursing and the person I report to . . .'
His voice trailed into silence.

'Kyle?'

'Damn.' He realized how exhausted he was, his eyes burned
from a combination of smoke, pollen, ash and lack of sleep.
*Should you really be talking to a reporter? But then again,
she's taking care of Grandma Alice, this total stranger is
taking care of someone you love, it's OK. Just be careful.
You still need a job.* A hollow pit in his belly, knowing he
had so much work to do, but with the central Nillewaug
complex uninhabitable – *you may not have a job.* Followed
by a more painful realization, and one he'd been trying to
ignore since the fire: *Grandma Alice, after all this work, has
lost her home. What am I going to do? What am I going to
do with Alice?*

'Kyle? What's wrong?'

'Where to start?' Throughout his life he'd had the unswerving
belief that in even the most dire situation something positive
can be found. But, so far, that silver lining had been elusive.
'Can I go off the record?'

'Of course.'

'Please, I don't really know you, but if you use my name
here . . . I just don't know. Although, I wonder if any of us
will have jobs. But I did get through to her.'

'To who?'

'Kayla Atwood, my boss. I'd texted her a bunch of times,
and she finally called back.'

'And?'

'And she told me that based on what had happened, and
that she'd just learned she was pregnant, she was giving notice.
She has no intention of coming back to Nillewaug.' He again

heard clicking. 'Please don't use my name, but there's no one steering this ship.'

'It sounds like you are,' she offered. 'OK, I'm on the Nillewaug website and I'm looking at the contact page. I see Delia and this Kayla person, and a director of Human Resources – Frank Stillman – under the tab for positions.'

'Frank's here, I saw him a while ago.'

'Seems like he'd be next in command,' she offered.

'Yeah, seems like, and again this has to be off the record. He's dealing with over two hundred employees who are all trying to figure out if they have jobs. He told me that with Kayla not here, I needed to take care of anything related to the residents. Mostly I think he's just scared. We all are.'

'What about upper management? Isn't there some kind of disaster plan?'

'Good questions. Yes, there is a disaster plan, which I'm trying to follow. But most of it is built around having an intact – or at least functioning – executive team. And right now we've got a CEO – Jim Warren – who hasn't shown his face, a CFO – Wally Doyle – who was here during the fire, but I haven't seen since. A nursing director who's sunning in Aruba . . .' He felt panic surge. *This is not helping.* 'Lil, I don't mean to be rude. But I've got to keep plowing through this phone stuff, and the other lines are buzzing.'

'Is there anything I can do to help?' she asked.

'You're doing it,' he said, and a wave of relief swept over him – *this is the silver lining.* 'I love my grandmother more than anyone in this world. Knowing she's safe makes all this other stuff manageable.' Emotion choked his throat. He bit the inside of his lip to regain control. 'But . . . you know if you do the story, you might want to touch base with the Red Cross. They've been a huge help, and I think if people want to donate or get clothing to residents, they're the ones to contact. Talk to them, see what they need, and make sure that's in your story.'

With her fingers on the keyboard and the phone on speaker, Lil heard the fatigue in Kyle's voice. *Get some sleep*, she thought, picturing the handsome nurse, with his soulful eyes,

who was so obviously devoted to Alice. 'Kyle, if at any point
– and please take this seriously – you want to crash here and
get a hot meal, we've got plenty of room. Even if you just
got a few hours of sleep.'

'Lil, I might take you up on that. But I have to get back to
work.'

She thanked him and hung up. Lil stared out her open
office window, bird chatter and the soft hum of the computer
the only sounds. Her thoughts on Kyle, and the Herculean
task of trying to account for each of the seven hundred
Nillewaug residents. This was so clearly not his job, not
anyone's really. And yet, in the midst of this awful disaster,
something which at the end of the day might well turn out
to be arson, here was Kyle showing humanity's other face,
the better face. No fanfare, no self-promotion, just one person
doing everything possible to help. Batting back a tear, she
began to write. It started with a couple of quick paragraphs,
inserting the bits she'd gleaned from Kyle – 'Thirty-eight
residents still unaccounted for . . . Kayla Atwood, Director
of Nursing, out of the country and unavailable for comment
. . . over two hundred Nillewaug employees uncertain about
their jobs'. And then she tracked down numbers for Jim
Warren, Nillewaug's CEO, and Wallace Doyle, the CFO.
Both men she knew. Actually, anyone who'd been in
Grenville long enough knew them, or at least knew of them,
two of the three Ravens of the Apocalypse – the small town
hyperbole for the high school students who'd led the town
to not one, but two state football championships over thirty
years ago. Back then, Lil was a new wife and new mother.
She let her thoughts drift – *you were pregnant, it must have
been with Tina* – strong memories of cool Saturday morn-
ings in the bleachers with Bradley. Like everyone else in
Grenville it was exciting, and the topic of tremendous conversation and speculation. People who knew nothing about
football, and she was one of them, were suddenly analyzing
plays, critiquing Coach Scott Monroe's training techniques,
and turning out for the Saturday games to the point that
additional bleachers had to be added. Those two seasons
had sparked a giddy hometown pride, with flags appearing

on every lamp post the day before a game, and banners strewn across the greens in Town Plot with encouraging words for 'our boys', or else urging residents to donate for better uniforms, or a new, and very expensive scoreboard and night lights. It was a bubble of enthusiasm and they all got caught up in it. At the center of it all were three gifted high school athletes – Jim 'Jimbo' Warren, Dennis Trask and Wally Doyle. It was like an unexpected gift. Something you never knew you wanted, but once you had it didn't know how you ever did without it. Something mesmerizing and so exciting about huddling up in the bleachers, wool blankets on their laps in the crisp snap of fall, Thermoses of coffee, or something stronger. The feeling of camaraderie among neighbors never stronger. But it was the game itself and those three boys. Jim's sure arm, Wally with his hulking grace protecting his quarterback as he searched for his opening. And Dennis sprinting downfield, not slowing as the missile found his sure hands. It was heart-in-your-throat exciting and ephemeral. Their senior year, when they won their second championship, was the last time Grenville made it to anything past Regionals. She knew it at the time, and maybe that's what was so special, the three Ravens of the Apocalypse were lightening in a bottle. And here, decades later, their names connected to Grenville's biggest tragedy. Caught by this strange symmetry she dialed Jim Warren's law office. A secretary picked up: 'Mr Warren is not in . . . can I take a message?' From there, on to Wally Doyle and another secretary: 'Mr Doyle is not in today, may I take a message?'

No you may not, she thought, hanging up, and wondering why neither man was at work on a Monday. Lil knew that if she wanted to have another serious story run, she'd need an interview with one or both of them. And time was running short. Not certain of the protocol, but certain she was stepping on somebody's toes, she called Edward Fleming. She waited, listening to a jazzy rendition of The Carpenters's 'Close to You', and then the editor-in-chief picked up. 'Good piece, Lil. What can I do for you?'

His words were clipped, and clear. He was a busy man, and

his every second mattered. But the compliment couldn't have been clearer. *He liked it . . . of course he did, he wouldn't have run it if he didn't.* Trying to match his efficiency of speech: 'Mr Fleming I want to do a follow-up piece on the fire.'

'Lil, this isn't your beat.'

Not realizing she had a beat, unless that's what the fluffy antique columns were, she persisted. 'I've got inside information.' She felt a pressure build, and had to restrain herself from rambling about how two of the residents were living with her, how she'd spoken with the nurse who appeared to be in charge and also was friends with a detective involved in the case.

'No promises,' he said. 'But get me one thousand to twelve-hundred words no later than two p.m.; if it's good and if it's important, I'll run it. And by the way, we've gotten numerous requests from other news services for your photographs. You'll be making some extra money off of those, not to mention the photo credit.' And without saying goodbye, he hung up.

'Lil?' Ada's voice from the front door.

'What's up?' She got up from the computer, while thinking through strategies to track down the ex-Ravens. She had less than two hours to get the story, write it up and send it in – *not much time.*

Ada was standing outside, holding the screen open. Behind her she could see Rose and Alice, both in long-sleeve shirts and sweat pants that they'd pieced together from their wardrobes. Alice had on her bedroom slippers and Rose had a pair of Ada's walking shoes.

'We're going out,' Ada said. 'Do you need anything?'

Lil felt a pang of guilt. 'Are you taking a cab?'

'No, Aaron offered to stay home from school.' She gave a wry smile. 'So considerate.'

'He is.' Lil laughed.

'We're taking his car. Figured we'd hit the post office and track down their mail, then off to Costco and get some clothes and groceries – they have nothing.' Conscious of the two women behind her, she whispered. 'Did you find out when and if they're going to be allowed to go into their apartments?'

'No, but I'm sure Kyle will know. But from the sounds of things it's not going to be today. You sure you don't want me to come?' Feeling horribly torn. *You're not really a reporter, Lil, what are you thinking? Your duty is to them; family always comes first.* 'My car's bigger,' she added, thinking of Aaron's partially restored and much-beloved 1968 Mercedes diesel.

'You got your column done?' Sounding like she was asking Aaron if he'd finished his homework.

'Yes, emailed in, and no word back from my editor, so I think it's good to go.'

'And now you're doing another piece on the fire?'

'Yes.'

She smiled.

'What?' Lil asked, unable to read her expression.

'Lil, I'm so proud of you. But if you want this story you're going to have to fight for it. It's national news, you need to stay here and figure out how your story is the one Edward Fleming will run.'

'You're sure?' Wondering if she'd somehow eavesdropped on the conversation with Mr Fleming. And realizing once again just how prescient she was.

'Yes, plus you know how I love Costco.'

'I do,' she said, wondering exactly how much stuff from the buy-in-bulk store she'd be able to cram into Aaron's trunk.

Ada glanced over her shoulders at Rose. 'Mom, I'll be with you in two seconds,' she said, and she closed the door behind.

'What?'

Ada wrapped her arms around Lil's waist.

Their lips met, and conscious of the closed door and her mother on the other side, there was a hurried excitement in their embrace. Ada giggled.

'I know,' Lil said, looking into her eyes and feeling the thrill of their still-young relationship. 'What if our parents find out?'

'I think she suspects,' Ada said.

'Are you going to tell her?'

'I don't know. I do know that I don't like this sneaking around, although . . .'

Lil felt Ada's fingers tickle her in a particularly sensitive spot at the bottom of her ribs. 'Stop that,' she gasped.

She reached up on her toes and they kissed. 'It is exciting.' And letting go she headed down the hall toward the front door.

Lil followed her out, savoring the feel of Ada's lips. She waved at Rose and Alice, as Aaron shouted up from the base of the goat path, 'You guys coming, or what?'

She watched as Rose took Alice's hand. The redhead looked back at Lil standing in the door and then at Ada who was heading toward the car. 'Which one's the boy?' she asked loudly, and then added: 'Are we going home?'

Stunned, Lil followed their progress to the waiting car. After years of caring for her mother, June, as she'd descended into Alzheimer's, Lil was used to strange moments of clarity and weird utterances. *But what the hell was that?*

They drove off, and Lil knew that she had to kick her ass into gear if she had a prayer of getting another piece into *The Register*. Ada was right, this was a massive story, and she'd gotten lucky – right place at the right time. Now it was a matter of making her own luck. Thus far neither Jim Warren nor Wally Doyle – at least that she was aware of – had commented on the fire. This was the angle she needed. She knew them both, knew where they lived – the ultra high-end Eagle's Cairn development. Grabbing her keys, she threw on a favorite navy blazer with patch pockets that kind of went with her jeans and sweats. At the door she hoisted her brown leather satchel, checking to make sure she had the camera, extra batteries, cell and paper and pen; and thinking of Fleming's words – *'If it's good and if it's important . . .'* – felt the clock ticking.

TEN

Wally Doyle had never felt such fear and desperation as he listened to Dennis's words through his cell. He stared dull-eyed through the second-floor windows of the guest/cabana house behind the pool. His thoughts oblivious to the budding spring woods.

'Dennis, don't, please. There's got to be a way.' His hand to his ear, the small prepaid phone mashed to the meaty side of his buzz-cut head. Tears streamed down his corpulent face, his eyes squeezing into red-rimmed slits.

'You'll come up with something. You always do.' His thoughts on his best bud. Dennis, the red-headed wild boy who'd picked him out of playground obscurity in first grade. Him, the fat kid – Wally the Walrus – and took him under his wing. And from day one: 'It's you and me, Wally . . . And don't you take nothing from no one.' His status as an object of scorn and taunts, shifting 180 degrees to where kids trembled at his approach, and readily handed over anything of interest in their lunch bags. *What kind of cookies are those?* Dennis would ask an intended victim, his chuckled answer always the same: '*Ours.*' They were a feared duo that not even the toughest kids would challenge. Wally cornering some scared nerd, his bulk making escape impossible, while Dennis danced around their face with lightening punches and a steady stream of taunts: '*Cry baby, pussy, faggot.*' Their pact revised a single time in Junior High when the Warrens moved to town, and their twosome became a threesome with the addition of slick Jimbo. And from there . . . local history took root. Playground bullying was fun, and, while none of them realized consciously what they were doing, they had a single goal: to be the best in everything, to dominate and annihilate any competition. 'You got to be first,' Jimbo would say.

To which Dennis would add: 'Second's just another word for

loser.' And while Wally could never keep up with his best buds academically, he made up for it with dogged determination on the playing fields. And it was there, in the peewee league of Pop Warner football that the three Ravens of the Apocalypse began their steady climb to small-town royalty, untouchable . . . until now.

'It's all gone to shit, Wally,' Dennis said, emotion choking the words. 'The cops picked up Jim a couple hours ago. And they've had a car outside your place, they're watching everything you do. They know everything. Just waiting till they have all their ducks in a row and then . . . bam bam bam.' He snorted. 'Three dead ravens. Shit!'

'He's too smart for them, Dennis,' said Wally. 'They're not going to find anything.' Never having heard this defeated tone in Dennis's voice. It had him freaked, even more than the two dark-suited men in the unmarked car now parked behind a forsythia hedge at the end of the drive. He'd first seen them when he'd left Nillewaug after the fire. At first not thinking much about the dark car behind him, but his nerves already wired from what he'd seen and what he'd done, making him hyper vigilant. *They're not following you,* he'd thought, glancing in the rear-view mirror. Then another turn, and another and they were still there. He'd even made a couple false turns, and they'd vanished. He'd told himself to chill, but as he'd pulled into Eagle's Cairn there they were again – *so screwed, did they see you do it? Do they know?*

'Wally, it's done.'

The silence scared him. 'Dennis? You're wrong. Everything's tighter than a virgin's pussy.' But as he spoke, Wally felt an agonizing doubt – *you're screwed.* And it wasn't just the bad thing he'd done at Nillewaug in the early a.m. of Sunday morning . . . it ran deeper. When the accounts would be examined for his Nillewaug clients, patterns of practice would emerge that might be construed as concealing funds. It was for the most part legal, but taken in total it would be considered fraud, as he'd learned at a recent symposium on estate planning. '*It's not the action, but the intention,*' the speaker had explained. And, as often happened, Wally got lost in the nuance. To him it was simple good-sense business, old people with money needed to get rid of that money before they died. *'They can't take it with them'* was one of his go-to expressions as he'd lay out strategies to eager sons and daughters of potential Nillewaug residents. *'There's no reason to wait for them to die to begin benefiting from resources they want you to have anyway . . . yes, very legal, and a number of ways to proceed.'* And for the most part he provided sound advice that saved families from watching fortunes get torpedoed by ruinous inheritance laws. Which of course led to the second big problem on his list, he should never have steered Nillewaug residents to his financial consulting practice. As the CFO of Nillewaug that was a conflict of interest, which no seminar on corporate compliance needed to point out. But there, as with so much over the course of his fifty-two years, he'd let Dennis and Jimbo talk him into something questionable. *'Way too much money to leave on the table,'* Jimbo had argued. *'Nillewaug is all about taking the worry out of getting old. And let's face it, a lot of that worry has to do with money. "Will I have enough?" "Will my children be taken care of?" What we're doing is helping people. And yes, if we profit by it, there's nothing wrong with that. It's doing well by doing good.'*

'I'm sorry I ever got you into this,' Dennis said.

'I'm not.' Wally sobbed, a tear landing on the remains of a mountainous platter of chili cheese nachos he'd devoured waiting for this call. Bits of sour cream, salsa and guacamole clung to the corners of his mouth, and three small spatters of bean dip had landed on his tautly stretched powder-blue polo shirt. 'You'll think of something,' was all he could say. 'We've been in worse messes.' Trying not to let Dennis hear his sobs as images of scary good times flew past. The sick-in-the-gut feeling of being pulled over by the cops in high school, the car reeking of pot, open bottles of beer and a nearly empty quart of whiskey stashed under the seat. A flashlight through the window: *'Have you boys been drinking?'*

Dennis in the driver's seat, smashed to the gills, his words slurred. *'No, Officer, not a drop.'*

But it was Grenville and they were the three Ravens. '*Just keep it to the speed limit boys, and get your butts home . . .*'

'*Yes, Officer.*'

'Not like this,' Dennis said. 'And no one gives a shit any more that we were the three Ravens; that tit ran dry years ago. Wally, people died in that fire . . . my dad is gone.' Dennis was crying. 'And they're going to try and pin that on us. Even without that, we're talking hard time. They'll take each case and multiply it out. I can't go back to prison. I won't. And I'm telling you, *you* won't last. You can't imagine what it's like in that place. The things they're going to do to you.'

'Maybe we could just hide someplace,' Wally said, knowing it was a stupid idea, but something calming about the thought of the two of them going off, someplace warm. 'Maybe Mexico.'

'They're watching us. We wouldn't make it past Hartford. I'm sorry, Wally. You know I love you. You do what you think's right, but I'm done. I think for Jen and the kids' sake you know what you have to do. But I'm out of here. I just wanted to call and . . . say goodbye. I love you.'

'Dennis . . .' Searching for anything to keep him talking, not to do this thing. But nothing came. He stared dully ahead, his tongue flicking at a peppery chunk of salsa caught between molars. 'Dennis . . . don't, please . . .' His fist clutched the phone as he heard the gun shot. 'No! Dennis . . . Dennis?' Frozen, he listened. 'NO! Dennis . . .' He looked down at the smeared platter with blobs of green, white and red, and then at his own dim reflection in the windows across from him. He was so fat, he'd stopped weighing himself when he'd passed three hundred and fifty pounds and the bathroom scale had maxed out. At one point, it had been muscle, like a refrigerator in motion, mowing down anything that got in the way. 'Wally the Walrus.' His beefy hand dropped the cell on to his desk. *Dennis* . . . an awful pain, like a hole ripped in his chest. Jimbo had been arrested and Dennis, beautiful Dennis with his red hair flopping over his eyes and that funny gap-toothed smile, which got especially big whenever he was talking him into something bad: '*Go on Wally, stick it in her.*' Dennis was gone. And there were men parked outside his house in a Ford with dark windows. Almost like they didn't care that he knew they were on to him. *Dennis . . .* unable to imagine life without him. That would be a life not worth living.

He freed the clinging tomato bit and swallowed. The fear, which had seemed overwhelming just moments ago was gone. He fished his keys out of his pant pocket, flicked through them and selected the little one for his bottom drawer. Sliding it open he looked at the loaded Colt. Dennis was right; there was no other way. He could survive prison, but life without Dennis . . . He lifted the pistol, feeling its heft in his hand. He looked across at the windows and watched his reflection raise the gun and put the barrel under his chin. Using his left hand to hold it steady, and checking in the window to make sure it was pointed up and toward the back of his head, he took a deep breath and as he let it out, he squeezed.

ELEVEN

Lil's eight-minute drive from Pilgrim's Progress to the Eagle's Cairn development ended with a question: 'Whose door do I knock on first?' Which was answered by the heart-skipping sound of a gunshot from the direction of the Doyles' imposing three-story Tudor revival. Her thoughts raised as she tried to locate the source of the shot: *the woods behind the house. What the hell?* And she was out of the car and running on the spongy spring grass, her leather satchel bouncing heavily against her back. *Maybe hunters,* she thought, *but it's too early and no one should be hunting this close to houses.* Her ears rang and her head, still tender from last night's whiskey, throbbed with each footfall. She tried to judge how far back in the woods it had come from. Not slowing, she spotted two men, one paunchy and fiftyish, the other trim, both in suits and ties racing across the lawn to her right. As they passed, the younger caught sight of her. 'You shouldn't be here.' He didn't break stride. His pumping arms affording Lil the glimpse of a holster. His warning did not deter her, as she rounded the brick house with its dozens of mullioned windows and half-timbered accents. *Obviously cops,* she thought as the younger man violently kicked the hinges off a six-foot-high wood gate that led into the pool area.

She hung back as the two men drew their weapons. Beyond the broken gate was a still-covered pool, expansive decks and a two-story smaller brick structure that matched the main house. It was a charming courtyard; the pool house with its mullioned windows and herringbone brickwork was like some fairy-tale cottage. Lil pulled out her camera and, keeping to the side of the open gate, sidled through. Looking at the LED, she snapped shots of the courtyard, with its tidy walkways and trimmed azaleas. She framed and clicked. A good shot of the older agent knocking on the door of the pool house. The younger man on the opposite side, his hand on the knob. It was unlocked, and they went in.

Trailing behind she caught a glimpse of a blonde woman in the main house – mid forties, thin lips. She was probably in the kitchen or a back-facing family room, one hand on the window frame, the other holding a phone. Without stopping, Lil shot image after image. *Jennifer Doyle* – putting a name to the face. She rounded the pool, her ears attuned to whatever was going on in the little cottage – actually not so small. While closed for the winter, she could see how the lower level was designed to open up as an outdoor kitchen and cabana. Much of the architectural detail like a stage curtain on sliding panels. She heard banging on the second floor. 'FBI, Mr Doyle, open the door.'

More banging, and the sound of a foot kicking wood. She thought of going in, and then noticed a side stairway partially concealed behind an outdoor shower. She ran up, and peered in the small-paned windows to an office. The scene inside was in perfect frame. 'No.' It was as though her brain suddenly split in half, part of her registering the horror before her and the other half hooked to the camera. She clicked fast, hoping the reflected glare from the windows wouldn't compromise the image. Her eyes fixed to the gory tableau.

Her mouth silently framed the name: 'Wally Doyle.' No one else it could be at over three hundred pounds – head thrown back with a good portion of his lower face ripped away. She shifted slightly to the left and caught a shot of dripping blood spatter on a framed photo of the championship Ravens, one of several. She gripped the doorknob to steady herself . . . and, not meaning to do it, the door opened. *Right place at the wrong time.* A passing thought – *just how many pictures can I fit on this memory card? Just keep shooting.* She zoomed in on Wally's pudgy hands still holding the gun, which had come to rest on his protuberant belly. Click click click. Not daring to move from the doorway, the blood oozing down the glass on the framed photo, a drop splattering the picture below, of . . . of course . . . Wally Doyle and the three Ravens of the Apocalypse, click click click. And Wally, his head thrown back, bits of tooth and bone glinting through his destroyed jaw, click click click. A platter of something on the desk in front of him. *Weird . . . A snack and then . . . kills himself?* Click click click, corn chip crumbs on the front of his polo shirt. A small black cell phone next to the snack. Click click click.

It was one of those strange points in her life, like walking down the aisle with Bradley or the surreal morning she awoke to find him dead in bed, where time loses meaning. Each second stretched and warped, she couldn't have been alone in that room for more than fifteen seconds. So many competing thoughts, as she stood in the doorway, click click click. Her finger and the dripping blood the only movement. A pit in her gut at the finality of his death . . . *Suicide?* Gun in his hand, shot under the jaw – '*Did it right*,' Bradley would have said, followed by: '*Damn shame.*'

Finally, with an angry bang the opposite door splintered, shuddered and the brass bolt ripped out of the lock plate. Click click click and she dropped the camera into her pocket, not wanting a repeat of what she'd gone through first with Hank and then with Mattie. She felt pangs of regret for shots she could have snapped as the agents, leading with their guns, entered Wally's office. For a brief moment the younger of the two stared down his barrel at her. 'You shouldn't be here.'

'I know,' she said softly. Letting his dark eyes get a good look at her, hands at her sides, just a middle-aged lady out for a stroll . . . or whatever. All the while squirreling away details, the faint smell of gunpowder, the position of the body, birdsong through the open door, the time on the clock – 12.22. *Lil, you have just over an hour and a half to get this story written and submitted.*

The older, heavyset agent was on his cell, breathing audibly, his face red, the back of his jacket deeply wrinkled, like he'd been sitting in a car for a long time. And weirdly, she thought of her oldest, Barbara, a Hollywood casting agent. Not her so much but the way she described people, all reduced to types for roles and potential actors. Her decisions fluidly based on the movie's budget and a multitude of tinsel-town variables she'd describe in gleeful detail after her second glass of wine. The younger man, even featured, tall, dark and handsome would be the star. And if Barbara were here, she'd rattle off first-name possibilities: Keanu, Benjamin, Brad, Leo . . . and the older out of shape guy, his wise mentor. Get some well-known name, but past his prime, maybe Brian or Danny, possibly Bruce. Lil noted that neither one checked Wally for a pulse. What would be the point? Dead is dead.

'Did you touch anything?' her leading man asked.

'No, just the door; it was unlocked.'

He nodded. 'Great. And you are?'

'Lil Campbell.'

'The reporter?'

She felt a rush of euphoria from his question. For the first time she wasn't Doc Campbell's wife, or June and Arthur's girl. 'Yes,' she said, not knowing if in fact that was true. *I mean really,* she thought, *I've had a single news story, and the rest . . . tips for haggling at the flea market, or how to read hallmarks on English sterling. Does that make me a reporter? But clearly this man saw my byline in the morning paper. He read my article.*

'Did you know him?'

'Marginally,' she said. And, nodding in the direction of the wall of framed photos: 'He was kind of a small-town hero a long time ago.'

The agent snorted. 'Yeah . . .' He caught sight of Doyle's cell. 'Dan, we need to check the history on that.'

His partner, still on the phone, looked at the cell, then at him and then at Lil. 'What's she doing here?'

'Reporter,' he said.

'Get her out of here.'

Lil's ears strained to catch the older man's conversation. The only words she caught: 'Crime scene . . . now . . . stiff.' And curiously: 'Not our job.'

'You need to wait downstairs, and don't go anywhere,' the younger agent cautioned. 'We'll need a statement.'

'Of course.' She moved slowly, taking a final look. The one door clearly had been locked and the side entrance open as she'd found it. If this had been a murder did she just screw up evidence by putting her hand on that knob? The other agent, now off the phone, was standing back. He looked at Lil, and then to his partner. 'Alex, get the camera.'

'Right.' He looked uncertain. 'How long till they get here?'

The older guy – possibly a paunched-out Bruce Willis – shrugged. 'You got someplace else to be?'

'Come on, Ms Campbell.'

'And your name?' Inching back through the open door.

He shook his head. 'Agent Brant.' He gave a crooked smile. 'Alex.'

Yes, very good looking, she thought, her eyes wandering to his ring finger – nothing there. 'Suicide?' she asked.

'Could be –' turning back to dead Wally – 'or else someone making it look like one.'

'I don't see a note,' she offered, trying to buy a few last seconds in the room, and noting his rumpled jacket . . . and how quickly the two agents had gotten there. 'You had him under surveillance.'

'Ms Campbell.' His expression was less friendly. 'Out, now, and don't leave, stay in the pool area . . . please.' He moved toward her, looking down at the door. 'Come on.'

Feeling like livestock being led through a paddock, she went down the stairs with Agent Alex – possibly Keanu – a close step behind.

'He must have been on the cell,' she offered. 'Which,

considering there's a regular phone on the desk, you have to wonder why.'

'Fishing, are we?' He chuckled. 'Why don't you wait over there, I don't know how long you'll have to stay. They probably won't get here for half an hour.'

'Who?'

'Crime-scene team, and a couple agents from a major-crime unit.'

'You're not?' she asked, wondering what Wally Doyle had done that warranted a surveillance team of FBI agents.

'No . . .' He looked at her, clearly aware she was hungry for this story. 'Fraud.'

'Interesting.' They were now at the bottom of the steps. Across the closed-up pool, with its tautly stretched black safety cover, she watched Jennifer Doyle emerge through the screen door. Her curiosity was off the charts. 'Fraud related to Nillewaug?'

'I got to get my camera,' he said, and left her.

'You know my husband was their medical director,' she nearly shouted after him. It was a blind stab, but he stopped dead, and turned.

'You were married to Dr Trask?'

'Norman Trask?' His answer not at all what she'd expected. 'Didn't he retire a couple decades ago?'

'Then Dr Stanley?'

'No,' she replied, seeing that this had him truly interested. 'My husband was Bradley Campbell. He was their first medical director. He felt there was something wrong about that place and didn't stay on long. I think Gordon Stanley took the position after him; I thought he was still doing it.'

'Did your husband go into any detail, about why he left?'

She felt her audience slipping, but what exactly had led Bradley to give up the lucrative side job? It was over ten years ago, and while there was little Bradley kept from her, there had been something strange about his turning down the Nillewaug position. 'I don't recall,' she said, regretting her lame answer.

'Well, if you do . . .' His head rose at the sound of a siren from down in the valley, and he jogged back to his car.

'Mrs Campbell?' Jennifer Doyle's voice from the back deck, where she stood looking toward the pool house. 'Is Wally . . .?' Her voice drifted.

'He's dead,' Lil stated simply, and watched Jennifer's face for the reaction. And while tempted to pull out the camera, she didn't.

Jennifer Doyle bit her lower lip and bobbed her head slightly. Something about her, lean to the point of anorexia – *Jack Spratt and his wife*. Her face a mask of worry, deep lines around her eyes and at the corners of her thin lips. Her collar-bones protruding from the scoop neck of her yellow blouse. 'Should I go back there?' she asked.

'I wouldn't,' Lil offered, walking around the edge of the pool, careful of the cords that held the cover bolted to rings in the patio.

Jennifer seemed frozen, her hands resting on the rail. 'He shot himself?'

'It looks that way,' Lil said, noting the signs of shock, her unfocused stare, the information not yet fully registering.

'They didn't give him a choice.' Her words were clipped.

'Who?' Lil asked.

Her gaze shifted from the pool house to Lil. 'Mrs Campbell, why are you here?'

Oh Lil, she thought, rapidly sifting through possible answers and finding one that was both vague and true. 'I heard a shot.'

She nodded. 'He wasn't as stupid as everyone thought,' she said. 'It's just . . . he was too trusting . . . I told him to take the deal. At least we would have come out of this, maybe been able to keep the house . . . maybe not. I told him it would have been OK. He should have taken it.'

'What deal? With whom?'

'I need to call the school,' she said. 'I don't want the boys coming home to this.' And without another word, she vanished into the kitchen.

Lil pulled out her cell to check the time – *who, what, when, where, why*? Handsome Alex had returned and was methodically taking photos, and through the open pool gate she spotted Hank Morgan pulling up in his Explorer, accompanied by Kevin Simpson. Hank saw her and rolled his eyes.

Moving fast in her direction. 'Getting to be a habit with you, Lil. And by the way, nice piece in *The Register*.'

'Thanks.'

'So.' He looked toward the pool house where agent Alex – *definitely Keanu* – was taking exterior shots. 'What happened?'

In under thirty seconds she gave him the facts she knew.

He sighed. 'Crap! More Feds.' And he went over to Alex. The men shook hands, and Hank went with the young agent up the side steps behind the shower.

'Crap indeed,' Lil muttered, not at all familiar with the complexities of police work, but realizing there were at least three layers of law enforcement now involved in charming little Grenville. On her list of things to do: get educated about investigations and police work. This, however, was no time for hitting the books. She pulled out her phone and for the second time that morning called Edward Fleming. His assistant told her he was in a meeting. 'It's important,' she said, wondering where this story fit in the hierarchy of things. *Is it really that important? Maybe you should wait for him to get back to you?* At what point, she wondered, would she use up whatever favors she had with the man? Clearly this was not what he wanted her doing, and yet . . . it's what she wanted.

He picked up. 'What is it, Lil?'

Using the fewest words possible she pitched the story: Wally Doyle, Nillewaug's Chief Financial Officer, shot dead, a probable suicide in the setting of a federal fraud investigation.

And then something strange; Fleming chortled. Not a little, but Lil pictured the normally straight-laced editor with his wire-rimmed glances snorting through his nose. 'And pictures, Lil? You got shots of the dead man, I'm assuming?'

'Yes.'

'Well done. So what's the problem?'

'They told me not to leave the scene; I don't know for how long. The Grenville chief of police just got here, but considering both the Feds and the state police are involved, I'm thinking this is going to chew up my afternoon.'

'Of course you can leave,' he said. 'They're not charging you with anything . . . are they?'

'No . . . at least I hope not. But . . .' It was difficult to put in words, and since the fire she'd been dealing with odd emotions. Things she didn't realize mattered, apparently did. It was not just that she was enjoying this sense of purpose, and of seeing her byline for something other than fluffy columns. There was something stronger, a forgotten hunger. She had wanted to be a journalist, and somehow she'd buried those ambitions; *apparently*, she mused, *buried doesn't mean dead.* It wasn't just that Keanu had instructed her to stay here, with some veiled threat that if she didn't there'd be consequences. Bottom line, she didn't want to leave. She wanted to catch every detail and glue it to the printed page. *Who what where when and why?* Her thoughts flipped through questions. *How does this fit in with Nillewaug? What exactly was Wally up to? Is that why he killed himself? Or did he kill himself?* And a weird excitement – *this is my story.*

'You don't have a laptop with wireless?' Fleming asked.

'No,' she admitted, feeling like a rank amateur.

'Get one,' he said, 'but here's what you do.' He laughed again, and she wondered if he'd just used up his quota for the year. 'This is the way it used to be. You're going to call my assistant, Fred Barrett, and read him your story. You do have a pad and paper, at least?'

'Yes.'

'OK. He'll type it up and I'll edit it myself . . . this time. The tricky part will be getting your camera out of there without arousing suspicion.'

'I'll call a friend. It shouldn't be hard. She can attach them to an email.'

'And, Lil . . .'

'Yes?'

'Get it to me fast and make it good.'

TWELVE

Ada scanned the aisle of freezer cases, spotting her mother and Alice in the distance. They were hovering around a woman serving samples of pot-stickers, a bag of which were in her oversized cart. With her monthly coupons in hand she was comparing the stock number for the frozen spinach pies with the one on the circular. Never much of a cook, and pretty much fine with living on cottage cheese, Greek yogurt, tea, Chinese take-out and Danish butter cookies, she was now confronted with feeding a seemingly bottomless teen and now her mother and Alice. She knew that Lil, who did the bulk of the cooking, was getting swept up in something new and exciting. Ada didn't need to be told how important this was. At the fire, she'd seen a side of Lil she'd only glimpsed before, her eyes intense her face flushed. And this morning, the unmistakable elation Lil had felt at seeing her story – and it was really good – on the front page. No – *she needs to do this* – wondering if maybe she shouldn't rescue the poor sample lady from Rose and Alice who were treating her booth like an all-you-can-eat buffet. Double checking that there was no limit on the coupon she grabbed four multi-pack boxes of frozen spinach pies and deposited them in her cart. She was pulling out a box of jalapeño pepper poppers to read the nutritional information when her cell buzzed.

'Is this Jimmy Olsen?' she quipped, seeing Lil's name on the caller ID.

'That's who I feel like,' she said. 'Where are you?'

'Costco, figured I'd stock up, and then try to do a walk-through late this afternoon in Mom's place and Alice's as well.'

'They're going to let you in?'

'I got through to Kyle and he said that on an apartment-by-apartment basis they're going to let families and residents do a quick go-through and see if there's anything they can salvage.

I'm also hoping to do some insurance photos. He doesn't think the Fire Marshall's going to want people in there for more than fifteen or twenty minutes. I'm not looking forward to it.'

'Ada, I hate to add to that . . . but I need your help.'

'Of course.' She listened as Lil told her about being the first on the scene of Wally Doyle's suicide. 'How horrible.' There was a pause, and for a moment Ada wondered if the connection had been broken. 'Lil?'

'It is horrible,' she finally said. 'And there's something wrong with me. Oh my God.'

'What?' Ada asked, pushing her cart out of the way of another shopper who wanted her share of spinach pies.

'Ada, he's dead, probably killed himself and all I can think about is being the first with the story. That's why I called you, I need you to come over here and get my camera, then pick out the best shots and get them to the paper.'

Ada smiled, loving the excitement in Lil's voice, her confusion, her passion. And then she looked up. 'Damn!' Rose and Alice were no longer in sight, likely having been cut off at the dumpling station. 'Lil, there's nothing wrong with you, other than we've both been going with too little sleep since the fire. Whatever emotions you need to feel about a man you barely knew killing himself will come. Don't feel guilty about this, or about getting this story.' Ada thought of Lil, how she'd looked that morning as she'd brought her her tea, so excited, giving her a quick peck on the cheek and then off to write. 'People can live their entire lives without real passion, or, if they find it, they somehow manage to run away from it, or snuff it out. The one thing we know for certain – and Lord knows we've seen enough of it lately – life is short.'

'It is,' Lil said. 'So I'm not a total ghoul?'

'I didn't say that, but a ghoul with a passion.' She added, lowering her voice, 'My ghoul.'

'So that's what they were singing.' Referring to The Temptations' classic.

'Yes, Lil,' she said and, catching the allusion, sang a quick line in a pitch-perfect alto: *Talking 'bout my ghoul* . . . let me round up Aaron and the ladies and I'll get there as quick as I can.' She hung up, glanced at the time, and, seeing none of her companions, dialed Aaron. 'We need to move fast,' she said. 'Find my mother and Alice and meet me at the checkout.'

'But . . .'

'Aaron, no buts, we've got a ton of things to do this afternoon, and I need your help. Please, just find them.'

Putting her weight into it, she maneuvered the heavy cart toward the front of the cavernous store. As she made a wide left, she saw Alice and Rose in a crowded throng around the kiosk for David's Cheesecake. 'Mom,' she shouted, as the cart picked up speed. 'Alice.'

Her mother, whose hearing aides had been lost in the fire, didn't budge as she pointed to a berry-topped custard tart, and indicated she wanted two samples. Alice waved. 'Hello, dear.'

Ada, unable to halt the forward momentum of the laden cart, yelled back, 'Alice, time to go home.' Seeing that didn't have the desired effect, she added, 'Let's see Johnny.' Moving a bit too fast now, it took all her strength to keep from hitting other shoppers or veering into a mountainous display of men's bathing suits. Digging in with her heels she slowed the cart, and, like a plane coming for landing, approached the shortest check out. The line moved fast, and, while waiting, she dialed Aaron again. 'I'm in check out *now*! Your great-grandmother and Alice are at the cheesecake booth. We need to move.'

'But they have the newest *World of Warcraft* and the price is better . . .'

'Fine,' she said, knowing a shake down when she heard it. 'Just get here, and bring Alice and Rose.'

'Thanks, Grandma.'

Looking at her cart, food to last a family for a month and some basic clothes for Rose and Alice, she rethought all that needed to get done. *Pick up Lil's camera, have Aaron load the pictures on the computer, email them to the paper, drop off and put away groceries, stop at the post office and try to track down Rose and Alice's mail and do change-of-address forms, locate Rose's insurance policy . . . probably can do that online.* And, thinking that if she didn't despise Jack – *yes Ada, be honest you can't stand your son-in-law* – he could be helpful with the whole insurance claim thing considering it was his company that had Rose's policy. Putting her smaller items on the belt, and leaving the larger ones in the cart with the bar codes facing up, she spotted her companions. 'Tremendous,' she muttered, seeing that Aaron wasn't the only one taking advantage of her urgency. He had in fact found her mother and Alice, and they in turn had decided the strapping seventeen year old made a good cheesecake-carting Sherpa.

'Did you get one of each?' Ada asked, as the stack of six oversized cake boxes landed on the conveyor belt, topped by a chit that the cashier handed to her assistant for Aaron's pricey – albeit discounted – video game.

'They're delicious,' Rose said, and added, whilst smiling at her daughter, 'Almost as good as the ones I got at Katz's . . . 'course I can't do that any more. Because someone insisted I move out of my perfectly lovely apartment into . . .'

'Fine, mother,' she said, wondering if between her and Lil's freezers they'd be able to store it all.

'I want to go home,' Alice said.

'We're going home,' Ada replied, trying to keep an eye on the flashing prices as the checkout woman scanned the bar codes. As she reached into her bag for her purse, her cell went off again. 'Aaron, can you get that?'

'Sure.' He took the phone.

She swallowed at the total. *$578.98? And over a hundred bucks in cheesecake.* Giving her mother a quick look. *Of course, cheesecake is delicious.* She handed over her American Express. As her goods were arranged into the cart, she caught part of Aaron's conversation. 'Who is it?' she asked.

'It's Kyle, he says that if we want to get into Rose and Alice's apartments we need to get there ASAP.'

'What?' she said, taking her receipt. 'Aaron, you push this thing, and let me have the phone.'

'Kyle, it's Ada Strauss, what's going on?'

'I just wanted you to know,' he said, sounding exhausted. 'They're letting a few people back into their apartments accompanied by fire fighters. I got clearance for both my grandma and Rose, but this is a time-limited offer. I overheard some guy from the insurance company telling the Fire Marshall his company wouldn't take any responsibility for injuries incurred as a result of people getting hurt. It's now or never for trying to retrieve anything.'

'We'll be there,' Ada said. And, feeling like a contestant on some bizarre game of *Beat the Clock*, told Aaron, 'Let's move.' She then realized her mother and Alice had strayed. She spotted them at the pizza window, 'Ladies,' she shouted, 'we're leaving, now!'

THIRTEEN

An hour later at Nillewaug, Ada's son-in-law and Aaron's father, Jack Gurston, couldn't have been in a worse mood. 'Moron!' Needing to get away from that dolt of a Fire Marshall. His eyes, red rimmed from smoke and ash, seemed set to pop from his harshly angled face, as he sat in the back of his Lexus, his navy suit reeking from burned plastics and accelerant. As a senior adjuster for The Clarion his primary objective was to contain the insurance company's exposure. But this . . . a nightmare and the kind of thing that could lose him his job if he weren't careful. *Moron, what the hell is he doing letting civilians back into that place? One fall and . . .* He knew he needed some rest, but what he needed and what The Clarion expected – although his Vice-President boss would never say it out loud – is get the job done and minimize The Clarion's payout.

And that's when he saw them. 'Fuck no!' Wondering if it was possible for things to get worse, but there his interfering bitch of a mother-in-law, her mother – whom he didn't mind so much – some old redhead in green sweats, and Aaron. His jaw tightened and he shut his eyes, the familiar rage always so close. *My son the fag. How could he do that to me? Not my son.* He knew that Rose lived here, at least she used to, so they wanted to get back in. Of course, and wouldn't it be great if the one who had a fall was his relative? Maybe his fag son. Wouldn't that look great? He glared at the quartet who were all clutching empty black garbage bags. They were headed toward a side entrance, like they were planning to just waltz back in. Moron Fire Marshall probably said it was OK. Or, thinking of Ada, who had no respect for how things were supposed to be, just assumed she could do whatever the hell she liked.

He shut his laptop and yanked open the car door, his long legs pumping fast as he broke into a jog and headed them off. 'What are you doing here?' Spittle flew from his mouth.

Ada turned, and Aaron's head shot around like he'd been struck.

Jack was breathing heavily, meeting Ada's witchy blue eyes. His gaze raked over Aaron, not wanting even to look at his son. The last words he'd said to him: '*You disgust me.*' 'What the hell do you think you're doing here?' he repeated.

It was Rose who spoke, her pale blue eyes looking up at him. 'Hello, Jack. I'm so glad you're here.' No irony in her voice. 'We were told we had a few minutes to go back and try to get . . .'

He stared at his wife's grandmother who he knew was in her nineties – the only decent member of the family. She so reminded him of his own grandmother, dead for over twenty years and one of the few people who he knew without doubt had loved him. 'I'm so sorry, Rose.' Realizing, through his layers of exhaustion, just how devastating this must be for her. He looked at the pathetic black plastic bags she was holding, obviously with the intent of retrieving what little she could of her possessions. Having been to hundreds of fires he knew that going back in the day after was fairly standard, unless the structure was unstable. Having already been through the building, he knew the concrete and steel infrastructure would not collapse, which might have made his job easier. What was driving him absolutely mad was the level of chaos. Rescue workers, fire fighters, boneheaded volunteers from half a dozen agencies, and cops – local, state, and in the past hour Feds in unmarked cars and dark suits. He'd practically screamed at the Fire Marshall, '*Who's in charge, here?*'

To be met by the man's infuriating answer: '*Depends who you talk to.*'

'You shouldn't go in alone,' he said, keeping his eyes on

Rose. Knowing that to look at either Aaron or Ada would make things worse. *In fact*, he decided, *pretend they're not there.*

'Would you come with us?' Rose asked. 'The firemen all seem so busy, and you look like you belong.'

He sighed, realizing she was right. That with his Clarion ID tag around his neck, no one would bother him. 'OK,' he said, knowing that if he didn't, word would get back to Susan, not that she'd say anything, just more of his wife's silent martyrdom. 'But just fifteen minutes.'

'In each of their apartments,' Ada said.

'Fine.' He gave her the briefest glance, noting she looked different from the last time he'd seen her, not quite able to put his finger on it, and really not caring. And then a quick look at Aaron. The kid looked healthy, tall, too good looking – *a fag.* He turned his back not wanting to drag this on a second longer than necessary, just get in, get out, and try to get through the day.

Inside Rose's apartment, Ada was shocked at the devastation, and wondered how her mother was holding up. *Horrible.* She stared at the wall of framed family photos that months earlier she and Aaron had hung. Most of the glass now shattered, the images obscured by smoke, as her mind put names to the filthy faces. Tears streamed as she pushed the ruined sofa – one she'd known her entire life – against the wall so she could get to the pictures.

'Let me help you.' Aaron grabbed the other end, and then scrambled up and plucked the pictures from their hooks.

'We should have brought gloves,' she said, her hands covered in ash, jagged glass everywhere. Looking back she saw Jack, tall as his son, helping Rose retrieve her important papers from a metal filing cabinet that had swelled in the heat; the drawers not opening. In spite of herself, grateful for his somber presence. Noting how he wouldn't even look at Aaron, but he was helping, and right now that mattered. He was even being kind to Alice, who stood still in the middle of Rose's destroyed living room, occasionally asking, 'Are we going home?'

'What are the chances he'd be here?' Aaron whispered as he wrapped pictures in filthy towels from the kitchen and gingerly layered them into his garbage bag.

Ada nodded, her thoughts skittering over the enormity of what had happened and what lay ahead. 'At least she wasn't hurt . . . not physically.' Her eyes wandering over her mother's possessions. Everything here having been selected from her Rivington Street apartment. Every dish, every vase, every piece of furniture connected to stories. The shattered Royal Doulton compote, with its scenes from Dickens, had been a wedding present. A clumsy ceramic pin tray made by Aaron's sister, Mona, in the fourth grade – she'd meant for it to be a mermaid, but the gaudily glazed lump, now blackened, looked like some horror show fish monster with breasts. It was of no intrinsic value, but Ada picked it up. 'I think this will wash clean.' And taking a ruined afghan that Rose had made from off her favorite arm chair, she carefully wrapped it.

'Did you bring a camera?' Jack asked.

Ada turned. 'No,' she said, wishing she'd held on to Lil's after she'd downloaded the photos and emailed them to the paper.

'I'll use mine and send you the pictures,' he said.

'Thank you,' she said, seeing a trace of humanity in a man she'd tried so hard to like, but couldn't. Always wondering what made her daughter pick such a bullying control freak, and not liking the answers. She went to the dining-room sideboard; its larger matching buffet sold to a used-furniture dealer when Rose moved out of the city. Straining to open the top drawer she found her mother's good silver, an ornate Victorian pattern with twisted finials that reminded her of pine cones. It had been a twentieth-anniversary present from Ada's father, Isaac, and was used every Sabbath and every family gathering since. The tightly closed drawer had protected the silver from the heat. *You can't leave this.* She grabbed one of the sofa cushions, unzipped the case and pulled out the stuffing. She then filled it with the heavy flatware. *Like a thief.*

'We have to leave,' Jack said, his tone gentle, one hand on Rose's back, while his other reached for Alice's elbow.

Rose turned back, her face and hands covered in dirt and ash. 'Thank you, Jack. I don't know what we would have done if you weren't here.'

'It's OK,' he replied, carrying her bag, and nudging her toward the door.

Alice turned and smiled. She looked down at his hand on her elbow. 'Are we going home?'

Ada watched Jack with the two women, trying to reconcile his unexpected kindness with the man she loathed.

He smiled at Alice. 'Yes, it's time to go home.'

Outside Rose's apartment they were met by Alice's grandson, Kyle in a pair of blue scrubs, his ID badge around his neck. He was holding a box of heavy-duty garbage bags. 'Thank you so much for doing this,' he said, looking at Ada who'd called him earlier. 'I just haven't had time.'

'Don't worry,' Ada said, 'we'll sort it out later. Aaron, can you haul all this out to your car, and if you don't think there's going to be room, take it back to my condo.'

'Not a problem.' He hefted two stuffed garbage bags and the pillow case filled with silver.

Ada looked at Rose and Alice; the two women were filthy. 'Mom, maybe you and Alice should go back home with Aaron? I'll help Kyle go through his mom's place.'

'I don't know.' Rose looked at Alice. 'Do you want to go back in there?' she asked.

The redhead shook her head no. 'I want to go home,' she said, and then to Kyle: 'Johnny, take me home.'

'That would be best,' Jack said, looking at Rose. 'Go home.'

'Do you think they'll let us back in?' Rose asked,

'I don't know,' Jack admitted. And they were interrupted by a man in a black flak vest, with a state police ID on his chest.

'What are you people doing in here?'

Jack spoke: 'These two are residents and I'm an adjuster with The Clarion. We're the underwriters for Nillewaug.'

'I'm a nurse here,' Kyle added, 'the residents were told it was safe for brief walk-throughs to get important personal items.'

The detective looked at Aaron and his bulging bags. 'Right . . . let me have your names, and who said it was OK? This is a crime scene. I'm going to need to know everything that's in those bags. And how do I know you're not looters?'

'Are you kidding me?' Ada said, feeling a pressure inside. 'Haven't these people gone through enough? Who the hell . . .'

Jack interrupted her. 'Detective,' he said, staring hard at the man's ID, and cutting Ada a look. 'Ada, please let me handle this. Detective Pelton, we got permission from the Fire Marshall, and I believe it's been extended to all the residents. He deemed the structure sound. It's possible he did not fully factor in the police concerns. I will be on site for the foreseeable future and will take responsibility for any personal items removed by these two residents.'

The detective shook his head, his expression was incredulous. 'They gave permission . . . you've got to be kidding.'

'I wish I were,' Jack said. 'I'd recommend whoever is in charge of the investigation coordinate with the Fire Marshall. Otherwise you're going to have a few hundred civilians tromping through your crime scene.'

'And you'll be here?' the detective asked.

'Yes.' Jack held his ID badge so the detective could get a clear look.

The detective looked hard at the ID, then up at Jack, Kyle, and the rest of them. 'OK, I guess finish up fast, and get out of here.'

'Appreciate it,' Jack said. 'Aaron, take Rose and Alice home, then bring the car back for your grandmother.'

Satisfied, or at least momentarily placated, the detective walked off. 'This is a nightmare,' Jack said, as Kyle turned the knob on his grandmother's apartment.

'Tell me about it,' Kyle replied. 'Six hundred displaced residents. Six hundred families who paid good money to have their loved one taken care of.'

'Or off their hands,' Ada added, as they walked down the hall into Alice's one bedroom.

'Probably best she doesn't see this,' Kyle said, as they got their first glimpse of the damage. Similar to Rose's everything reeked of smoke, and anything plastic – from soda bottles to a set of unbreakable dishes Kyle had gotten for his demented grandmother – were melted into unrecognizable blobs. The once cream-colored carpet was soaked and blackened, the ends of the synthetic pile, which was supposedly heat resistant, had curled and melted into caramel-colored tips that crunched underfoot.

Kyle led them into the living area, at first glance containing nothing of tremendous value: a pair of stuffed chairs and a couch in a matching floral upholstery – all ruined. A flat-screen TV, the metal back still standing, but the rest a shiny black puddle.

'Did she have renter's insurance?' Jack asked.

'No,' Kyle said, walking to a framed photo on a coffee table. 'I couldn't see the point. She has so little.' He picked up the picture, the glass intact and thick with grime.

Ada stood next to him. 'Who are they?' Looking at the image of two blonde women, and two toddlers, one with dark hair and the other a strawberry blonde in matching outfits with penguins on their chests.

'My family.' He shook his head. 'That's Alice about thirty years ago, and then me, Kelly and my mom.' And, shaking open a bag, he wrapped the photo and gently placed it inside.

'You're a twin?' she asked.

'Fraternal.'

'No men in the picture,' she noted.

'Just me. My mom never married.'

'So who's Johnny?' Ada asked.

'I guess he's my grandfather, but women in my family have trouble hanging on to men. I never met him. And Alice never discussed him.'

'What's wrong?'

'Nothing, just sad. This whole thing is so sad. And now . . .'

Ada trailed behind him as he took pictures, opened drawers, and then led her into Alice's bedroom.

Kyle glanced back at Jack, who was taking photos of the destroyed apartment. 'She didn't have renter's, so why bother?'

Jack seemed torn, and then said something that surprised Ada. 'Depending on what caused the fire, she might be able to get a settlement.'

'You mean from the facility's policy?' Ada asked, turning back from the hall.

Jack stared at her. 'Maybe. It doesn't hurt to document what's been lost, and make an inventory.'

'No,' she said, and for a brief instant could swear she saw something like compassion in his eyes. 'Makes sense.'

He looked away and went back to taking pictures of Alice's ruined home.

In the bedroom, Ada helped Kyle go through drawers and the walk-in closet. She noted how neat the room was in spite of the water and smoke damage. The two clothes chests tightly shut, their contents folded. The furniture a once blonde-wood mid-century suite, the finish now blackened and bubbled to an alligator-skin texture. She said little as Kyle went through the drawers and sorted through his grandmother's things, filling a bag with clothes that could possibly be salvaged. 'I'll swing by and launder these.'

'Don't be silly, you've got more than enough to do.' Feeling an odd sense of intruding into a private world, as he pulled out stacks of silk underwear and surprisingly fancy . . . *provocative*, bras and lingerie.

He glanced back at her, as he slid neatly folded stacks of satin teddies into his bag. 'In her day, Alice was kind of a hottie.' He smiled. 'I guess if there's any silver lining in her Alzheimer's it's that she doesn't realize it's no longer true. She's quite a flirt.' In a tall chest, next to her neatly made bed, which was covered in what had once been a pale pink matelassé spread, he found her jewelry. He stared in. 'What should I take?'

'Here. I'll double bag, just dump the whole thing in. We don't have time to go through it,' Ada said, looking at the hodgepodge of mostly costume pieces, but some gold bracelets, and neatly stacked velvet boxes.

'Thanks.'

'Don't forget her bills and anything financial.'

'Right.' Kyle stood by the bed and slowly turned, surveying the room. 'I kept all that stuff in her kitchen.'

Ada followed, hoisting a half-filled garbage bag, her thoughts unquiet. 'She likes things neat.'

'Yes,' Kyle said, as they passed Jack in the living room. 'I think it has to do with all the chaos in her life. At least in her home she could have some kind of order. Even now, if anything's out of place it drives her crazy. She might not remember what it is, but she knows where it belongs.'

'A place for everything . . .' Ada murmured, trying to remember her Harry as his dementia had worsened; he couldn't have cared less where anything was. In the end, that was the least of it, as she'd needed to do everything for him, feed him, bathe him . . . Alice's dementia was advanced, but somehow her ability to keep a tidy home, and fold her clothes as precisely as a store clerk hadn't been affected.

'You would have fit right in,' he said, as he opened a drawer next to the refrigerator in the tiny kitchenette.

She held her bag open. 'Just dump it in, you can sort it later.' Looking at the contents, mostly bills and the ubiquitous statements from Medicare like her mother received with the words: 'This is not a bill' emblazoned over the cellophane address window. 'She still handles her bills?'

'Are you kidding? That was the first clue I had that something was seriously wrong. She stopped paying them. Had them addressed, stamped and ready to go, but the last step of taking them to the mailbox left her mind. I got a call from her crying in the middle of the night that the power went out. So I'm thinking the lines are down. I called the electric company to find out when her power is expected to be back up only to find out she hadn't paid her bill in four months.' He put the empty drawer back and began to go through the cabinets, pulling out a favorite mug. He grabbed a Tony the Tiger cereal bowl. 'This was mine,' he said, 'and this was Kelly's,' he added, on finding a second with a brightly colored Toucan Sam.

'How long ago did that happen?' Ada asked, noting how at home Kyle was in his grandmother's kitchen.

'Let's see, she's been here five years, probably close to seven years ago. It took me a little while to figure things out. And once I started digging . . .' He gave a humorless laugh. 'You can't imagine the mess, like an onion, you get through one layer and suddenly something else appears you'd not anticipated.'

'I do know,' Ada said. 'My husband had dementia. His doctor said it was a combination of Alzheimer's and little strokes. I didn't have the bills to deal with – I've always handled those – but everything else. And driving. Oh my God, that was the worst. He wouldn't stop driving, even when I hired someone to do it . . . and we lived in New York.'

'That can't have gone well,' he said, stepping back, his gaze wandering over the space. He shook his head. 'I tried so hard to get her into this place, every cent she had, everything I could scrape together, and now what?'

'You can't think about that,' Ada said. 'She can stay with us for as long as you need.'

'No,' Kyle said. 'You've been more than kind, but that's no answer, and we both know it. I'll figure something out.'

'There's no rush. We have plenty of space . . . What about your mother?' Ada asked, wondering why it had fallen to Kyle to care for his grandmother.

He stepped back, his eyes sad and tired. 'She's dead. Well, I think that's about all for now.'

Jack appeared. 'We should move.' Glancing at Ada, he said, 'I'll email you copies of the pictures.'

'Thanks,' she said, noting how he wouldn't meet her gaze. 'Aaron should be back soon.'

Jack stiffened, the corner of his mouth twitched. 'How's he doing?'

Ada bit back her first impulse – *ask him yourself, he's your son!* 'Fine, his grades are good, he seems happy.'

Jack nodded. 'Good,' he said, his curt tone making it clear that was all he wanted to know.

Kyle, with one plastic bag over his shoulder, and the other in his hand, looked from Jack to Ada. 'Aaron's your son?'

Jack looked at Kyle, a wariness crossed his face. 'Yeah.'

'He's a good kid,' Kyle said.

Jack squinted, and his mouth twisted like he'd just eaten something sour. 'Come on, we need to get out of here.'

FOURTEEN

Mattie Perez stood at the entrance to Delia Preston's fourth-floor corner office. Her nose, used to the stench of burned wood and plastics, sniffed carefully, searching for nuance – *is there something else here?* Her mind racing, knowing that if they couldn't come up with something solid, Jim Warren would be out before nightfall. She reached for her Visine, her eyes tearing from the ash and pollen. Stepping into Delia's office, she widened her focus, taking in the long view through shattered windows, the glass edges alive with rainbows. But her mind wasn't focused on the panoramic views of budding trees and rolling hills bursting with the first green of spring. Behind and to her left stood Jamie, who knew when to stay silent.

Mattie raked her gaze back over Delia's spacious office, with its singed and soaked Berber carpet, leather chairs, sleek Herman Miller furniture and tattered drapes. On the desk was a melted computer and monitor, with a matching pool of plastic that had once been a printer. She studied the floor-to-ceiling shelving unit with rows of awards, those made out of plastics having melted, a couple with glass or crystal orbs mostly intact, albeit blackened. One glass case had survived, and inside was a display of crafts made by the residents, a tatted doily, two small still-life water colors, and a row of ceramic frogs. All of which had been here when she'd first come to Nillewaug last fall. At the time she'd had suspicions about Preston. There was something too cozy about Grenville and how old people flocked here like some kind of golden-years Mecca. Nillewaug was a piece of that illusion, a comfortable and secure place, with everything taken care of. But something about it had felt rotten, too much complicity throughout the town. And fortunately for Delia the prior case had veered in another direction and suspicions about Preston had been tabled. Now, she replayed the scene, remembering the polished administrator with her blonde upsweep and flawless make-up. The cracks in her veneer had come when Mattie had pushed to speak with the powers behind Nillewaug, Delia's boss, Jim Warren, who, thanks to some very quick work on Mattie's part – 'Your honor, we have his fingerprints on the probable murder weapon' – would not be getting released, at least not yet. But unless they found something damning . . . he'd walk.

Last fall Delia and Nillewaug had come under scrutiny when connections were made to the town's high-end antique dealers, who were being murdered. At the time it was clear that Delia was part of a cozy group of Grenville professionals – realtors, antique dealers, lawyers, and financial planners – who referred well-heeled elderly clients to one another, like a flock of vultures. After the case had been solved, there was no need to dig further.

'Jamie,' she said, breaking the silence. 'Let's put together what we know. What happened in this room?'

The young detective collected her thoughts. 'At roughly four in the morning, in the middle of a fire, someone broke that window and pushed Delia Preston's dead body through it. According to the M.E. she had been murdered roughly four hours before that by a single blow to the head. We have a likely murder weapon,' Jamie said, referring to the crystal-and-steel trophy – *Best Assisted-Care Facility in New England 2010*, presented by *New England Magazine* – Mattie had found earlier. The foot-high award – euphemistically called a tomb-stone – had been wiped with an ammonia solution, but not well. It still contained traces of Preston's blood and skin. As Jamie presented the case, Mattie reflected that regardless of how obnoxious Arvin the Medical Examiner could be, he'd been spot on with his estimation of something grapefruit sized.

'Said murder weapon,' Jamie continued, 'has five partial prints on the base – Preston's, Jim Warren's, the bonded cleaning woman, and two unknowns.'

Mattie had hoped that Warren's fingerprints would be enough for the Feds to hold him. But it was flimsy, she knew it, the judge knew it, and Warren's attorney – *'He accepted the award at a banquet in front of two hundred people, of course his fingerprints were on it!'* – most certainly knew it.

'Keep going,' Mattie said, knowing all this but finding it useful to run the evidence.

'Based on his being under surveillance, we know that Warren met with Preston four hours before she was killed. He arrived at eight oh-two and left at nine forty-eight. At least two hours before her death. Mattie, if she was the whistle blower on this fraud thing, why didn't they have a wire on her?'

'Good question. It wasn't a planned meeting; they didn't have time. But maybe she wasn't being as cooperative as they'd hoped. At least between the lines that's the impression I got. So Warren contacted Delia at her home, was insistent they meet at Nillewaug. Why there, why not somewhere else? And why on a Saturday night?'

'I don't know,' Jamie said.

'He was freaking out,' she added. 'Just learned – or at the least suspected – that his megabucks fraud scam was coming undone.'

'Yes, two agents show up at his law practice on a Saturday afternoon and subpoena boxes of records. The shit was hitting the fan. But according to Fitzhugh and Connor he didn't know he was under surveillance, and could only guess at why they wanted those records. At least that's their take. But Warren was sketchy on the phone with Preston. He might have known he was being watched . . . and possibly tapped.'

'He was angry,' Jamie added, having listened to the taped conversation that the agents had shared. Warren phoning her at home, insisting they meet in her office. 'He knew something, and knew enough to not say it on the phone. So why meet at all?' she asked, and then added: 'He didn't kill her, we know she was still alive when he left . . . maybe it was just a booty call. Saturday night, guy's feeling horny. He more or less admitted he was having an affair with her.'

'Yes, and Arvin said she'd had sex within hours of her death. But I don't buy that's why he wanted to meet her, or at least not the only reason. He wanted something and he believed it was here. Or he needed information. Or maybe he knew it was her that had contacted the Feds, and he wanted to shut her up.'

'All possible,' Jamie said. 'So he shows up, and not long

after she – or he – entered the passcode and turned off the security system.'

'Yes, and because it's all on the same line and through the same company, the fire alarms and audible alarms, as well.' Mattie pulled out a thin pair of gloves and mentally divided the room into cubes, like squares on a piece of graph paper. She focused on apparent hot spots, where something could be hidden. She started with the modernist desk, pulling out drawers, looking behind them, under them for scribbled passcodes. 'Why take down the security system?' she asked. Not finding anything of interest. She let her eyes wander to the broken windows behind the desk, then the bookshelves, awards, trophies and framed photographs – Preston shaking hands with local politicians, her sleek blonde do, her practiced smile and crisp suits. The epitome of a woman executive: confident, attractive, and feminine.

'She was a nurse,' Jamie said, now standing by the bookcase and reading the inscription on a bronze plaque. 'That's what the M.S.N. is for – Master of Science in Nursing.'

'Yes,' Mattie said. 'Do you think that's important?' Liking the way Jamie was trying to piece things together.

'Something from this morning,' Jamie said, picking up the plaque. 'I'm trying to understand the workings of this Medicare and Medicaid business, but it seems that a big part of it has to do with faking the bills. And in order to do that you need a doctor and a nurse signing lots of forms.'

'Right, we have dead doctor Trask who everyone thought was retired, but is apparently staying in practice.'

'At least his pen hand is,' Jamie added. 'And Preston signing off as the nurse. It's a tight loop. And according to the agents it was being done at a level that flew below their radar. So why drop a dime on herself? She had to be raking it in . . . or someone was. Why would she call the fraud hotline?'

'We don't know,' Mattie said, her eyes wandering toward the open door of Preston's private bath and the keypad to the security system on the wall next to it. 'There's a lot we don't know.' She felt a wave of frustration. It wasn't just the early stages of a murder investigation, but there were too many hands stirring the pot, and while agents Connor and Fitzhugh had been courteous, they'd not been forthcoming. Gingerly, her gloved left index finger touched the keypad, as her right hand pushed back the bathroom door. *How nice to have your own office bathroom*, she mused, noting the once white, but now ash-covered towels, the veined marble vanity with nickel fixtures, the walk-in shower and a framed art deco poster for Veuve Clicquot with a flapper riding a bicycle and a glass of champagne in one hand. The image held her attention, the glass not shattered by the heat, still perfectly centered on the wall – *too perfect*. She touched the edge of the frame, feeling how solidly it was held to the wall. She tugged; it didn't move. 'Right.' Her gloved hands moved up the side of the picture. Midway on the right she found the latch, pressed it down and the picture slid to the right, revealing a generous wall safe. She smiled at Jamie. 'Well at least now we know why they wanted to bring the security system down. You'd have to do it to get into the safe.'

'So how do we get in?' Jamie asked.

Mattie pulled back on the door, and, to her surprise, it opened. As the two of them stared into the steel box, Mattie's cell rang.

'There's nothing in there,' Jamie observed.

'But there was.' Mattie pulled out her phone, and looked at the caller ID. *What now?* 'Hello Lil.'

'Mattie, I hate to bother you, but I'm doing a second piece on the fire and the murders, and I'm struggling to make sense of things. I understand that Jim Warren was arrested, but not for murder or arson but for fraud. Can you comment on that?'

'Lil . . .' Mattie's gaze fixed on the three empty steel shelves inside the safe. 'I can't.' But then added: 'How long did Ada's mom live here?'

'Few months.'

'Is she on Medicaid?' Mattie asked.

'Of course not. She's not rolling in it, but Rose has money, and certainly Ada does,' Lil said.

'Right, everyone in this place has money . . . or at least had it. When Ada was getting Rose in here who handled the contracts?'

'That's part of what I'm trying to figure,' Lil said. 'The

contracts were drawn up through Jim Warren's law office, but somehow Wally Doyle had a hand in the financials. Every Nillewaug resident and their family had a consultation with him. Ada didn't think much of it, felt it was a little shady.'

'How so?'

'You'll have to ask her, but he was trying to get Rose divested of her assets.'

'And then a few years later,' Mattie said, understanding the elegance of the scheme, 'she'd qualify for Medicaid and they'd start to bill, saying she was receiving nursing-home care.'

'So that's it,' Lil said. 'Oh my God, how much money is that? Nillewaug is massive. Do you know it's one of the largest assisted-care facilities in New England? And if they were systematically impoverishing the residents, at least on paper, and then billing Medicaid . . . That must be why he did it. He knew they were on to him. He was going to jail.'

'What are you talking about?' Mattie asked. 'Who did what?'

'You don't know? Wally Doyle killed himself less than an hour ago. I'm at his house. I was the first to see him. He must have panicked, knew they were going to arrest him.'

Mattie looked at her phone. 'He's dead? You have got to be kidding.' Anger surged. 'Why the hell didn't someone tell us?'

'I don't know,' Lil said. 'It does seem like a lot of different agencies involved. What I've gathered is both Wally Doyle and Jim Warren were being investigated for a financial scam at Nillewaug. I bet that's why Bradley walked away. He must have known, or at least suspected.'

Mattie felt like she'd been sucker punched. 'Lil, are you certain it was suicide? Did you actually see him pull the trigger?'

'No, but I was there in seconds. Would you like me to tell you what I saw?'

'Please,' Mattie said, and she listened as Lil gave a succinct report of the gunshot and the scene inside the pool house. She asked a few clarifying questions, and then, thinking about Lil's article in the morning paper, said, 'You took pictures, didn't you?'

There was a pause. 'I did.'

'Jesus, Lil,' she said and, despite the horrible sense of the investigation being out of control, laughed. 'What happened to Doctor Campbell's widow? Such a lovely lady.'

'She was,' Lil quipped. 'But this one's better. It's fascinating, right now I'm sitting in Doyle's backyard watching a real crime-scene team in action.'

'Yours were the first photographs weren't they?'

'Yes.'

'You handed them over to the agents?'

Another pause.

'Lil?'

'I gave them to Ada to get to the paper.'

'Of course you did.'

'In my defense,' Lil said, 'they didn't ask for them, and it's part of my job . . . So, I'll go with the fraud angle. I always wondered what happens to reporters if they're just wrong about something.'

'You might find out,' Mattie said. 'I need those pictures, and I'm not going to be the only one.'

'Of course,' Lil said. 'But they're still mine. Supposedly, once I give a statement I can get out of here. So anytime you want to meet is fine.'

'This feels like a negotiation,' Mattie commented, looking at the empty safe in Preston's bath.

'It is. But Mattie, if there's any way I can help . . . There's something else, which you've probably already picked up on, but it seems glaring and I'm using it in my article.'

'What?'

'Whatever's going on, both in terms of the Nillewaug scam and these murders, suicides, whatever . . . it all goes back to the Three Ravens of the Apocalypse. Jim Warren the quarterback is in custody being investigated for fraud, his partner – ex-linebacker, Wally Doyle, also under federal investigation is an apparent suicide, and our running back's father is one of the dead at Nillewaug. But not just one of the random dead . . .' She paused. 'The fire started in his apartment.'

'You spoke to the Fire Marshall?'

'Sam? Of course, plus his preliminary report is public

domain. Mattie, one last question . . . was Dr Trask somehow mixed up in this fraud thing?'

'Possibly.'

'Good word,' Lil said, 'reminds me of a bad medical joke Bradley used to tell.'

'Let's hear it,' Mattie said.

'What's a radiologist's favorite shrub?'

'No clue.'

'It's a hedge . . . "Can't rule out this, possibly that, couldn't say with certainty . . ." So . . . why exactly do you think Dr Trask was "possibly" involved?'

Mattie answered Lil's question with one of her own. 'When you worked with your husband did you do any of his billing?'

'Tons of it,' Lil said.

'Medicare and Medicaid?'

'Absolutely, lots of the former and very little of the latter. Grenville's a wealthy town, not many here qualify for Medicaid.'

'And he'd sign off for any bill submitted?' Mattie asked.

'Of course, without the MD signature no claim would get processed.'

'There's your answer, Lil.'

'Trask was signing off on patients at Nillewaug? That's insane. He was retired . . .'

'Apparently not. Good luck with your story, Lil.'

'And you with your investigation.'

FIFTEEN

Lil hung up with Mattie and checked the time on her phone. Fleming had told her to call in the story no later than two. It was ten of. 'Crap,' she said, glancing over her notes, consisting of seemingly random information and impressions. From the comfort of her wicker chair she viewed the players in Wally Doyle's lovely pool area. She felt like an audience member, largely ignored by the dark-suited men and women. Occasionally, they'd remind her that she had to give a statement before leaving. But she was low on their priority list and it wasn't clear who was running this show. Certainly not the two agents – whom she'd dubbed Keanu and Bruce. They'd seemed eager – relieved even – to hand off the lead to a second pair of agents, a man and a woman whom she'd not yet cast with their Hollywood types. 'Stop it, Lil.' She needed to focus on the story, but was finding it hard. *Like, what the hell do you think you're doing? You're no reporter.* She took a deep breath, and tapped Fleming's number. His assistant, Fred, whom she'd never met, answered.

'Mr Fleming said you'd call. We need to hurry if this is for the evening edition.'

'OK, let's start with this,' she said, staring at her notes and pretending a confidence she did not feel. '"*When deadly smoke and flames swept through the assisted-care facility of Nillewaug Village early Sunday morning, leaving five dead, six hundred homeless and dozens still unaccounted for, the specter of arson was raised. This suspicion, and the finding by the state's Medical Examiner that Delia Preston, M.S.N., the administrative director of Nillewaug, was the victim of homicide, has touched off a multi-agency investigation, which includes local, state and federal authorities. But while the Nillewaug fire, the largest and deadliest in Grenville history, has been brought under control, the story has spread. Early this afternoon the facility's CEO, James Warren, was arrested. Hours later its Chief Financial Officer, Wally Doyle, was found dead from a single gunshot wound to the head at his Eagle's Cairn home, an apparent suicide.*" That wasn't bad, she told herself – *who, what, when, where, why . . . Just get out the story, Lil.* 'OK, new paragraph, "*As the death toll and mystery shrouding the disaster expand, facts are starting to emerge. While still preliminary, the results of Preston's autopsy indicate she was killed by blunt trauma to the head prior to the fire.*"'

Lil had a vivid flashback, picturing Preston's broken body lying on the ground, her skirt hiked up, her head twisted, the strangely erotic glimpse of her stocking tops and garters, like something out of a vintage girly magazine. Women don't wear things like that for themselves. *Who was she dressing for?* She looked at her cell and heard the click of keys over the line. '"*One early line of investigation, and possible motive, centers around fraud allegations, involving improper billing to Medicaid.*"'

As the words spilled from her lips, doubts hounded her – *do you know this for certain? Is this libel? Hedge, Lil.* Paragraph by paragraph she talked through the story, imagining that she was telling it to Ada, trying to anticipate her questions, and finding that for every sketchy fact she was able to report, dozens of unanswered questions queued behind. Occasionally Fred would interrupt for clarification, but mostly he typed and she talked.

When she got to the small-town connection between Doyle, Warren and dead Dr Trask, Fred asked, 'Have you spoken to his son, Dennis?'

'No, but as soon as I finish here I intend to track him down.'

'Pity you don't have a quote from him, you know, something about his father.'

'I know.' She looked up from the phone to see the female agent in her dark navy suit approach.

'Ms Campbell? I'm Federal Agent Rebecca Cook, I need to take your statement.'

'Of course,' Lil said, and instead of thinking how her daughter might cast the stern-faced woman in her early forties, she tried to come up with quick descriptions for her story – *seasoned veteran,* being what she settled on. 'Fred, I've got to go. Do you think that's enough?'

'I do. I'll get it to Mr Fleming,' he said, then hung up.

Lil felt a wave of relief as she met this new agent's gaze. 'I'm ready.'

A button was pressed on a tiny digital recorder, and the questions began. 'Why were you outside Mr Doyle's house?'

'I'd come to get a statement from him about Nillewaug for an article.'

'And you knew him?'

'Not well, but socially, yes.'

'When was the last time you'd seen him?'

'A couple weeks ago in the grocery store.'

'Did you talk to him then?'

'No,' Lil said, not sharing her memory of spotting the obese man at the deli counter of the local family-owned grocers. It had been lunch time and he'd been in front of her. Lil felt ashamed remembering the thoughts she'd had at the time as morbidly obese Wally Doyle had ordered two large submarine sandwiches. Each one of which had to be over a thousand calories.

'When *did* you last speak to him?' Agent Cook asked.

'About four months ago when my friend's mother was moving into Nillewaug.'

'And what are their names?'

And so it went, as she shot question after question, Lil studied Agent Cook. The way she'd let her go off on brief tangents, but then bring her back to Wally Doyle. She honed in on the meeting with Ada, Rose and Wally Doyle around the time of Rose's move. 'Why would the Chief Financial Officer meet with a resident?' she asked.

'We were told it was part of the intake process.'

'I see. Did residents meet with other parts of the leadership structure?'

'It was Mr Doyle, Ms Preston and the director of nursing, Kayla Atwood.'

'And you were there because?'

Her question trailed and Lil smiled. *Oh what the hell.* 'Ada and I live together. She doesn't drive, so I was playing chauffeur. But I stayed outside when they met with Mr Doyle.'

'Did your friend tell you about the meeting?'

'She did.' Remembering how Ada and Rose had been left with strange impressions after their forty-five minutes with Mr Doyle.

Agent Cook gave a small smile, and nodded. 'And?'

'Ada told me it had felt like a sales pitch.'

'Explain.'

'Again, I wasn't in there, but she said that Mr Doyle was pushing to get her mother's assets divested, beyond that you'll have to talk to her.'

'Why would he do that?'

'You're asking me to speculate?'

'Yes, and I suspect as a reporter you've drawn some hypotheses.'

'What I've gathered is they were trying to impoverish the residents, at least on paper, and then after the look-back period had passed, bill Medicaid for nursing-home services, while continuing to bill the families for the monthly fees. This is why Nillewaug was under investigation and why your colleagues had him under surveillance.' And that's when a light went off. 'Can I ask you a question?'

'It depends,' she said, lips tight, clearly not wanting to lose time.

'If Wally Doyle was being watched, who else was?' Deliberately keeping quiet about what Mattie had told her about Jim Warren's arrest. *But really,* Lil thought, *if the two of them warranted federal agents, why not Delia Preston?*

'Sorry.' She shook her head. 'I can't tell you that. OK, let's go back to earlier this afternoon. With as much detail as possible walk me through your every step.'

Thirty minutes later, Agent Cook clicked off her recorder and thanked Lil for her time. As Lil walked back through the gate she had a guilty twinge. *You answered all her questions truthfully, and yet . . . you held back. Why?* Realizing that part of it had to do with Agent Cook's unwillingness to share information – *it's not her job. You should have brought up the three Ravens connection.*

She slid behind the Lincoln's wheel, adjusting the mirror to survey the view of Eagle's Cairn. She looked down the crushed-shell drive that led to Jim Warren's house, the brick chimneys the only part visible. She wondered if he knew that Wally was dead. And she wondered if he had something to do with it. With two Ravens accounted for – one dead and one under investigation for fraud – she considered her next move. Find Dennis Trask. *Where would he be on the Monday after his father died?* She pulled out her cell and Googled Dennis's dealership. Several options popped up and she touched the screen activating the call for 'corporate head-quarter'. 'Is Mr Trask in?' she asked when the receptionist picked up.

'Who should I say is calling?'

She disconnected, put the car in drive and shot for the expressway. As she drove, her thoughts skittered over everything she could remember about Norman Trask, his lovely wife, Kate, and their three sons. She knew that Bradley and Dr Trask would occasionally refer patients to one another, and they'd see them at church. Like everyone she knew the small-town gossip about Dennis, high school star, out of control and ends up in jail. His mother dies while he's incarcerated – *did that have something to do with it?* And then he gets out and turns his life around. She knew, too, that Bradley, as the medical consultant to the high school sports teams, had treated Dennis for minor injuries. And then she recalled a conversation with Bradley at one of the games; they'd been in their usual front-row fifty-yard-line seats – courtesy of his being the team's medical consultant. *'Something's off about that boy,'* he'd said.

She'd asked him *'What do you mean?'* as Dennis had plucked Jim Warren's spiraling pass from the air and sprinted toward a touchdown. Only now she couldn't recall Bradley's answer, probably obliterated by the screaming in the stands. But she pictured him shaking his head. *What did you know, Bradley?*

Two exits later and she took the left for the Bedford Turnpike and automotive mile, the stretch of dealers on the outskirts of Grenville. Because it's close and convenient, and most makes are represented, it's where pretty much everyone in town bought their cars. It's where she'd purchased the Lincoln after Bradley's death, and then replaced it with a newer model after it got totaled last fall. As she headed toward Trask Toyota, she noted something. The name Trask was in front of half a dozen dealerships – Trask Nissan, Trask Buick/Oldsmobile, Trask Saab/Audi and Trask Mitsubishi. Even Trask Lincoln/Mercury, which when she bought this car was still Maybury Lincoln/ Mercury. Clearly Dennis Trask was doing well, and had taken over dealerships in adjacent lots. The BMW and Mercedes dealers hadn't yet sprouted the Trask name, but other than that . . . *Interesting.*

She took the left into the Trask Toyota lot, and parked in front of the expansive showroom. She glanced at a shiny blue Prius, having thought on many occasions that with escalating fuel prices she should ditch her guzzler. Problem was, Lil and Ada loved the guzzler; it's what Bradley always drove, albeit in black, and it could fit six comfortably. Plus, as she knew from experience, it could withstand both head-on and side collisions without getting the occupants fatally squished.

Shouldering her bag she headed through the showroom and breezed past a salesman in a crisp navy suit and starched white shirt. She didn't have a clear plan as she made toward a corridor with a sign that read 'owner', on the way passing a waiting area with magazines and the morning paper with her cover story and pictures of the fire. She wondered if Dennis had seen it and was thinking through the options of how to get the man to talk to her, when her gaze shifted to the right, and there he was, moving fast through a side door.

'Dennis!' Lil shouted, having not really looked at him in a few decades, but remembering the strapping red-headed athlete he'd been. But now, still well over six foot, where he'd been all lean muscle he had a comfortable middle-aged spread. His charcoal-gray suit jacket unbuttoned, his burgundy tie clipped to a white shirt that bulged over his belt. Most of the red gone in his silvery buzz cut.

He turned, stopped. 'Mrs Campbell?'

'Dennis,' she said, going over to him, extending a hand. 'I'm so sorry.' Taking his hand, and holding it in both of hers. She could see he was taken aback, common courtesy forcing him to respond.

'Thank you,' he said, 'it's pretty awful.'

'I can't imagine what you're going through. Your dad . . . I'm so sorry. And then poor Wally.' Her eyes fixed on his, gauging his response. His shoulders sagged and he glanced toward the door.

'Thank you. He was a good friend. I've got to go.'

'Of course,' she replied as dozens of questions shot to mind. Foremost of which was: *how the hell did you know Wally Doyle is dead?* 'Do you know when the funeral is?'

He turned, met Lil's gaze. He squinted. 'My brother's arranging it, I'm certain it will be in the paper.' And quickly added: 'Wally's wife, Jen told me about Wally . . . in case you were wondering. I've got to go.' And he abruptly turned and exited the dealership.

As she watched him leave she spotted Mattie and her tall

young partner approach him as he was opening the door of a dark green Lexus. Mattie showed her badge, as Lil fished out her camera. And then realized Ada had it. 'Damn,' she muttered, touching the camera app on her phone. The resolution wasn't good enough, not to mention the glare through the dealership windows. Nevertheless she started to shoot while heading in their direction. She was out the door and closing in when Mattie spotted her.

'Sorry, Lil,' she said. 'No reporters.'

There was no mistaking the rage in Dennis Trask's face as he glared first at Mattie and then at Lil. *If looks could kill,* Lil mused, *we'd both be dead. But why me? What did I do? Was there something in the article?*

'Are you arresting him?' she asked, as her right thumb touched the screen to take a shot.

'No, Lil, just questioning. And sorry,' she said with finality, 'no reporters.'

SIXTEEN

Dennis Trask trailed the detectives in his Lexus, for a drive that ended in the familiar lot of the Grenville PD. 'Just questioning,' he reminded himself, and then ran the evidence to support that conclusion. The short boxy woman detective saying they wanted to ask him about his father and the fire, and offering him the choice of driving with them or following behind. If this were to end in an arrest they'd never risk him in his own vehicle. '*Of course,*' he'd said, '*anything to help.*' Running, he knew, would be stupid, like painting a target on his back. *And for what?* Not that he hadn't done quite a bit that was outside the law; he flipped through recent infractions, mostly with prostitutes of legal age. He always checked ID and the girls would never report him, no matter how badly they got hurt. And his financial schemes, especially with Wally and Delia dead, were untraceable. The one potential weakness, and why he intended to get more information than give, had to do with his good buddy Jimbo Warren. It made him nervous knowing Jim was in custody, but unlike Wally, Warren was smart. The question was, would he keep his mouth shut or, if given the chance, cut a deal and rat him out?

He parked and got out of the car, and gave a sad smile in the direction of the female detectives. The curly haired short one nodded back, and the freakishly tall young one with the ponytail was already heading toward the door. *Both dykes*, he mused, *what other woman becomes a cop?* Or thinking about the few mannish female prison guards he'd met – *had to be dykes*. But the young one, maybe a few years younger and he'd do her. *Bet she'd struggle*, he thought, checking her muscular forearms and ridiculously long legs. *Pity she's not blonde.* He took a deep breath and felt the afternoon sun on his face. Looking at the brick police department felt like old times, trying to remember his last visit inside over thirty years ago.

He strode toward the door the short detective was holding for him. 'Thanks.' He walked in noting the battered oak counter and waxed linoleum floor. To the right were the holding cells where he'd spent several nights waiting for his dad to pick him up, and once . . . well, that had been a real bad time. Knowing that he'd done something stupid and nothing his father or the attorneys at Windham, Porter and Smith could do about it. Third DUI in Connecticut was a mandatory year in prison, no exceptions and off he'd gone to Osborn.

'This way,' Detective Perez said, leading him to the left.

He followed, checking out the two uniformed officers and the clerk behind the counter. None of them old enough to remember him.

'Hello Dennis,' said a familiar voice and he looked up to see Hank Morgan. 'I'm sorry to hear about your dad.'

'Thanks.' A surge of fury and fear behind his eyes, as memories flooded in. *Screw you, Hank, you've got nothing on me. I did not start that fucking fire, but I bet I know who did . . . and once I know for sure, they will pay.*

'Can I have someone get you a water, a coffee?'

'Coffee would be good,' he said, meeting Hank's sad expression with one of his own. *What a difference a few decades make*, he thought, remembering a much younger Hank Morgan when he'd been Grenville's first chief of police.

He took a seat at the long table in the interview room, noting the clock was different and the chairs had been replaced with a set of black chrome and vinyl stackers. The two women detectives sat on the other side and Hank settled at the head of the table. The receptionist from behind the front counter appeared with a carafe of coffee and disposable cups.

'We realize you've got a lot on your plate,' Detective Perez began. 'But as you're aware we have a multi-fatality fire and a homicide.'

'Lil Campbell's article said it was arson.' Dennis gritted his teeth, wanting them to see outrage. 'If that's true, my father was murdered. So yes –' tears in his eyes – 'I have a lot on my plate, but nothing is more important than catching my father's killer. So ask your questions.' His words were choked and bitter.

Mattie nodded. 'When did you last see your father?'

'Saturday morning,' he said, and he described their routine of Skyping. And sensing the detective's next question as to why he didn't just visit his father, he added, 'It was less stressful for both of us. I hated to see the way he lived, and he hated that I hated it. So we Skyped once a week and then I'd take him out with my family for Tuesday night supper. That way we could pretend the problem didn't exist.'

'The hoarding?'

'Yes, and he couldn't stand that word. To him it was all necessary. The place was disgusting. When my mother was alive she managed to keep it contained, but after her death . . .' Dennis stared at his hands, the memory of the fire too real, the call from Wally: *'Dennis, it's bad.'* He looked at Hank and then at the short detective who appeared in charge. 'What makes you think it's arson?'

Detective Perez held his gaze. Her words were slow and measured: 'Too coincidental with the murder of Delia Preston, and the presence of accelerant.'

'You know I was there?' he asked, figuring the best approach was to be honest . . . at least where he could.

'Yes, according to several witnesses you were instrumental in helping many of the residents out of the building.'

'I couldn't get to him,' he said, remembering the awful frustration. 'It was too hot, and the smoke; I couldn't breathe. I tried . . .'

'Your father?'

'Yes, it was too hot on the second floor, I tried . . . it was too hot. I kept hoping he'd made it out before I got there. I tried, when I opened the door to his hall, like a wall of heat; there was no way. I ran around the outside as the first fire trucks arrived. I showed them where his apartment was; the windows were blown out, and there were flames and the smoke was so thick. I knew then that if he hadn't made it out he was gone.' Tears of rage and frustration flowed. 'The smoke was black, that's why you think an accelerant was used.' He looked at her, not wiping his cheeks.

'It indicates the presence of hydrocarbons – gasoline, kerosene.'

Dennis shook his head – *yes, give information to get information.* And slowly, using the back of his hand he wiped his tears. 'You think it was him that started it? My father would never do something like that . . . not deliberately. And yes his place was filled with solvents. Turpentine, denatured alcohol, the oils he used for lubricating and cleaning the clocks. I kept telling him to get rid of it, that it was a fire hazard. But it was useless, just made him mad. And all those fucking journals . . . It started in his apartment; is that what you're saying?'

'It looks that way, Dennis,' Hank said.

'How did you hear about the fire?' Mattie asked.

And Dennis knew this was where he needed to tread softly. *Say the truth the whole truth and leave out the bits that can cause problems.* 'Wally Doyle called me.'

'At what time?'

'Before four a.m.'

'Not after?'

'No,' he repeated, watching the gears turn behind Detective Mattie Perez's dark eyes.

'You realize that was before the first nine-one-one call.'

'I do now; I didn't then.'

'Do you remember the exact time?'

He stopped, remembering the call pulling him from a deep sleep. Annoyed to hear Wally's voice, pissed that he'd used the house line and not the disposable cell he kept for their conversations. But in this case, probably best to have left a record. 'I'd say three forty-five, but I'm sure you can check with the phone company.' Suspecting she already had.

'Why would he call you?' she asked.

Dennis looked at his hands and at the cooling cup of coffee before him. He pictured Wally, and felt a pang of loss. Mostly for what Wally represented, a man who would literally die for him. 'We were like brothers. In fact, he was closer to me than my own. Of course he'd call. I'd just assumed he'd already called the fire department, or . . . he probably didn't think he needed to.' He looked at her. 'The place had sprinklers and alarms, aren't those supposed to trigger a call if there's a problem? Why didn't that happen? Why didn't they go off?' And without being told he knew the answer, and suspected the culprits, one of whom – Delia – was dead. *What were she and Jim playing at?*

'Tell me everything you can about that call,' she said.

Dennis remembered the terror in Wally's voice, the pitch high and breathless, like air through a dog's squeeze toy. '*What am I supposed to do, Dennis? Tell me what am I supposed to do?*' 'He wanted me there. I told him to get everyone out, to stay calm and that I'd be there as fast as I could.' Most of which was true, the part he omitted: '*Make sure you've emptied the safe.*'

'Was there more?' she asked.

'No, I don't think so. I hung up, threw something on and drove over.' He'd floored the accelerator for the ten-minute drive, and, as he'd approached Nillewaug, saw smoke rising from behind the central residence. As he'd turned down the long drive to the facility he'd been shocked at the sight of flames over the roof. And then sirens, but from behind him. 'It was all wrong,' he said. 'I shouldn't have gotten there before the fire trucks.'

'What was Wally Doyle doing there?' Detective Perez asked.

He looked at her, a quizzical expression on his tear-streaked face. 'He didn't say . . . I don't know.'

'Do you find his being there at three forty-five in the morning unusual?'

'Very.'

'And he didn't say why?' she persisted.

'No, maybe someone on staff called and said there was a problem . . .' He stared ahead, questions hammering at his thoughts. Good question, Detective – *what the fuck was Wally doing there?* When he'd arrived the fire was blazing, and the hottest spot was the back windows of his father's second-floor apartment. 'It doesn't add up.'

'No,' she agreed, and then abruptly shifted topics. 'What was your relationship to Nillewaug?'

'Other than getting my dad in there when it opened, I invested a million dollars.'

'Back in nineteen ninety-nine?'

'Yes.'

'And your return on investment?'

'Solid,' he said.

'How solid?' she asked.

'Nothing the first two years, then a steady five to ten percent annually. Which, considering the crap economy, is damn good.'

'A million dollars is a lot of money. What made you decide to put it in Nillewaug?'

Her questions were starting to annoy. All of this she already knew; she was gauging his veracity. But one of the myriad things he'd learned in prison was that his natural tendency to lie had to be resisted. Lies, of which he told many, needed to be perfect. Lying for lying's sake was for kids and fools. 'Several reasons,' he said, keeping his tone even. 'I know and trust Wally and Jim. Grenville, as you're probably aware, is a Mecca for wealthy retirees and when they showed me the business plan, it seemed rock solid. And, it was at a time where I knew my dad had to downsize.' In spite of himself, he smiled – 'Like that was ever going to happen. I figured I could move him in at the beginning, get one of the best units.'

'At a discount?' Mattie asked.

'Yes,' he said, 'my dad loved nothing more than a good bargain.'

'How long ago did he retire?' she asked.

What is she doing? A twinge of rage like razors down his spine: *it's a trick.* 'According to him he never fully retired, just stopped performing surgery.'

'What does that mean . . . not fully retired? Was he still seeing patients?'

His blue eyes narrowed, while his tone stayed pleasant and conversational, a good citizen, a grieving son. 'He closed his surgical practice a year or two before moving to Nillewaug. I know that he kept renewing his license and went to conferences. Beyond that he told me about doing some consultation; I don't know the details.'

'Would you describe him as wealthy?' she asked.

'He was comfortable,' he said, trying to figure where she was going. *Of course, she's trying to establish motive.*

'Do you know his net worth?'

'Couple million I suspect.'

'But no longer in his name.'

He nodded. *Yes, she's either done her homework or is good at guessing.* 'When he moved to Nillewaug his financial adviser recommended we – me and my brothers – put the money into a trust. At the same time Dad did all the other legal stuff like power of attorney, updated his will and made one of my brothers his health-care proxy in case anything happened to him.'

'Wally Doyle was his adviser?'

He shook his head and sighed – more grief, but not too much. 'Yes.'

'And you didn't find that odd, or a conflict of interest?'

'Because he also worked for Nillewaug?' he asked, letting her know he understood where she was going and had nothing to hide.

He looked at Hank seated at the head of the table. 'While it's not as small as it used to be, this is Grenville. We don't think about things like that. Yes, it's probably not a good idea to have a friend or family member as your financial adviser or your attorney or your doctor, but we all do. End of the day it's a matter of trust and who has your back.' *And thank God he'd finally cut the strings on his hulking puppet.* He imagined fat Wally trying to field these questions, and the others that would most certainly follow. Like, *where did you come up with the idea to divest Nillewaug residents of their assets?* Or, *how did you know to stay below the thresholds for the number of residents you'd bill to Medicaid?*

'So on paper,' she continued, 'your father had very little in the way of assets. Even the bank accounts he had access to were under your brother Robert's name.'

'Yes.'

Detective Perez glanced at her young partner. 'What's the total so far, Jamie, of the cash found in Dr Trask's apartment?'

'Sixty-five thousand dollars.'

Dennis stared at the tall young woman and then back at the detective. His expression incredulous, but not overdone. 'What are you talking about?'

'You weren't aware that your father had a considerable amount of cash in his apartment?'

'No.' He stared at his hands, his brow furrowed. *Dad is dead, Delia is dead and Wally is dead, the only one left who knows is Jim – what have you been up to Jim? Did you kill my dad?* The only possible answer that made any sense was *yes.* With that realization, like a match on gasoline, his rage ignited. *Hold it together, Dennis, smile.* 'I know little about my father's day-to-day finances. All of that's handled by my brother, Robert. I have no idea why Dad had that kind of money.' *You're a dead man, Jim. Dead dead dead.* All doubt erased. Jim had killed his father . . . and Delia and then tried to bolt. *Dead dead dead.*

The young detective cleared her throat. 'And then there's the bonds.'

Dennis froze, his mind's eye picturing Jim Warren's body riddled with bullets. 'What bonds?'

'Fifty thousand dollars in old US bearer bonds,' Detective Perez said.

'Why would he have those?' Dennis asked, knowing exactly

where those bonds came from, and why his dad had so much
cash. All his life a seemingly endless supply of untaxed
liquidity that had bought Dennis's freedom on more than one
occasion.

'Good question. Do you have an answer?'

'No.'

'Or where that cash was coming from?'

'I don't.' But of course he did. Knowing how each week
Delia would give his father a couple thousand dollars for signing
off on stacks of bogus treatment plans for hundreds of Nillewaug
residents. His dad knew it was fraud, but rationalized it away.
It's no big deal, he'd say, *look at all the taxes these people
have paid. They deserve to have their care underwritten by
the government. It's peanuts. And if you think about it, the care
they're getting here –* ' never including himself – '*is better than
a nursing home.*'

'And you had no knowledge of your father's finances?'

'Just what I told you. You need to speak to my brother,
Bob.' Picturing his staid oldest brother, an orthopedic
surgeon like his father and a kiss-ass through and through.
But the truth, which was abundantly clear to all three
brothers, was that while dad had little time for Dennis
growing up, he was without doubt the favorite. If asked why,
his older brothers would mumble something about Dennis's
athletic abilities or his early school achievements – they
would be wrong.

'From what you said your father's estate is considerable.
Didn't you mind being marginalized in the decision making?'

'I didn't see it that way, and frankly, I don't see what
bearing this has on the investigation of my father's murder.
Detective Perez, if I'm under suspicion in any way, just come
out with it. This dancing around is getting us nowhere. I know
that you know I have a criminal past. You know I did a year
at Osborn and that I had my felony expunged seven years
after I got out. I'm sure Chief Morgan has told you about all
the stupid shit I did when I was a teenager. To say I was a
steady customer here would be an understatement. When it
came time for my dad to move to Nillewaug, and to do all
of that financial planning, I didn't want anything in my name.

My brothers and I have a long history; they don't trust me. And I don't blame them.'

'And obviously,' she said, 'a man who can invest a million dollars with friends is not hurting for money.'

'Correct.' Seeing where she was going, he beat her to the next line of questioning. 'My dad gave me a sizeable loan when I got out of prison. It paid for my first car dealership in exchange for a series of promises.' Despite the situation, he smiled, remembering those long-ago conversations with his dad, most of them during his weekly visits at Osborn. Those hours were some of his most treasured memories. *'We're more alike than you might think, Dennis,'* his father had said. And that had been the truth, although never before spoken. *'The difference,'* his respected surgeon father had explained, *'is you let people see your wild side and it scares them. I keep mine hidden, even from your mother. We both know how much better you are than everyone else, smarter, stronger, faster.'*

It was during those talks that Dennis had shared with his father that things weren't quite so hidden. *'I know about you and your women, Dad. The receptionist you paid off, the girls when you're at your "conferences".'* There was more, having spent hours perusing his father's financial statements and the books for his surgical practice, realizing that what his dad reported to the IRS was roughly a third of what he had coming in. And then there was always cash and bonds in the gun safe, which Dennis had learned how to break in to when he was eleven. Stacks of cash from patients who, for whatever reasons, didn't want to go through their insurance companies and paid for procedures in cash. And now the detective, while raising questions, had clarified several. Finding that much cash in his dad's apartment 'A' made sense and 'B' ruled out robbery. He fidgeted with his Styrofoam cup. 'My dad wanted me to straighten up, and we negotiated what that would entail. It worked out pretty well.'

'How much was the loan for?' she asked.

'Five hundred grand for a down payment on the Toyota dealership, and then a second loan for the same when I wanted to get the lot next door. But after a few years where he saw I wasn't slipping back into my evil ways . . .' He shot Hank a look. 'And yes, I did have a couple slips that I'm certain our Police Chief will tell you about, but eventually my dad told me to forget about the money.' A tear tracked down his cheek. 'He told me that he'd paid for college for my brothers and that this was no different. I went to Osborn and they went to Yale and Stanford.'

'What about enemies?' Mattie asked.

Dennis stopped. Years of dealing with cops, judges and attorneys had trained him never to jump at an unclear question. Instead, taking a page from all the attorneys who'd prepped him over the years, he parroted her question. 'Enemies?'

'Your father, are you aware if there was anyone who'd want to harm him?'

'No. My dad was well liked. If he had an enemy I didn't know about it.' He knew this was untrue, but the irony was that the man who killed his father – Jim Warren – was far more friend than enemy. He wondered if his dad had suffered, and knew that if these officers didn't lock him up here and now, he wouldn't rest till Jim had paid for what he'd done. Thinking of the how gave him a tingle of excitement.

Detective Perez turned to Hank Morgan. 'Did you have any questions?' she asked.

To Dennis it felt like she was checking in with the local Police Chief – *God, he looks old.* He waited, thinking of his dad, of how many times he'd been called by Hank in the past. Always showing up, never doing what Jim's dad would do – *'Leave him there overnight, knock some sense into him.'* He wondered what was running through Hank's head. There had been lots of situations, but so far in the past. All the kids he'd shake down for their lunch money or just for the fun of it. Occasionally one of them working up the balls to try and fight back, but with Wally and then Jim at his side it never went well for them. As a kid he'd get a thrill when the calls would come from angry parents, teachers, or the vice principal – *'The principal in charge of vice,'* Jim would joke. Listening in the hall as his mother fretted and made excuses.

'Are you certain it was Dennis? It must have been some other boy.' Her feeble attempts at discipline. *'You have to be punished. When your father gets here . . .'*

Hank looked at Dennis. 'Dennis, were you aware that Jim and Wally were in some kind of financial trouble with Nillewaug?'

Interesting, Dennis thought, meeting the Police Chief's gaze. This does feel like old times, that weird sensation that Hank Morgan knew more than he was telling. Hank could play the hick cop, but he was no fool. It was a trap and for the first time in the interview he didn't know how to avoid it. 'I didn't,' he said, going for the simplest lie possible. But as it left his lips he knew that Hank knew it wasn't true.

'Who told you about Wally?' he asked.

'What about him?'

Hank cocked a brow. 'His . . . death.'

'Jen,' Dennis said, suddenly feeling like he was falling back in time and was once again the smart-mouthed drunk teenager in the holding tank. *And why did he say 'death' that way?*

'Of course. You ever see Bill Stankus?'

Dennis fought the impulse to smirk. 'No,' he said, remembering one of the dorky kids he'd terrorized from elementary through high school. Stinky Stankus, the name he'd been given after peeing himself in fear in the third grade.

'Roger Clayton?'

'Sorry, no, not since junior high.' *What is he going for? Gayton* Clayton was the biggest fag in town, now supposedly some big deal Broadway producer. Clayton was also the first kid that landed a then twelve-year-old Dennis in real trouble. It hadn't been his fault. Prissy little Clayton had overreacted when Dennis had done his usual routine. It had been after school, and maybe it was the purple puffy-sleeved shirt Clayton was wearing that day, but the kid had it coming. They'd rode home on the same bus, Clayton getting out a few stops before Dennis. But on that day, Dennis, without Wally or Jim, had followed Clayton. Middle of the afternoon, no one around. He'd felt the kid's fear, as he'd tried to pretend Dennis wasn't steps behind him and just kept walking. 'Hey, Gayton,' he'd shouted, when the bus pulled away, 'have you always liked to suck dick?' And then Clayton had said something smart-assed – *no*, he thought, trying to remember. Maybe he'd just begged Dennis to leave him alone. As if that was going to happen.

And Dennis was all over him, not really meaning to hurt him, just the fun of watching him cry, his hands over his face, falling to the ground. Dennis kicking his books into a clump of poison ivy and then stomping Clayton, something about that feeling so right. Looking around the wooded street, no one watching. Kicking him again. 'Get your hands out of the way.' The kid holding his belly, trying to cover his face. 'I said, get your fucking hands out of the way!' A kick in the gut, a kick in the back. The kid blubbering, begging him to stop. Kick kick kick, and then a woman's voice: 'What the hell do you think you're doing? Leave him alone! I'm calling the cops! Leave him alone!' Even the memory of it causing his pulse to quicken, standing over Clayton, knowing the kid's life was in his hands. But now, looking up at Hank, those familiar eyes the way he was watching him.

Hank turned to Detective Perez. 'Roger Clayton wound up with a broken wrist and nose. His parents were going to press charges, and for some reason they ended up changing their mind, pulled their kid out of the public-school system and sent him to private. Why did they change their mind, Dennis?'

Dennis felt the last thirty years of trying to keep his nose clean get stripped away. 'My dad settled with them.'

'Yes,' Hank said, 'a nice way of putting it. You got sent to detention for less than a week. Your dad cut them a check, and despite my strong recommendation that they go through with the case the Claytons begged off. Didn't think it would be in their son's best interest. I don't think I've ever seen a kid so frightened. His parents told me for a couple months he wouldn't leave his house. You'd really done a job on him.'

'Why bring this up?' Dennis asked, trying to get his bearings. Wondering what any of this had to do with Nillewaug or his father.

Hank's expression was unreadable. 'Detective Perez asked if your father had enemies. I suspect he did. You certainly do. Human nature is what it is. Yes, your dad paid off the Claytons, but do you think Roger ever forgot what you did to him?'

Dennis stared back. 'You think Roger Clayton had something to do with my father's murder?'

'Of course not,' Hank said. 'He's a success. He left town and never looked back. But his parents weren't the only ones to get paid off, were they?' And he turned to Detective Perez. 'The funny thing about Dr Trask was his ability to talk parents into dropping charges. But the kids,' he said, looking back at Dennis. 'The three of you did some real damage to some of those kids. I've always wondered . . .' The corners of Hank's mouth turned down and his eyes looked hard. 'Vicky Binghamton.'

Dennis felt like he was seventeen again. Knowing he was in deep shit and there was nothing his dad could do about it. Frightened, but exhilarated too.

'Who's Vicky Binghamton?' Perez asked.

'Prettiest girl in town at the time. Fifteen years old when Dennis and his two buddies decided to get her drunk and gang rape her.'

Dennis knew to say nothing, but every detail about that glorious night crisp as a new twenty. It had been a pre-game rally party at Jim Warren's house. It was Jim who'd invited the blue-eyed blonde-haired sophomore, with her long legs and full young breasts. She'd had a huge crush on quarterback Jim; it might even have been reciprocated the way Jim talked about her – '*I've never met a girl so beautiful.*' She was hot, a ripe peach waiting to be plucked. Sitting there Dennis looked between Hank, Detective Perez, and the young detective. They were staring at him. 'Charges were never brought.'

Hank snorted. 'Of course not. What a shock, and then Vicky and her mother – who was your father's receptionist – left town. I always wondered what that one cost. Or was it a three-way settlement? I have to say, Dennis, the fact that your father had all that cash on hand . . . bearer bonds, it's cleared up something I've always wondered.'

Detective Plank looked across at him. 'What's that?'

'Whenever parents wanted to bring charges against Dennis it almost immediately turned into a settlement discussion. But what never made sense were the amounts. The Clayton settlement just covered medical expenses and maybe a year of private school; it didn't seem enough. I'll check, but it was maybe fifty grand. It seemed too small, especially where there was an attorney involved. So now I'm thinking the bulk of the settlement happened under the table. Which makes sense, because then not only did Dr Trask get Dennis out of any immediate trouble, he's now involved the parents in doing something illegal.'

'Because they're not declaring that money on their taxes,' Jamie added.

'Yes.' Hank glared at Dennis. 'Altogether, Dennis, how many settlements were there?'

'I don't know. It was a long time ago; my dad never told me the details.' And that wasn't a lie. Although he could guess where cash had exchanged hands, but how much and how often – no clue. '*You don't need to know, son,*' his father would say. '*Just don't do it again.*'

Dennis's tears flowed anew as he realized that the only people on this earth who loved him unconditionally, certainly more than his wife and his two greedy sons, were gone. '*I won't, Dad. I promise.*' Neither he nor his dad putting any stock in that promise.

'Now,' Hank said, fixing Dennis with a cold stare. 'Why don't you tell us about your relationship with Delia Preston?'

SEVENTEEN

L il's cheeks burned and her inner adolescent screamed as she listened to Edward Fleming's critique of her article over the phone. 'Not rigorous, Lil. Not by a long shot. I had to go with it, though, but there are too many holes. You just don't have the experience. I've put Daryl Bent on the story. I'm sorry. I told him to call you for some background material.'

She stared at the monitor on her desk, as the late edition of *The Brattlebury Register* appeared. She fought back her first and second impulses – yell at Fleming and beg him to reconsider – and went with her third option. 'Mr Fleming, I'm the first to admit I'm new at this. Can you tell me what's missing?'

'You asked more questions than you answered, Lil. People need to go away understanding the story; it's basic reporting. And where there are holes, you have to fill them with something, and not speculation. When you read it, you'll see I edited out most of your "unable to say" and "authorities won't comment"; that stuff has to be done with a light hand. Don't get me wrong, you had some good stuff, and the pictures of Wally Doyle were tremendous, but after reading your two features, the reader doesn't know what happened at Nillewaug. Instead, they've got this rambling conspiracy, with no motive, and not enough facts. The stuff about Medicaid fraud was tremendous, but where's the proof? How much money? For how long? How did it work? I mean this is *Journalism 101*. And with the exception of the woman who got pushed out the window we don't really know if the other four dead were murdered or was it just a freaky coincidence. You have the local Fire Marshall and the one from the state hedging on their reports and nothing in final form. You told us in the first story there was accelerant, but we still don't know if that was incidental or deliberate. Was the fire set or not? And how the hell did you miss the piece about the alarms not working or being shut off? I don't want to read about something as significant as that in my competition.'

The only consolation in this miserable call was that Lil didn't have to be there in person, feeling on the verge of tears. Struggling to keep her voice neutral, she had to say something. 'All of what's in there is true. The confusion and ambiguity is part of what's going on. There are three layers of law enforcement, whose efforts from what I can see are not co-ordinated. And as I mentioned in the story –' feeling battered and defensive – 'the first federal agents on the scene of Doyle's suicide were investigating fraud allegations, and did little more than secure the scene while waiting for an FBI homicide team. On top of that you have the investigation of the fire – both local and state – and a swarm of insurance adjusters all with their own agendas.'

Fleming interrupted, his tone impatient. 'Lil, just stop. Step back from the story and you've got the biggest assisted-care facility in this part of the state, largely uninhabitable with six hundred residents homeless. Not to mention a major employer, with hundreds of employees. This is what should have been in your story; the crisp reporting of facts. You were OK in the first piece, but this second one . . . The story is too big, you're too green and you don't know how to focus. I'm sorry. A seasoned reporter would run the story that's complete, or nearly complete. You're attempting the whole thing, and it's too much.'

'Eyes too big for my stomach,' she offered, trying to understand his critique.

'Yes. It doesn't mean that speculation isn't important. Of course it is, it's just not the story; it's the reporter's work.'

Sensing he wanted to end the call, she made a plea. 'Could you give me another shot? I've got the connections, I know this town.'

There was silence. 'I can't, you had your shot and you blew it with that last piece. I won't be put in that position again. I need to know that my lead story – this story – will be set for the morning edition. I know Daryl will do that, and I want you to pay attention to how he does it . . . Tell you what, take one of the side stories, one that you think is important and work it through. If it's good and it adds something, I'll run it. If not, I won't.' And he abruptly said goodbye and hung up.

She wanted to argue, but instead listened to the dial tone, and stared at the monitor. Preoccupied with his words – *I won't be put in that position again* – she didn't hear Ada in the hall.

'You OK?' Ada asked, coming up behind her.

'My story sucks,' Lil said, feeling like she'd been punched in the gut.

'Says who?' Ada pulled up the wooden rocker and sat next to her.

Lil told her about Fleming's comments and of being pulled off the story. 'I feel like a kid who's just gotten an "F".' Her eyes shifting from Ada back to the screen and her story that had just been posted. 'Crap,' she added, reading the headline and the lead:

Nillewaug Village Chief Financial Officer Dead from Suspected Suicide
– Lil Campbell, correspondent

A single gunshot rang out in the exclusive cul-de-sac community of Eagle's Cairn just after noon today. Wallace Doyle, financial adviser and Chief Financial Officer (CFO) for the Nillewaug Village assisted-care community was dead from a catastrophic, and apparently self-inflicted, head injury. Discovered in the pool house behind his stately home by this reporter and two federal agents just moments after the gunshot was heard, he was found holding a handgun . . .'

Lil shook her head. 'He's right. This is garbage.'

Ada read over her shoulder. 'They picked the picture I thought they would,' she commented. It was an image of Wally Doyle, his head tilted back, and the framed photo of the three Ravens with blood splatter behind him. The angle obscured most of the gore from his mangled jaw; it told the story without being gross.

Lil felt numb. 'He said the pictures were good.' She forced herself to read on, noting how many times she used words like *apparent, possible, speculation, hypothesis, unknown, uncertain.* Her prose was little more than a magician waving his hands; Fleming's words ate like a cancer. *What do you think you're doing, Lil? You're no reporter.*

'It's good, Lil. I don't know what he was talking about,' Ada said.

'Thanks,' Lil replied, turning to look at her, knowing she was trying to be supportive. But Fleming was the authority and he essentially said it sucked. 'So how are *you* holding up?' Lil asked, realizing that she'd been so self-absorbed since getting out of bed this morning, she'd had little time to check in on Ada and her various charges.

'Tired,' she admitted. 'I think my mom has more energy than I do. She and Alice are like a pair of wind-up toys that just keep going. They're taking a walk around the lake.'

'Is Aaron with them?'

She laughed. 'No, he said he needed to take a nap before dinner.'

Lil pushed back from the computer and looked out the single window in her office at the woods behind their condos. A buzzing caught her attention. 'There's a fly in here,' she said. The buzz stopped, and then started again.

'In the window,' Ada said.

Lil got up and pulled back the curtain edge. Her pulse quickened; it wasn't a fly but a large black and orange wasp, maybe a yellow jacket.

'Keep it away from me.' Ada headed toward the door, wary due to her dangerous allergy to any kind of bee bite, for which she had to keep an epinephrine injection near her at all times.

Lil grabbed a wad of tissues from the box beside the computer and, keeping her eyes on the buzzing insect, went for the kill. She crushed and felt its body crunch between her fingers. 'Weird,' she said, opening the tissue to look at the gooey corpse.

'What?'

'The Hornets were the team The Ravens played in their second state finals. I guess what's weird is how the fire and Wally Doyle's suicide bring such a tragic ending to an otherwise positive bit of town history. Poor bug.'

'Poor my ass,' Ada said. 'That thing could kill me. And you keep coming back to these Ravens.' She pointed at the computer screen and the picture of Wally Doyle.

'So?' she asked, still badly demoralized by Fleming's comments.

'Lil, snap out of this.' Ada stroked her cheek. 'You just had two feature stories back to back, and finished your column. Give yourself a break.'

'I hate it that he's right. And I don't want to give up on this story.'

'Then don't, you're in the middle of something and you've got to figure it out. My money's on all the connections to the football team. It's too much to be coincidence. There's something there, and you're the one who's going to find it.'

'I don't know,' Lil said, letting Ada's words sink in. 'For years I was Bradley's wife, his helpmate, office manager, pseudo-nurse, mother, chauffeur for Tina and Barbara. All of that was great . . . or at least OK. But it's like a part of me was put away. I remember reading *The Feminine Mystique* when I was in my twenties, and thinking how so much of it was true, but didn't apply to me. I wasn't unhappy or unfulfilled. Being part of Bradley's medical practice was meaningful. He used to say how lucky he felt being able to make a living at helping people. And I loved that about him and about the practice. I guess I never realized how much, and when he sold the practice and we moved here . . .' She struggled to find the words. 'I remember packing up the house and thinking, OK, now we're going to a retirement community. Is this it? Like my life is winding down and I've missed something important.'

'Of course I get it,' Ada said. 'For me it was being the power behind the throne. The woman behind the man. Harry was a showman, and Strauss's would never have been the success it was without him. But he had no head for figures, and he trusted people he shouldn't have. All of which fell to me. And I loved it! When we sold out, I brokered the deal.' She shook her head. 'There was lots of writing on the wall, we were getting edged out by the big chains, didn't have nearly the bargaining power we needed and I knew that his health was slipping. He didn't want to sell. I wore him down. I had to.'

'Do you miss it?' Lil asked.

'I don't. I loved it at the time, building a business and watching it grow and knowing that it was our doing. But it was time, we made out great and it's not something I'd do again. I like my life here . . . my life with you. But it's your turn now. You have a passion for writing, you need to do this.'

Her words were like a balm. 'Fleming told me to take one of the side stories.'

'Then do. But go with your strengths. This is your town and you know everyone involved in this story. And screw the bastard, don't let him get into your head. If you get the better story, he'll have to use it.'

'I don't know about that.' There was a banging at the front door, and then the bell rang. 'Coming,' Lil said, spotting Rose and Alice through the window, still in their mismatched borrowed sweats and new walking shoes. 'What's up?' she asked, opening the door.

'Is my daughter here?' Rose sounded winded.

Ada followed behind. 'Mom?'

'I've made a decision,' Rose stated, a glow in her cheeks from her walk by the lake. 'I don't know why you didn't think of this before. But I like it here. This is so much nicer than that death trap you dumped me in. Don't you agree, Alice?'

The demented redhead turned at the sound of her name. 'Yes, it's pretty.'

'Wouldn't you rather live here?' Rose asked Alice. 'All these walking paths, and we met such lovely people at the lake.' She turned to Ada. 'Why didn't you tell me there was so much to do here? Did you know they have bus trips to the city twice a week, and it's only forty dollars including lunch and a show? And the grounds; it's like living in a park . . . you must pay a fortune in common fees. How many gardeners do they have?'

Alice smiled. 'I like the ducks.'

'It feels like home,' Rose continued. 'This woman we met by the lake, Candace . . . do you know her?'

'No,' Ada said, her expression wary.

'Nice lady. Used to be a travel agent. She was saying they offer water aerobics. My orthopedist was saying that would be the best thing for my arthritis. Remember how much I used to love going to the Y? Candace said you have two Olympic-size pools, and that the health club is free to residents. Is that true?'

'It is,' Ada said. 'Do you want to buy a condo here?'

'Why would I do that?' Rose smiled at her daughter. 'You're obviously not living in yours. I can see that. It's just Aaron. Why couldn't Alice and I move in? There's three bedrooms. It's ridiculous having them empty like that. We'd each take one and Aaron has his.'

'Which one's the boy?' Alice asked, looking at Lil and then at Ada.

'They have a point,' Lil said, trying to ignore Alice. 'At least for the short run.'

Ada stared at her mother. 'Of course you can stay as long

as you need to, Mom. There's no question about that. But Alice's family might have other plans . . .'

'Please,' Rose said, 'it's just her grandson, Kyle, and his sister in Manhattan. And you saw that poor boy; he's got enough on his plate without having to worry about his grandmother. And he said his sister is a big-shot realtor in the city.' Rose's voice lowered to a whisper. 'No way in hell she's going to take care of Alice.'

'Kyle's a good boy,' Alice said with enthusiasm. 'Are we going home?'

'We are home,' Rose said.

'Oh goody!' Alice's face lit with joy. 'Goody goody goody.'

'But, Mom . . .' Ada looked panicked.

Lil looked at Rose and out-of-it Alice, and an idea took root. She had two displaced Nillewaug residents living with her. This was a story, or at least it could be. The more she thought about it, the better she liked it. A chance to get away from the reporting of numbers – six hundred displaced, tens of millions in damages and all of the factoids that, while important, robbed the story of its deeper meanings – people had lost their homes, their sense of security and, in five instances, their lives. 'Rose, would you let me interview you for the paper?'

'Of course, Lil. But why would you want to write about me?'

'Lil?' Ada looked at her. 'What are you thinking?'

'I think I found my story. Could we do this now?'

'Sure.' Rose took a couple of steps toward the rock garden and bench. 'But someone has to keep an eye on Alice, and Aaron's sleeping. Ada? Could you?' Rose looked at her daughter. 'Ada, don't look so scared. I know you're trying to think of reasons why I can't live here. But it's the logical solution.' She then turned to Lil, her expression serious. 'Lil, I'm old, but I'm not stupid. You and Ada need to make the decision. Whether or not you decide to tell me what's going on is also your choice, the both of you.'

'OK then,' Lil said, not knowing how to respond, as she realized Rose had guessed that Ada and she had moved beyond best friends. 'Ada, could you stay with Alice while I interview your mom?'

'Of course.'

The two women's eyes met, and Lil went to Ada. Her voice low: 'I think she knows about us.'

'Probably,' Ada replied. 'And she still wants to move in. Do you think she's right? It makes sense, at least for now.'

'I'm OK with it. In some ways this place is a better fit for her than for us.'

Ada nodded, deep in thought. 'Let me get Alice better settled. I think at any rate she'll be with us for a bit. We'll talk later.'

'Good.' Feeling the eyes of the two older women on them, not to mention their across-the-path neighbors, Lil resisted the urge to kiss Ada. It rankled as she realized that when Bradley had been alive, a quick peck as they parted on the walkway would have been standard. Here, with Ada, it would be cause for gossip. 'I love you,' Lil whispered.

'Same here, I think we're about to find out if that's enough.' She turned back toward her mother and Alice. 'Hey, Alice, let's get you set up.'

Rose let go of Alice's hand. She smiled as she looked at her demented friend's pink walking shoes. She glanced at Lil and shrugged. 'I got black but she insisted on the pink.'

'You went practical,' Lil offered.

'Or blah. Can we chat outside?' She looked toward the stone bench in the middle of the rock garden with its tidy evergreens, budding crocus and tender iris shoots.

'Of course, almost no one sits out here.' Lil thought about running inside for her recorder or at least a pad, but something told her to not lose the moment.

'What a waste,' Rose said, settling her stocky frame on the bench. 'Perfect height for me.' She sighed. 'Isn't that funny?' she added, looking at the condo across the way.

'What?' Lil followed her gaze.

'I just saw the curtain in that window move.' She smiled and waved in the direction of Bernice Framm's kitchen. 'This is what living in the country is supposed to be. I'm glad to be out of that place.'

'What was so bad about it?' Lil asked, realizing that this was the first time Rose and she had had any kind of real conversation without Ada around.

'Where to start?' She turned and Lil was struck by the depth of her earnestness. 'It was . . . is . . . a place to die. It's lovely and the food was good, but lipstick on a pig and it's still a death house. An abattoir for unwanted grannies.'

Lil chuckled. 'You don't think that's a bit much?'

'No. Everyone was so old . . . and yes, I have no illusions about my own age. But it's one thing to know you're ninety, but another to live in a world where you're constantly reminded of it. The dining hall was the worst.'

'How so?'

'The conversation, and I tried. But all anyone wanted to talk about was how no one visited, and of course . . . their bowels.' She stared down the path, through her thick glasses her eyes were magnified and seemed unfocused. 'Those were the two themes – depressed and constipated. The food really was good, though. But it was getting to where I'd just as soon stay in my apartment and microwave frozen dinners.' She shook her head. 'I don't blame Ada, though. I know it sounds like I do. In case you haven't noticed, Lil, it sucks getting old. And New York was getting bad. I couldn't leave my apartment alone any more. Between my eyes and my hearing, it was too much. I never told her, or my other children . . . last fall I got mugged.'

'That's terrible. What happened? Were you hurt?'

'It was stupid and it happened fast. I went to the pharmacy, and didn't feel like waiting for them to deliver. Some kid with a hood over his head followed me out and grabbed my purse. Like an idiot I didn't let go.' She shook her head. 'I was so mad, he broke the strap of my favorite bag and then pushed me hard. I was lucky I was close to a building; if I'd fallen I would have broken my hip. He was swearing at me, like he hated me. He couldn't have been more than sixteen, probably Aaron's age. I can still picture him. There was spit flying out of his mouth. I screamed at him, "What's wrong with you?" My bag ripped open and he grabbed my purse and my prescriptions and ran. Probably thought I had some good pills . . . hope he enjoyed my diuretic.'

'Did you call the police?'

'Why? It was done. I had twelve dollars in my purse, and

when I got home I cancelled my credit card, and called my doctor to ask him for new prescriptions. But that was the last time I left my apartment alone. I hated feeling that way, frightened to go outside.'

'Why didn't you tell Ada?'

'Because it would just have become more fuel for the "what to do about Mom" discussion. I'd pretty much resigned myself to staying in my apartment until they carted me out in a box. The nurses came, although even they were making trouble. When I had my heart attack last year and stayed with Ada, they'd told me if I couldn't walk and get around my apartment they wouldn't come. There was a whole list of things I had to be able to do, or they'd refuse to reopen my case. They said they couldn't take on the liability.'

'I remember,' Lil said. 'There was a checklist.'

'I was so frightened. It was my last bit of freedom. If I couldn't do each of those tasks, I was convinced I'd land in a nursing home. It was humiliating. I'm a grown woman and suddenly I'm being graded on can I get in and out of bed, out of a chair, on and off the toilet. Can I wipe my own butt? And in the end –' clapping her hands in front of her – 'say what you will, but Nillewaug for all of its fancy furniture and ridiculous prices was a nursing home. At least it didn't smell like piss.'

'But everyone depressed and constipated.'

'Yes . . . and one other thing, dirt poor.'

'Excuse me?' Lil perked at the use of a description not generally applied to the affluent residents. 'That place was not cheap.'

'You ain't kidding. My buy-in was close to four hundred grand, and that was after Ada bargained them down from over five. And the monthly fees were three thousand five hundred.'

'That kind of argues against poor. Your typical Nillewaug resident had to have a sizeable nest egg.'

'Exactly.' Her teeth clenched. 'That was the other topic of conversation, and boy did that place feed on it.'

'What do you mean?'

'Money and fear. You're lucky, Lil. And I know Ada's set, and because of her I don't worry about it too much; it's not like I'm going to end up on the street. She put up most of the buy-in for Nillewaug. If it had been my money, I would never have done it. But money was something that got talked about a lot. And boy did those people play on it.'

'The Nillewaug Promise?' Lil asked.

'Yes, the promise.' Rose's mouth twisted. 'I got sick of hearing about The Promise. "Don't worry, you're set until death you do depart." But people did worry . . . a lot. And they were angry.'

'About?'

'About being poor, about losing control. We were all encouraged to sign things over to our children, or in some cases our grandchildren.'

'So on paper people would appear to have nothing.' Lil thought about Fleming's criticisms of her last story. Yes, she'd brought up the Medicaid fraud angle; what she hadn't done was explain it. 'Did that happen to you?'

'I don't have much. Ada's the one with money. But some of the other residents were loaded. We're talking CEOs, family money, or just people who'd invested well and saved for retirement. You'd think that getting us in there and then hitting us up for those monthly fees would have been enough, but that was just the beginning. Is this what you wanted to hear about?'

Lil nodded.

'Good. The day I moved in there was a thick packet on the kitchen counter and an invitation for "three complementary sessions" with the fat man – Mr Doyle. I imagine it has something to do with why he shot himself. Something wasn't right.'

'Do you have details? Or know who would?'

She rocked back slightly catching the sun on her face. 'Trusts; he pressured a lot of the residents to sign their assets over to their children. I can give you some names, and I know that they weren't happy about it. Felt like they were forced into doing it. Others . . .' She looked toward Ada's condo door. 'Like Alice, if someone gave all her money away, would she even notice?'

'Her grandson would.'

'Yes, but think about it, Lil. Kyle would do anything for Alice.' She chuckled, and mimicked Alice: *'He's a good boy.*

But how many children and grandchildren are just waiting for their inheritance? What if some fat guy in a suit with a bunch of degrees behind his desk told you that you didn't have to wait for grandma to kick the bucket?'

Lil was struck by Rose's savvy, and felt slightly ashamed for not having noticed her keen intelligence sooner. 'So collusion between prospective heirs and Nillewaug. It's a good theory, Rose, and not far from what I've been thinking. What I need is proof.'

'That could be tough. Considering Doyle's dead, and . . .' She shuddered. 'And Ms Preston too. I dreamed about her last night, only she wasn't falling from Nillewaug but from the Trade Center. Nine eleven was the first time I ever wanted to leave New York. It wasn't long after that Ada and Harry moved into this place.'

Lil had never made that connection, but, thinking back, she and Bradley moved in 2002 and Ada and Harry took the adjoining condo a few months later. Before then they'd had a town house in Brooklyn Heights. Ada rarely spoke about 9/11, and whenever it came on the news she'd be shaken by it. The general reason she gave for the move was Harry's deteriorating health, his heart and lungs and a rapidly progressing dementia. They'd both married men considerably older than themselves, and moving here in their mid fifties had made Lil and Ada two of the youngest in Pilgrim's Progress. But to hear Rose, she wondered if part of Ada's exodus from New York had to do with that awful day – living in that part of Brooklyn, one stop from downtown Manhattan; it must have been terrifying.

'Do you think someone is trying to clean house?' Rose asked.

'It's possible,' Lil said, noting how quickly Rose's mind shifted topics . . . like her daughter's.

'You do know that the fat man wasn't the brightest bulb in the box?'

'You don't think he was competent.'

'I thought he was reading a script,' she said bluntly. 'And once he knew that I had no real money, no "assets to protect for my children and grandchildren" . . . He used that phrase a lot. And don't get me wrong, I am blessed in my family,

love them dearly, but if I had a lot of cash I'd blow it on trips
to the casino. Which, I cannot believe Ada neglected to tell
me, are perfectly possible given that Pilgrim's Progress has
weekly trips to Foxwoods and Mohegan Sun. Do you go?'

'I don't, but back to Wally Doyle. He wanted you to put
your money into a trust?'

'Yes. And it was clearly the point of the interview, like one
of those horrible salesmen trying to trick you into a time share
by offering you a free vacation. Everything else had been a
lead up. I remember having to stop him to say I had no money
and he was wasting his time. That it was Ada who was under-
writing that ridiculously expensive place. It's strange . . .'

'What?'

'It's almost as if he didn't believe me. Although –' she
clicked her tongue – 'that's not quite it . . . he had trouble
accepting what I was telling him, and kept pushing the trust.
He could set it up, he's sure my children would want it . . .
I told him "no" repeatedly. But thinking back, I could see how
just his persistence would get most people to say yes, just to
get him to shut up.'

'Hard sell.'

'Very. But I don't think this helps your story much. And I
doubt Alice would even remember meeting Doyle. And honestly,
I don't think she has much money, either. You need to talk to
someone who actually went for it.'

'You're right,' Lil said, remembering what Kyle had told
her about his grandmother and how he'd arranged for her to
stay at Nillewaug. 'You have someone in mind?'

'Maybe if I saw a list of names.'

'What's the matter?' Lil asked, seeing tears through Rose's
glasses.

'It's nothing. I was in that place for four months and didn't
really make friends. Maybe I never gave it a chance, but I was
so angry. It's funny, I lived all my life in an apartment in New
York that wasn't much bigger, but moving to Nillewaug . . .
it felt like prison . . . or worse. The place before you die. I
know that I don't have a lot of years left. Even just talking
about Nillewaug – and what a pretentious name – it makes
my chest ache.'

Lil cut her a worried look.

She cracked a smile. 'No, I'm not having a heart attack. But heart sick, in a place like that there's no hope. You're there to die, and before you go they're going to strip you of anything worth taking. Like cows to slaughter . . . it was an abattoir.'

'Really?' Lil laughed.

'I do love my crossword puzzles. Do you get *The Times* delivered?' she asked.

'No.' Thinking it wouldn't be a bad idea, if for no other reason than to study the reporting and prose styles of the reporters, Lil told her she'd get it started.

Rose shrugged. 'I don't think I was much help.'

'No, you were.' And that was the truth although not in the way Lil had anticipated. But again she was left with more questions than answers. She thought about Wally Doyle, pushing past the horrible images of his mangled face. Seeing his fat frame stuffed in a navy suit, sitting next to his pretty blonde wife at church, and then remembering him in the dark purple-and-white Raven's uniform, an unstoppable behemoth. Rose had made a critical observation – Wally wasn't that smart, certainly not the type to mastermind a complex financial fraud. Jim Warren on the other hand – absolutely. And Dennis Trask with his sprawling empire of car dealerships – without a doubt. Even Delia Preston, although she was likely more of a cog in a larger machine. Still, there was something about Delia, remembering the fierce intelligence that shone beneath her polished exterior. All of it snuffed out, and someone trying to make it look like an accident.

Ada called out from her condo, 'Lil?' She was carrying a stack of papers. Behind her, Alice followed, having changed into a pink tracksuit that still had the size sticker on the leg and her matching pink running shoes. 'You need to see these.' And she handed Lil a stack of forms.

After years in Bradley's office, Lil immediately recognized the Medicaid statements. They all bore Alice's name, reassured the recipient 'This is not a bill' and then itemized services billed over the prior month. In this case 'Skilled Nursing Facility' i.e. a nursing home at the per diem rate of a hundred and ten dollars – thirty-three hundred for the month. Lil's pulse quickened, realizing that this was potentially a smoking gun. 'Rose, Alice was your next-door neighbor at Nillewaug, correct?'

'Yes.'

Lil looked at the redhead who stood transfixed by a clump of yellow and white daffodils that had bloomed overnight. She thought back to last fall. 'Ada, do you remember when we met with Delia last year?'

'Of course, why?'

She stared at Alice; this was not someone who could be deemed capable of living on her own. She needed constant redirection, would be unsafe around a stove, probably need some help dressing. Although so far that hadn't seemed a huge issue. 'Rose, the building you lived in was considered independent living?'

'Yes, why?'

'Something doesn't make sense . . . didn't Delia specifically say they wouldn't take someone who had dementia as a resident?'

Ada nodded. 'She was vague, said something about "a significant degree of". But then –' and she too looked at Alice – 'maybe it wasn't so bad when she moved in. Delia did say that once they took someone they'd provide care for the long haul. Maybe she wasn't showing signs when she moved in. Or maybe Kyle was able to keep it under wraps.'

'Maybe.' Still holding the forms, Lil felt connections take hold.

Ada commented: 'I wonder how much money's involved with this Medicaid scam. Just for Alice, thirty-three hundred a month, just shy of forty grand a year. How many people in that building were they doing that for?'

'It wasn't a nursing home,' Lil said. She scanned down to the signature lines and next to the space for *attending MD/ DO* the name: *Norman Trask, MD*. A supposedly retired surgeon signing forms for patients who weren't in a nursing home – *what was in it for him?*

'Sure felt like a nursing home,' Rose said, looking at Ada.

Lil's head swam as the line of investigation she needed to

pursue took shape. Get a list of the residents, find out how many were on Medicaid, try to contact either them or their families, download policies and definitions for nursing homes, get the rules for Medicaid eligibility . . . And something else . . . 'Ada?' She walked away from Rose to the far side of the little stone wall that provided the border for the seating area. Ada followed. 'I don't think Kyle's been entirely honest with us.'

'About?'

'Think about it. His grandmother is too demented to be in her own apartment. She's getting billed nursing-home-level care for services she's not receiving. He must have known about that. What if?'

'What if he's part of it?' she stated. 'It seems he would have to have known something. But he seems so nice. In my heart I can't believe he's faking that. Look at how hard he's trying to help people, and how devoted he is to Alice.'

'Maybe. Or maybe he's trying to cover his tracks . . . Ladies?' Calling back to Rose and Alice. 'I need to make some calls. Ada, are you all set?'

'We're good,' she said. 'Do what you need to do.' A worried expression crossed her face. 'This is giving me the creeps, Lil. Maybe you should leave this to the cops. Call Mattie and tell her about this.'

'I think she already knows. She was the one who told me that they were investigating fraud. I think I'm just catching up.'

'No.' Ada persisted. 'Someone killed Delia, lit fire to a building with six hundred residents and God knows what else. Lil, I'm worried. We have to be careful. Whoever's behind this is not fooling around.'

Lil felt her fear, and realized she was right. The rational part of her mind was saying – *this is none of your business, this is dangerous.* 'I want to find out what happened. I need to.'

Ada gave a crooked smile. 'I know. And you want to be the first with the story.'

'Yes.'

'Good. So how can I help?'

EIGHTEEN

Kyle Sullivan gave a weary smile to the Latina cleaning woman as she exited the fourth-floor conference room in the Safe Harbor Pavilion, aka the Alzheimer's and dementia building. Inside were law-enforcement agents, four in suits and the tall silver-haired local Chief of Police. Next to him was a short woman in a navy suit, whom he recognized from after the fire.

He watched the cleaning woman as she headed down the hall and felt badly for her; she was probably out of a job having worked in the now uninhabitable central residential building. Several brief conversations with the facility's HR director, Frank Stillman, had left him confused, angry and scared. As the only available member of Nillewaug's executive team Stillman – from Kyle's perspective – had largely thrown up his hands. *'How am I supposed to know?'* he'd told Kyle after one of the other nurses had asked if there'd be paychecks on Friday. *And how the hell*, Kyle mused, *did this land on my shoulders?* He pictured his glamorous sister, Kelly. She'd make some quip about his bleeding heart and *'God-given right to save the world, while simultaneously making yourself miserable. You're a fucking saint, Kyle,'* she'd say. *'One of the last good guys . . . and we all know what happens to them.'* And she'd mime a gun to the side of her head and pull the trigger.

The cleaning lady stood by the elevators. As she got in, their eyes connected briefly; she shrugged. He wondered what her name was, having passed her countless times over the last five years. He didn't know it, and wondered if that made him racist – *maybe a little*. He thought back through all the hospitals and health-care facilities he'd worked in, first as a trainee, then as a registered nurse, and now as a nurse practitioner. How many cleaning and hospitality women had he passed, most of them with skin darker than his or with thick accents from Eastern Europe. While rarely discussed, there was tremendous institutionalized prejudice in health care, where almost all the top jobs went to white men, and up until a few years ago nursing was for women. And again old conversations with Kelly played in his mind. *'Become a doctor for God's sake. They're the ones with power. Why would you become a nurse? It's kind of a faggy thing to do Kyle, do you have something else you want to tell me?'*

'No Kelly, I'm not gay.' Beyond that, there was no point in trying to explain something she'd never understand. Yes, he could have gone to medical school, but nursing, actually taking care of people – physically, emotionally, even spiritually – was what he'd always wanted to do. But now, running on two hours sleep since Saturday, he was less certain.

There was more, too, as he stared at the closed conference-room door; an almost unbearable anxiety. So much that needed to be done. The phone hadn't let up since the fire, and he felt a crushing guilt at having put it on the answering machine last night. He'd pleaded with both of the night nurses to take incoming calls. *'Are you kidding?'* one had responded, and the other had clearly stated: *'Sorry, not my job. And not yours either, Kyle.'*

The door opened and a tall young woman in a gray suit appeared. 'Mr Sullivan, we're ready.'

Kyle followed her into the familiar room, with its brass-edged walnut table and comfortable mauve chairs. The vertical blinds were cracked open letting in a soft light.

He was shown to a chair in the middle of the long side of the table facing the windows. Across from him were two men, one black, one white, both with close-cropped hair and dark suits. To their left was the short, curly haired detective he'd seen the morning of the fire and her tall partner. Grenville's uniformed Chief of Police was at the other end. In the corner at a forty-five-degree angle from him was a youngish man with a camera on a tripod. Introductions were made, and as Alice had taught him as a child, he repeated each name as he shook their hands – 'Agent Fitzhugh, Agent Connor, Detective Plank, Detective Perez, Chief Morgan'.

Not knowing what to expect, Kyle reassured himself: *just tell the truth and then you can get back to work.*

Detective Perez nodded to Agent Connor and began. 'Mr Sullivan, how long have you worked at Nillewaug?'

'About five and a half years.'

'And you're a nurse, correct?'

'Yes, I'm an APRN.'

'And that's a special type of nurse?' she asked.

'I'm able to do things an RN can't.'

'Such as?'

'Prescribe medication, prescribe certain treatments, as well as do everything that an RN is able to do.'

'How is that different from being a doctor?' she asked.

Kyle met the short woman's gaze. 'It's not so different. The scope of what I can do is not as extensive and there are certain medications I'm not allowed to prescribe.'

'But you need to practice under the auspices of a physician, correct?'

'No,' he said, having explained the vagaries of his licensure many times. 'In Connecticut the statute merely states that there's a *collaborative* relationship with a physician.'

'Interesting,' Detective Perez said, and proceeded to get his background information, and where he trained. 'So if you grew up in Queens and went to school at NYU, how is it you ended up at Nillewaug?'

'Nillewaug had placed an ad in *The Times*, specifically looking for APRNs. It seemed like a good opportunity, plus I've always been drawn to geriatrics.'

'Your grandmother is a resident here?'

'Yes, Alice Sullivan. She's a lot of the reason I decided to work here.' Remembering how Kelly had found the ad in *The Times* jobs section. One of the few times she'd actually shown an interest in his career. Although he suspected it had more to do with Alice's rapid decline and Kelly's fear that it would impact her lifestyle. 'Alice has Alzheimer's and there was no way I'd ever place her in a nursing home. I know too much about those places and I couldn't do that to her. When I called Nillewaug for information about the positions they were very eager to have me interview. They use APRNs almost exclusively here.'

'Instead of physicians?' Agent Connor broke in.

Kyle's anxiety pinged, was something about this wrong? 'More like in addition to. We do have a medical director, Dr Stanley, and then various specialists come as needed.'

'What about Dr Trask?' Connor asked.

'Who . . .? You mean the man who died in his apartment? He was just a resident.'

'Then why,' Connor continued, 'would he be signing treatment plans for other residents?'

Kyle met Connor's gaze. 'I don't know about that.' He paused, trying to think through the mountains of biannual treatment plans and quarterly updates he'd written over the past two and a half years at Nillewaug. 'I'm reasonably certain that all the treatment plans, at least the ones I'm aware of, were signed by Dr Stanley.'

Connor made a note on his yellow legal pad. 'Did Dr Stanley actually see every patient?'

'No,' Kyle said, knowing that he and the other two APRNs did the intake evaluations and ongoing treatment.

Connor made eye contact with Kyle. 'Did he see *any* of the patients?'

Kyle was startled at the direction of Connor's inquiry and answered truthfully: 'I don't know.' It was a moment of clarity, like a curtain thrown open. *Did Doctor Stanley see any of the patients?* Throughout nursing school, and in his job as a visiting nurse before Nillewaug, he'd never questioned the crushing bulk of daily paperwork. He knew that his bosses cared more for the thorough and timely completion of forms than they did for the quality of the care provided. Never once had he been criticized for his handling of a case, but should a box go unchecked, or a diagnostic code be missing from a billing sheet, there would be someone insisting he correct the deficiency before shift's end. Even more than that was the necessity that every treatment plan be signed, following a statement that the care provided was deemed *'medically necessary'* by a physician.

Connor clicked his tongue against the inside of his mouth. 'Did you ever see Dr Stanley with a patient?'

'No.' And over the next fifteen minutes Kyle answered

questions about how treatment plans were left in Dr Stanley's mailbox. He'd come in two or three times a week, sign them and leave. On occasion Kyle would call Dr Stanley about a particularly worrisome case. He was always cordial, but those brief discussions left him with the sense that he was annoying the man who invariably told him to follow whatever course he felt best.

'And you just worked in this building? The Alzheimer's unit?' Connor asked.

'Here and the long-term care and rehab building – Maple Creek.'

'But not the residential complex?'

'No, that's not a skilled facility. I would have no reason to be over there, other than visiting my grandmother.'

'How much money do you make a year, Mr Sullivan?' Connor asked.

'Somewhere around a hundred thousand,' Kyle answered, and then added: 'I do a fair amount of overtime.'

Connor nodded. 'Why is that? Do you need the money for something in particular?'

Kyle felt a tingle down his spine. *Have I done something wrong?* 'They're always short on nurses.'

'And your expenses are considerable, aren't they Mr Sullivan?' Connor asked. 'The monthly fees for your grand-mother are over three thousand dollars.'

Kyle looked at Connor, his face unreadable. Behind him his tall partner was now standing, staring at him. *These are traps,* he thought, the realization causing him to pause. These two federal agents knew how much money he made and also knew what his expenses were and were not. 'I don't pay monthly fees,' Kyle said. 'When I came to work here it was mostly because I was looking for a place for my grandmother. They cut me a very good deal. I didn't think there was anything wrong with it . . . I still don't.'

'What was the deal?' Connor asked.

'We could buy in at a much reduced rate for one of the smaller units and they'd waive the monthly fee. In exchange I signed a five-year contract. The other two APRNs made similar agreements.'

Connor nodded. 'Those are tremendous perks. What would you say they're worth?'

Kyle remembered the relief he'd felt after that first meeting with Delia Preston and Kayla Atwood. They'd clearly wanted to hire him, and Delia knew why he wanted the job. *'We've got your grandmother covered. There's nowhere else she'll get better care. Literally, this is the best assisted-care facility in Connecticut, probably New England. The food is great. It's a secure facility, and as her dementia worsens, it's nothing we can't handle. Plus –'* and the look she'd given him, as though reading his every thought – *'you'll be here. It's a win win. We get a dedicated and caring APRN and you get a wonderful place for your grandmother to live.'* At the time he'd felt relieved and grateful. The salary was nothing to write home about, and the other benefits were barely at par, but this . . . 'It's worth a lot,' he finally said. 'And I'm not just talking about the money. But let's see . . . the fees would have been around three grand a month and one-bedroom units have a buy-in of two hundred fifty thousand and up.'

'What did you pay for the unit?' Connor asked.

'A hundred . . .' And beating the agent to his next question: 'They let me finance it over five years. And there was wording in the contract that the discounted one hundred and fifty was a loan that would be forgiven over the course of five years. There was a progressive schedule, where each year a larger amount was subtracted. But if I left before the contract was up, I'd be responsible for the whole thing.'

'That's a strong incentive to stay.' Connor cracked the barest of smiles.

'You're not kidding,' Kyle agreed. 'But I didn't mind. It seemed like a Godsend.'

'And you never asked yourself why they were cutting you such a good deal?'

Kyle shook his head. 'No, there's a nursing shortage, this place has always struggled to keep its nurses and APRNs, and, considering what they were asking me to do, it was a great deal, but not suspicious, if that's what you're getting at. They get every cent out of me they put in.'

Connor looked at the short female detective, and, like players passing a ball, she asked the next question. 'Why don't nurses stay?'

'These are tough jobs, and because we're always under-staffed there's an expectation that people will work doubles, like I did the night of the fire.'

'Someone called out?' she asked.

'Yes.'

'Can't you refuse to come in?'

'Theoretically, yes. In truth, someone has to be here.' This is the part that kicked his guilt high. 'That night I was the only nurse on duty for Safe Harbor and Maple Creek.'

'That seems a lot,' she commented.

'It is. That's why nurses don't stay. In the time I've been here I don't think they've ever had a full roster. I was supposed to cover one hundred beds that night in two separate buildings.'

'Is that even legal?' she asked.

'I don't know,' he admitted. 'If the health department caught wind . . . there were two aides on, but still, even for third shift the ratio – at least the one they promise in their brochures – is never supposed to be higher than thirty to one, which is still high.' As the words left his mouth, he realized why he hadn't known about the fire. When his first twelve-hour shift had ended at eight, he'd been confronted with the not infrequent specter of a night trying to stay on top of one hundred nursing home patients. Admittedly most would be asleep, but in the Alzheimer's unit there were always wanderers and a couple of screamers. He'd not seen the fire, because he'd never had the chance. When he'd finally heard that first siren, he and an aide had been attempting to clean and then coax a wiry and incontinent ninety year old back to her room.

To Kyle it seemed the questions would never end. As Detective Perez finished one line, Agent Connor would pick up the next. At one point he looked down to find a cup of coffee, and several times he thought about the work piling up for him, and whether or not anyone would show up for next shift, and what would happen if they didn't? What would happen if he just left? The Nillewaug Promise had been broken. Alice had nowhere to live, and the kindness of those two women would surely reach an end. And then he thought of the spreadsheet on his computer, with the names of all six hundred Nillewaug residents in the burned building. Finally, all of them accounted for and the information passed along to the Red Cross, the Health Department and most importantly to their families. As he entertained the fantasy of walking away from Nillewaug, maybe taking Alice and going back to New York, he knew that wouldn't happen. Yes, the fire was out, but six-hundred people in need of assisted living were homeless. The immediate disaster was passed, but in its wake was something larger. As the questions shifted from one direction to the next, he was forced to confront painful truths. The worst of these was brought home by Detective Perez, whom he sensed had first-hand knowledge of the struggles he'd gone through with his grandmother.

'Help me to understand this,' she began. 'Your grandmother has fairly advanced Alzheimer's?'

'Moderate, not advanced.'

'But still . . . why would they have agreed to take her into the assisted-care residence when what she required was something higher? You said earlier that she needed a nursing home.'

'I didn't want them to know how bad it was,' he admitted.

'So you lied?'

'I did, but she still dresses herself, takes care of her hygiene. Obviously she can't cook or handle a checkbook. But when I saw how much support they had in place, it seemed doable.'

'Your grandmother wasn't the only one, was she?'

Kyle paused, not entirely certain what she was asking. 'With dementia?'

'Yes,' Detective Perez prompted, 'with significant dementia living in the assisted-care residence and not one of the nursing-home buildings.'

'It's true,' he added, 'but I didn't think there was anything wrong with that. I still don't. People are much happier feeling they have some autonomy. My grandmother liked her apartment after she got over the shock of the move. I was doing everything I could to keep her from going into Safe Harbor.'

'How,' Agent Connor interjected, 'is it possible for people with a "moderate" amount of Alzheimer's to execute the kinds of contracts and other legal documents Nillewaug required?'

The question stopped Kyle cold. He thought about Nillewaug before the fire, walking the beautifully maintained grounds, seeing residents, many of them with ankle bracelets, many of them with aides whose sole purpose was to keep them from wandering off. 'I don't know. I wasn't involved with that.' Remembering how cavalier Delia Preston had been when he'd fretted over trying to bring Alice to Nillewaug. *'She's demented,'* Delia had said with a laugh and a conspiratorial wink, *'she won't remember what she did or didn't sign. None of them do. It'll be fine. Just fine.'*

NINETEEN

Ada stared at the computer screen in the back office and toggled through archived documents from the local papers. Lil was out interviewing the family of the woman who'd died on the roof of Nillewaug, and Rose and Alice were napping back in her condo. The printer hummed as she made hard copies of articles that referenced the championship Ravens: Wally Doyle, Dennis Trask, and Jim Warren. Most of it was mundane reporting of high-school athletics, but throughout were hints of the excitement, state records broken and hyperbolic lines like: *'Our three Ravens are flying straight to the state championships.'* More than the mediocre prose she was struck by the photos, crisp action shots of Dennis Trask, both feet off the ground, plucking a ball from the sky, Wally Doyle sacking an opposing quarterback, and one beautiful image of Jim Warren just as he'd snapped a ball, a hulking Doyle in front of him, his mouth open as though screaming for the opposing line to try and get through to his quarterback.

Over thirty years later this picture was like some creepy
metaphor for Nillewaug – Wally Doyle still protecting his
quarterback. She startled when she saw the team photo that
had been in Lil's piece, only hers had been dripping with
Wally Doyle's blood. The photos gave her pause, remembering
the obese man who'd tried to pressure her into having Rose
divest her assets. How many at Nillewaug had gone for that?
The underlying message clear: 'Why wait for Gran to drop
dead? Get her money now.' Strangely, there was no byline for
the photos. Whoever had taken these, on beyond knowing their
way around a telephoto lens and high-speed photography,
obviously had access to the team and the players.

'Not so helpful,' she said as she perused another search,
this time accessing the Grenville High School website. She
marveled at how times had changed to where parents were
encouraged to email their child's teachers and with a password
could check to see if homework had been handed in and the
latest test and quiz scores.

She clicked the menu option for 'Year Books' and a pull
down for years appeared. She smiled, calculated back and
detoured from the Ravens to pull up Lil's 1968 senior class
yearbook. She flipped through the electronic pages stopping
on the images of a very young Lillian Herrington. She was
editor of the school paper, sang in the choir, played a flapper
in the senior production of *The Boyfriend* and under her
portrait: 'Most likely to: become a reporter for the *New York
Times*.' 'Could still happen,' Ada mused, studying the lovely
young woman with long blonde hair, who hadn't smiled for
the photographer.

She moved the cursor back to the drop down and stopped
on 1976 and 1977 – the championship years. And as she noted,
the heyday of the Farrah Fawcett flip.

'Interesting,' she said, coming upon some of the same
photographs that had been in the paper, only here they gave
credit to Samuel King. 'All right.' Scrolling through the
pages she found young Mr King in the photography club
and on the staff of the school paper. *And this is useful, how?
And why do I know that name . . .? Lil's article.* She reached
across the desk to a neatly folded stack of papers with Lil's

first piece on the fire. Sam King was Grenville's Fire Marshall. 'Again –' thinking out loud – 'why does everything tie back to those football players, this cannot all be coincidence.' Wondering where she could get her hands on copies of the high school paper, or if they even still existed. A half-formed suspicion made her reach for the phone. It rang twice. 'Lil?'

'Ada, what's up?'

'I had a thought, are you still at your interview?'

'Just finished, I was about to head to the next. I think I've got this fraud angle nailed. The trick will be explaining it in a way that doesn't make my readers' eyes glaze over.'

'That's great, but I still think the meat in this story is with the connections between your three Ravens. You want another? And I don't know if it's important.'

'Shoot.'

'Your Fire Marshall – who when Mattie was here I clearly heard her say he was pushing to have this labeled an accident – was the team photographer.'

'Sam King, I'd forgotten about that. He was like a team mascot. He got some amazing shots . . . huh. In his preliminary report he did call it accidental. The state's Fire Marshall wouldn't commit.'

And that's when Ada heard the front door bang open and her mother's voice.

'Ada! Ada! Where are you?'

'Something's up,' Ada said. 'We'll talk later. It's just –' searching for the words – 'this fire happened for a reason, my money is on arson, and it all feeds back to your Ravens. Yet your Fire Marshall, who was clearly in tight with those three, wants to call it an accident. It doesn't sit right.'

Rose's voice shouted from the foyer. 'Ada! Where are you?'

'We'll talk later. Love you, Lil.'

'Back at you, call me if you need me.' And she hung up.

Ada pushed away from the computer, as Rose entered in a breathless panic.

'What?' Ada asked.

'It's Alice,' Rose stammered.

'Where is she?'

'I was taking a nap,' Rose said, her eyes wide behind her thick glasses. 'I didn't hear her leave.'

'How long were you asleep?' Ada was on her feet and racing back to her condo. She made a quick circuit, checking the bedrooms, the bathrooms and the living room, opening every closet as she went. Her pulse pounded – *this is a nightmare. The door was locked. When did you last see Alice? Noon? One?* Staring at the kitchen clock – it was almost three.

'Not more than an hour.' Rose trailed after her daughter. 'She can't have gotten far.'

Ada nodded, sensing her mother's distress. 'This isn't your fault,' she said, not certain if that were entirely true. Then again, they'd all agreed to look after Alice, if blame were to be placed . . . 'We'll find her.' And she was out the door. She stood at the top of the walk and looked down at the quiet street below. The late-morning sun warmed her face. 'Alice,' she shouted, 'Alice.' Turning slowly, she saw Bernice Framm's face in the corner of her kitchen window. Normally, Bernice's snooping was a source of annoyance, but now . . . She looked directly at her, and, making eye contact, walked to her front door. 'Bernice,' she called, knocking and ringing the bell.

'Hold on,' said a startled and unhappy voice, 'I'm coming.'

Ada waited, trying to decide her next move. Lil was out with her interview and Aaron was in school. She thought about calling Kyle. If she couldn't locate Alice quickly, she'd have to inform him. After an agonizing wait, Bernice's door cracked open.

'Yes?' Bernice, who'd spent fifty years as the secretary to Grenville's mayors did little to hide her dislike for Ada. 'What can I do for you?' Her mouth pursed.

Ada had wondered at Bernice's animosity. She'd said few words to the woman in the years they'd been across-the-walk neighbors, but from the beginning she'd sensed her ill will. *Was it because she was from New York, Jewish . . . gay?* But now was not the time. 'The red-headed woman who's been with us the past couple days; she's wandered off, have you seen her?'

Bernice's eyes narrowed. 'There are rules about the number of guests we're allowed.'

Ada was taken aback, and fought down her first impulse, which was to throttle this woman who'd spent her working life as the gatekeeper to the town mayor. A position that, according to Lil, she'd used as her personal throne of power, blocking access like a linebacker. Keeping a calm smile – at least what she hoped passed for one – Ada shifted tack. 'Thank you, Bernice, and yes I'm aware of the guest rules. I have a three-bedroom unit and between my grandson, my mother and Alice, both of whom we've taken in after the Nillewaug fire – where they lost everything – I'm still below the four-person limit.'

'They were in the fire?' Bernice's eyes lit, the whiff of gossip overcoming her dislike.

'It was horrible,' Ada admitted, realizing two things. First, Bernice already knew her two visitors had been in the fire and second, parsing out information was the key to getting Bernice's help. 'And this place, every road looks like every other one. Coming from Nillewaug where everything is laid out, they don't have a prayer.'

'And the streets have no names,' Bernice added, shaking her head and warming to a favored topic. 'You'd think they could at least name the streets instead of just putting up the numbers for the units.'

'So true,' Ada said. 'Anyway, I was hoping you saw her, she can't have wandered far.'

'I don't know,' Bernice said, her tone pessimistic. 'I might have seen her, but it was over an hour ago.'

Ada followed Bernice's gaze. It led not down the path to the road, but in the other direction past the circular seating area to an unpaved hiking trail through the woods. And sure enough, when she squinted she could see faint footprints in the layer of yellow pollen. 'Thanks, Bernice.'

'Will she be OK?' the woman asked. 'Does she have health problems?'

'She's fine,' Ada said, imagining that Bernice would have preferred something juicier, like: *she has a rare exploding heart condition, I'm certain she'll have detonated by now.*

'That's good,' Bernice said, her expression resuming its resting state of pinched disapproval.

'She is a bit confused,' Ada added, thinking it best to give her something.

'Like Alzheimer's?' An uptick in Bernice's voice.

'Yes, sadly.'

'Oh that's just terrible. Should I call security?'

'If it's no trouble,' Ada said, knowing that this favor would cost.

'No trouble at all . . . but can't they just locate her with the bracelet?'

Ada startled. 'Of course.' She looked at Bernice and felt a bit ashamed for not having thought of that herself. Yes, since the fire, the bracelet hadn't been connected to whatever system Nillewaug had used, but . . . 'Thank you so much, Bernice,' she added, a bit more effusive than was normal. 'If you call security, her name is Alice Sullivan. I'll try to see if the bracelet is functioning. Thank you so much.' Pulling out her cell, she headed toward the wooded path. Entering the sun-dappled woods she tried to think of what she'd say when Kyle picked up.

'Hello?'

'Kyle, it's Ada. I don't want to worry you, but your grandmother has gone for a walk and we're trying to locate her.' There was a crushing silence, and Ada imagined what he must be thinking of her and Lil after they'd agreed to keep Alice safe. 'Kyle?'

'I'm here,' he said. 'How long ago?'

'About an hour,' Ada admitted, always a firm believer in full disclosure. Her gaze on the path's gentle upward slope, the visibility good as the trees weren't yet in leaf. 'She's wearing a bracelet. Any chance it's still working?'

'It should,' he said. 'It's GPS, hold on and I'll get the number for the monitoring service.' He read her the phone number and gave her Nillewaug's access code. 'I'll be there in five,' he said.

'No,' Ada said, her fingers rapidly entering the numbers into her cell. 'We've got security notified and I'll call the monitor people. We'll find her, Kyle. She's on foot and there are just so many places she can go.'

'I'm on my way.'

Before she could argue further, his phone clicked.

'I've got another call coming,' he said. 'I'll see you in a few. If you find her before I get there, call me.'

'Of course,' Ada said, as the line clicked off. 'Terrible, how could this happen?' she muttered, while calling the monitoring company. A woman with an Indian accent answered. Ada quickly described the situation with Alice.

The woman asked for the account number. 'Yes,' she said, 'the bracelet is operating. You can locate her with your GPS.'

'What GPS?' Ada asked.

'Do you have a smart phone?' the woman asked.

'Yes,' she said, and wondered what would have happened if her phone wasn't so clever.

'Not a problem. Just go to the App store.' She gave her the name of the company's GPS application. 'Download our app to your phone and punch in the access code. It will then ask you for Alice's name and date of birth, which, if you do not have handy, I can give to you. Alice will be the red bull's-eye on the screen and you will be the green arrow. It is very simple to operate . . . and a bit of fun, like a game.'

Ada thanked her, not seeing the 'fun' in any of this and sitting on a bench beside a copse of laurel, did as instructed. Waiting for the app to load, she hiked up the slope, her eyes scanning the periphery in case Alice had wandered off the path. Her emotions an anxious gurgle of guilt and fear. *Why did we leave her with my mother? Because she asked you to. Why did we take her in the first place? Because it was the right thing to do. What if something's happened to her?* The bar on the app reached completion and a picture of a house with the words 'Safe Home' appeared on the screen. She touched it lightly with her finger, and then carefully entered the code and Alice's information. The screen blinked twice, and like something on an old video game a red bulls-eye and green arrow appeared. Between them a dotted line let her know Alice was roughly half a mile away. With the phone in hand, she pictured the layout of Pilgrim's Progress and had a good idea of where she'd gone. And saying a silent prayer – *please let me find her.*

Dear God, please let her be OK – she broke into a jog and darted up the path.

Kyle Sullivan hung up with Ada, and wondered what new horror faced him on the other line. This day— *No*, he thought, *since Sunday, like a dream . . . a waking nightmare.* Where, when you think things can't get worse, they do. The cell showed it was Kelly calling. He thought about not answering, but knew his twin would keep on trying.

'I've been thinking this over,' she said, before he'd even said hello. 'I'm coming to get Grandma.'

He pictured his beautiful sister, Kelly, and her glamorous SoHo loft, with soaring windows over West Broadway and mid-century Danish furniture. 'What are you talking about?'

'I've been a self-centered bitch, as usual.' Her tone dramatic. 'And as usual you're too much of a good guy to say it. I'm coming to get Grandma Alice and nothing you can say changes things. It's time I stepped up, at least till things calm down.'

A long list of objections flew to mind and hovered on Kyle's tongue. He bit the inside of his mouth. *Where to start?* But then, the thought of seeing Kelly, of desperately wanting someone to talk to, and maybe for the short run, if she threw enough money at it, she *could* take care of Alice. Of course she had no clue what was involved, but he could tell her, let her know how to hire aides, how to work around Alice's funny emotional quirks, how to distract her – *maybe this could work* – knowing in his heart there wasn't a chance in hell. As his concerns pushed from his brain to his mouth, he stopped himself – *are you insane, man? Let her help.* 'How soon can you get here?' he asked.

'I'm on my way.'

TWENTY

Not for the first time today, Lil asked herself, *What are you doing?* It was late Tuesday afternoon, her nerves jangled, as she sipped black coffee in one of the two window tables at the Brown Bear diner. Her back was to the kitchen and she gazed out at the colonials on Main Street – mostly antique shops now, but private homes when she was growing up. She glanced at the clock over the door – nearly four fifteen. *He said he'd be here by four. Is he even coming? He clearly didn't want to.* She felt discouraged, frustrated and humiliated and wondered if this wasn't just setting the stage for more of the same. The last couple of hours spent on her cell with families of Nillewaug residents, seeing if anyone would be willing to discuss how it happened that their once well-off elder relatives had come to fall below the poverty level and meet Medicaid eligibility. It was while pursuing this thread she'd received a soul-crushing call from her editor. 'What are you doing?' he'd asked. 'The fraud story at Nillewaug is way too big for you. Didn't we agree on that? That's the problem here, you're so green you don't know what you don't know. And what's worse,' he'd continued, 'you're muddying the water for Daryl who can actually handle this story. You need to back off. Stop calling these families. Obviously there's something going on, and all you've done is made it harder for Daryl to get the story.'

The call had deteriorated further. She'd tried to explain, but every time she began to speak, he'd interrupt. He was furious. But why, she wondered, was he so mad? *What have I done that's so bad?* Even here, people had come up to her and told her how good they'd thought both of the stories had been. Were they just being polite? The call had ended with Edward Fleming throwing her a scrap. 'You want a piece of this story. Here, find out what the plans are for the displaced residents – that's it, Lil. Stay away from Medicaid fraud, from arson, from homicide. Just report on the homeless, how many, where they are, and what the plans are. Can you do that?'

'Yes.'

'Good,' he'd said, and hung up.

She'd wanted to scream back that he could take his friggin paper and . . . *But really, where would that get you? Out of a job, most likely.* While she certainly didn't need the pennies they gave her from the weekly column and whatever added cash she'd get from these articles, having a real job, with a real paper, was a rare thing. Especially now where all the papers were shrinking, reporters were losing their jobs, and increasingly people looked to the Internet for their news.

The waitress, thankfully not the one who'd been here last fall when she'd had her heart attack, refilled her coffee. 'You sure I can't get you anything, Mrs Campbell? A piece of pie, maybe?'

'No thanks.' Lil's cell rang. Figuring it was the Fire Marshall, cancelling after all and putting a demoralizing cap on her afternoon, she looked at the screen; it was her daughter, Barbara. 'Hi sweetie,' she said, her voice lighter than her mood.

'Mom . . .'

'What's the matter?' Immediately tuning in to her worried tone.

'Are you at your computer?' she asked.

'No, I'm at the Brown Bear waiting for someone, who's probably going to stand me up.'

'Ada?'

'No, why?'

'Mom, there are photos of you and Mrs Strauss on a website called Grenville4Grenvillians.com.' She paused. 'I got a Google alert and . . .'

'What are you talking about?' She was aware of the website, which frequently posted embarrassing tidbits about local officials. But this, trying to piece the information . . . 'What the hell is a Google alert?'

'It's where you get notified whenever something or someone you're interested in gets posted on the web. I have a few dozen of them for projects I'm working on, for myself, the kids, Carlton, and I did one for you.'

'Why?'

'Lots of reasons, mostly to try and stay on top of what people are saying in the press. With the kids it's another way to make sure they're not getting into something they shouldn't on the web.'

Lil had a sick feeling. 'What kind of pictures?'

'It's nothing pornographic . . . but someone's been watching the two of you.' Again there was hesitation.

'Just spit it out.'

'There's one of you kissing, another of the two of you holding hands . . . and someone obviously got one of the two of you in bed . . . together.'

The sick feeling blossomed, a combination of rage and fear, blood rushed to her cheeks. 'Why . . . who?' Immediately thinking of their across-the-walk neighbors – Bernice, Clayton.

'I just got the alert, because they actually included both of your names with the latest postings. But it's not the first time they've put up photos of the two of you. If I scroll back, looks like the first ones went up on Monday . . . Mom?'

'Yes?' And suddenly, a moment Lil had been putting off was at hand. While Ada and she had certainly not hidden the nature of their relatively new relationship from their respective children, their unspoken approach had been 'if they don't ask, we won't tell'. Ada's grandson, Aaron was the only one in their lives who knew they were a couple. Now, apparently so did anyone in Grenville . . . or anyone who accessed the website, such as her daughter in LA. 'It's true, Barbara.' She looked up as the bell over the diner's front door jingled, and Sam King in a dark green blazer with a Grenville patch on the left side of his chest entered. 'Barbara, I've got an interview to do now, thanks for the heads up. I'll give you a call later and we can talk.'

'Mom, you know I love you, but . . . are you gay?'

Aware of her surroundings, and Sam as he approached, she lowered her voice: 'It's complicated. We need to talk. I love Ada. So whatever that makes me.'

'What am I supposed to tell the kids? Stuff like this gets around, once it's on the web . . . this could go viral.'

'But who would care?' Lil asked, realizing that obviously

someone did. *Who would do this and why? And how the hell could they get a picture of the two of us in bed?* Immediately picturing the sliding glass doors that looked out on the woods behind their condos. They often left the curtains open at night to catch the sunrise. How easy it would be for someone to walk around back and . . . her heart was racing.

'People do care,' Barbara said. 'You have no idea how much. They won't tell you to your face, but you're going to find that people treat you differently.'

Lil forced a smile and looked up at Sam, now standing at the edge of the booth, his gaze furtive as he looked from her and then back to the door. 'Just a second,' she told him, sensing he wanted to be anywhere but there. 'Barbara, I have to go.' The news that she and Ada were now cause for scandal and Barbara's closing words had her shaken. *And what were these pictures?* She hung up. 'Hi, Sam. Thanks for coming.' Knowing full well that she'd strong-armed him into this meeting, by leading him to believe she had compromising information. 'I'm sure you've got to be crazy busy with this Nillewaug mess.'

'You have no idea.'

'Sit, please.'

'I don't have long,' he said, and he eased his big gut into the booth. He glanced around the restaurant and pulled a Manila envelope from inside his jacket; he slid it across the table. 'You wanted this . . . It's a copy of Nillewaug's emergency plans.' He looked up at the waitress. 'Coffee.'

'Thanks.' She opened the folder, her thoughts on Barbara's bombshell – she needed to see those pictures, and more importantly, *I have to warn Ada.* 'Sam,' she said, searching his face – *does he know?* But all she saw was someone she'd known for decades, who seemed a bit older than the last time they'd chatted, and whose brown eyes were hooded from lack of sleep, and what was likely the biggest case in his career. Beyond that she knew he was a flawed man whose wife eventually left him because he couldn't keep it in his pants and whom she now suspected of some complicity in the Nillewaug disaster. 'Two seconds, Sam, I need to make a quick call.'

'You want me to leave?' His tone hopeful.

'No, please sit. I'll be fast.' She was out of the booth, cell in hand, her finger pressing the screen for Ada's cell. Aaron picked up, as she stepped outside the diner and stood in the shadowed doorway.

'Lil, I'm so glad you called. Grandma wouldn't let me get in touch with you. Where are you?' he asked. 'We've got a situation here.'

'What's happening?'

'Alice's granddaughter drove up from New York and is taking her back with her. She's pretty upset.'

'Alice?'

'No, Kelly, the granddaughter. I guess when I was at school Alice got out of the condo and wandered off. Grandma found her, but . . . it's kind of a mess. Kyle's here too. Oh, and Lil . . .'

'Yes?'

'You heard about the blog postings?'

'I did. You've seen them?'

'Everyone's seen them,' he said.

'How's your grandmother taking it?'

'I'll put her on . . . they're not that bad, though. Nothing pervy, kind of sweet actually. But you've been outed.'

'Great.' She looked back at Sam; he seemed lost in anxious reflection as he sipped his coffee and then checked his watch.

'Lil?' Ada's voice, like a balm on Lil's troubled mood.

'Ada, what's happening?'

'Put it this way,' she said drily, 'it's been a busy afternoon. My mother took a nap, and Alice took a walk . . . a very long walk. Which, thank God, she's all right and thank God again for that ankle bracelet.'

'Where'd she go?'

'I found her at the lake watching the ducks. Of course I had to call Kyle, and he was fine with it, but apparently his sister Kelly freaked. She drove up from New York. And now she's insisting that Alice go back with her. Which honestly –' her tone dropped to a whisper – 'right now that would be just fine. What are we going to do?'

Lil wasn't certain what part she was asking about. 'They're her family,' she said, taking a stab at the first layer, 'let them decide. At least she wasn't hurt. Have you seen the web postings?'

'Yes.'

'What's up there?' Desperate to get on-line and see for herself.

'There are two entries. Yesterday's has a picture of the two of us holding hands. But today's . . . Lil, someone was outside our bedroom taking pictures. It was last night. If it weren't totally creepy and very frightening I'd say it was a cute picture. You look sweet when you're asleep, of course my mouth is wide open . . . do I snore, Lil?'

'Sometimes . . .' She could tell Ada was trying to keep her tone light. 'What does it say?' Tempted to pull up her web browser, but the last time she did that while on the phone, she inadvertently disconnected the call. 'Can you read it to me?'

'Hold on.'

She stared through the plate-glass window feeling pulled. From across the street, she saw Belle Evans who ran the multi-dealer shop where Lil had worked briefly last fall. She waved, thinking Belle had seen her; she didn't wave back. *I guess she hadn't seen me, or . . . did she just snub me?*

Ada came back on line. 'I've got it in front of me. Yesterday's post under the picture of the two of us holding hands: *"From Doctor's wife to hand-holding dyke. And we all thought she was such a proper lady. Guess she had us fooled."*'

'Where was the picture taken?'

'It's just outside our condos from yesterday morning; it had to have been Bernice or Clayton.'

'That was my thought, and the second posting, what does it say?'

'*"Lesbians in our midst. Doctor's wife Lillian Campbell in bed with retail tycoon Ada Strauss . . . literally. Is this the Grenville we want? What next? A Gay Pride Parade down Main Street?"* If this were New York,' Ada said, 'no one would care.'

'I know . . . but it's Grenville. Ada, I'll be home as soon as I can. I've got Fire Marshall Sam, and he clearly does not want to be here. But he knows something, and he's scared of what I know.'

'Which is?' Ada asked.

'Not nearly enough. I feel like a fraud.'

'Get him to talk,' Ada urged. 'Make him think you know something. The more I read about those Ravens the more I think I understand. Three teenage boys given the keys to the town – and now thirty-four years later they're still running the place, committing major fraud, systematically milking old people out of their life's savings, getting their families to collude. I think Mr King has important things to say. Remember, Lil, when all else fails, men like to talk about themselves.'

'Right,' she said, and they hung up. Lil went back inside the restaurant that smelled of bacon and fresh-baked bread. She looked at Sam, wondering if this was a dead end. Already bracing herself for Fleming's critique. She slid into the worn red upholstered booth, and pulled a pad of paper and pen from her bag. Her first thought: *put him at ease, don't scare him away.* 'What can you tell me about the plans for all of the displaced Nillewaug residents?'

He looked up from his coffee and shook his head. 'Other than it's a fucking nightmare, excuse my French.'

'No apology necessary, and please continue. Tell me about the emergency plan, and thanks again for making a copy for me.'

He looked at her from over his coffee, his expression wary, like a child at the doctor's waiting for the needle. 'This all has to be off the record, Lil. And you're not taping it.'

'OK,' Lil said, feeling like he could bolt at any second.

'All right. For starters, it's useless. The plan only covers the two nursing-home units, neither of which had to be evacuated. So really, it has almost no bearing on what's happened.'

'There was no emergency plan for the residential complex?'

'Nope, and by law they didn't need one . . . except . . .'

'What?'

'Well . . .' He leaned over. 'And this is what you want, isn't it?' His voice choked. 'There's a lot that wasn't kosher about that place. And it's all going to come out. You know that, you put a lot of it in your articles, but one thing you didn't have, and heads are going to roll because of it. Someone signed off on the entire facility as being a nursing home.'

'Which it wasn't,' Lil added.

'Not at all. Official word back from Hartford and the Health Department is that "a mistake was made" in the number of beds considered skilled. There was no mistake. Someone got paid off. Someone high enough up so that "*the mistake*" would remain undetected.' He reached across the table and flipped open the folder. 'Here,' he said, pulling out a copy of a license issued by the state. 'See, right there, "capacity seven hundred". It should only be for one hundred . . . And catch this, Lil. What they're saying is that the seven instead of a one is a typo.'

His candor was surprising. He was giving her a scoop, and Lil could already imagine Fleming's response – '*You can't handle this, Lil . . . too green . . . don't know what you don't know.*'

Screw him! She met Sam's gaze, he seemed like a man resigned. 'Aren't licenses renewed annually?' she asked, remembering how each year Bradley would send a check and get the new certificate to post in his office.

'They are. Every year since two thousand, when Nillewaug was first licensed, there has been a "typo" on their certificate.'

'For eleven years?'

'Apparently.'

This information was too good not to use, and no way in hell was she giving it to the reporter Fleming had assigned to the bigger story. 'OK, if it's licensed for seven hundred, even if it's a typo, then shouldn't the emergency plan extend to all seven hundred residents?'

'Yes, absolutely.'

And that's when she realized two things, Sam, as the Fire Marshall, would have been aware of the 'typo' on Nillewaug's license, and he'd obviously said nothing . . . for over a decade. Feeling like a nugget of gold had dropped in her lap, she attempted to pull the interview back to shores where he'd feel safer. Not once losing sight of her and Ada's suspicion about the Ravens, which was likely where the mother lode lay. 'How bad has it been trying to get people into safe shelter?' she asked, noting how he wouldn't meet her gaze, while wondering how she'd track down whatever state employee had made that initial 'typo'.

'Bad.' Clearly relieved by this new direction, he educated her in what becomes of people dispossessed by fire. He explained how it was in everyone's best interest to make Nillewaug habitable ASAP. 'The structure is sound,' he said with conviction, after the waitress had filled his coffee a third time, 'but the damage . . . extensive. The clean-up is massive, and very expensive.' He leaned in again, and not for the first time, she regretted not taping this. 'The insurance companies don't want to pay.'

'Of course they don't want to pay, but beyond that? What are you saying?'

'Here's the deal. Nillewaug is insured through Clarion Mutual. Then you have the residents who had various insurance through a couple dozen companies. Now, here's where it starts to split apart. Samples from Dr Trask's apartment clearly show there was accelerant. The question becomes, was the fire started deliberately, or was it an accident, likely from spontaneous combustion of the various solvents he used on his clocks?' He looked at her. 'That was my conclusion and I stand by it. One of his piles of rags fell to the floor, he didn't see it, and four hours later it ignites. It happens a lot. Some of the smartest people I know are total idiots when it comes to home safety. But in something this big, the state comes in and they're saying arson can't be ruled out, which makes the insurance companies nervous. Especially The Clarion that's on the hook for tens of millions. So what do they do?'

She shook her head, noting how this was a topic where Sam seemed comfortable. 'Not a clue.' Wanting to keep him talking, while thinking how to steer back to deeper waters.

'They bring in their own investigator, who took samples. And he's not alone. I took samples. And . . . because it's a big fire, the state Fire Marshal took samples. And . . . because the Feds are somehow involved in this mess, a team from ATF showed up and they took samples. Which means, we now have four separate sets, to be interpreted by four different labs, and we will most likely get four different results.'

'Samples?'

'From where the fire started. And though I'm certain it was caused by spontaneous combustion, at least one of those three other investigators will lean on the side of arson. And, considering we have a homicide that occurred around the time of the fire, arson becomes increasingly suspect. All of which leads to a lengthy, and very expensive, process. And I'm not even getting to anything criminal. Before checks get cut to the victims, there will be a tremendous amount of jockeying, about who should pay. Which, if it doesn't get resolved, will mean a longer time before people can actually get their places cleaned and they can return. And here's a fun fact, Lil. If it is determined arson, and the homicide is related, then all the deaths will be considered homicide. In Connecticut, arson homicide can warrant the death penalty.'

'That is interesting. And in the case of arson don't you mostly look to whoever will profit the most?'

'Yes.' Holding up his empty coffee cup, he flagged the waitress. 'People burn their places for the insurance money. But . . . you always have to look for your nut case. Because just when you're convinced it's greedy Jim Warren – and he is a bastard – it'll turn out some fire bug set the whole thing just to watch it burn. Or, God help us, there'll be a pyro on the fire department who set it so he could play the hero.'

'Are you kidding?' Her interest perked at the mention of Jim Warren, and clearly no love was lost between the men.

'Wish I were. It's the bane of every fire station, and at least once in every fire chief's career they get burned by it – no pun intended.'

'That's not what happened here, though.'

'No,' he said. 'If it weren't for Delia Preston getting murdered I'd put my money behind Doctor Trask getting careless. I still think the fire and the murder are two bad things that happened independently . . . then again I don't know the whole story.'

'So why's Jim Warren a bastard?' she asked.

His expression darkened. 'Crap . . .' He stared at the table, and the silence stretched. Finally, he met her gaze. 'He's not someone to mess with. He's dangerous and for all of his surface charm the man is a snake . . . no, I shouldn't say that. Snakes are good, keep the vermin down. There's not a damn thing that's good about Jim Warren.'

His vehemence surprised her. 'Sam, where did all that come from?'

'Lil . . .' He stared at his coffee, apparently deciding about something. He looked across at her, his expression intent. 'What I'm going to tell you can't be repeated. I need your word on that.'

It reminded her of things patients would tell Bradley. Desperate to unload some painful truth they'd wait until he'd reassured them of total confidentiality. Occasionally he'd make some provision – '*As long as you're not planning to kill someone . . . including yourself.*' But mostly his reply: '*It will never leave this room.*' And that's what she said to Sam. 'It will never leave this room.'

He let out a deep breath. 'I'm not the only one who knows this, which doesn't make it better. Or the fact that we were all kids, or that I was completely in awe of The Ravens and Jim and Dennis Trask were big stars. This happened so long ago, but I've never forgotten. At the time I assumed there'd be arrests and a trial, we all did, but then nothing. Days, weeks, months and it's as if nothing happened that night. I thought it would be like on a TV show where detectives would pull us out of class and ask us what happened. You ever regret something, Lil? Something you did or didn't do that just stuck with you . . . always wondering what if I'd had the courage to say something?'

'Sure,' she said, not wanting to break his flow. He was clearly tormented, and she reached across the table and took his hand. 'Just go ahead.'

He glanced around the empty dining room, the waitress in back with the cook. 'It was a party at the Trasks'. I don't think there were any adults there, in fact I'm sure of it. I can't remember where Dennis's parents were, I know they were at the game – maybe there was another party; there must have been. Last game of the regular season and we were ten for ten and going into the play-offs for the second year in a row. We . . . they . . . were unstoppable. Thirty-four years ago and I can still see what she was wearing, one of those tube top things; it was blue-striped and a tight denim mini skirt. She was so pretty. I kind of had a crush on her. Me and probably half the boys in school. And she was smart, just not about Jim Warren. But he really liked her, had been saying he was her boyfriend. What they did to her . . .'

'Who was the girl?'

He stopped, and then said, more to himself, 'In for a penny . . . Vicky. Vicky Binghamton.'

The name was instantly familiar, but Lil didn't match it to a teenager in a tube top and short denim skirt. Who she remembered was a little blonde-haired girl, with china-blue eyes playing in the kiddie corner of Bradley's waiting room. 'What happened to her?'

'They got her drunk. The three of them, but it was mostly Dennis and Jim, playing with her, flattering her. She was so wasted, the three of them on the couch with her like she was a toy. Someone should have stopped it . . . I should have tried. I knew what they were doing was wrong. We all did, but no one said anything. No one even tried . . . and then they took her upstairs. And that's not even the worst part.'

A tear trickled down Sam's cheek. 'She was screaming, screaming for them to stop. No one went up to help her . . . and someone turned the music up so we couldn't hear. She was only fifteen.'

Lil sat taking in the story, and the hollow expression in Sam's eyes. He'd been carrying this around a long time, and maybe it had nothing to do with the story. Then again, front and center at the rape of Vicky Binghamton – Wally, Dennis and Jim. Thirty-four years later a fire in Grenville and a woman is murdered and there they are again – the three Ravens. 'What happened to her? To Vicky?'

'She left school. And left town. I saw her once after . . . after they did that to her. It was after school, she was with her mother and they were cleaning out her locker. Her entire face . . .' His mouth twisted and tears squeezed from his eyes. 'It wasn't just a rape. They beat her. She was such a beautiful girl, bubbly and so full of life. But the look in her eyes . . . empty and frightened. They should have gone to jail for what they did. To this day I can't figure what happened.

They say that in cases of rape it goes unreported over half the time. That's what it would have had to have been.'

'Did you speak to her?' Imagining the scene, and sensing there was more.

'No, and after she was gone it wasn't discussed. At least not by anyone I knew. There were dozens of us at that party. We all heard; we all knew. And no one said a thing.' He looked up, his mouth twisted. He grabbed a napkin and dabbed his eyes. 'You can't imagine how disgusted I felt with myself. It's the one thing in my life I'd give anything to do over. Why didn't I stop it?'

'Was it just her and her mother?' Lil asked, wracking her brain for an image of Victoria Binghamton and her mother. But all she could see was that little girl with a giant picture book.

'I think so,' he said, staring at his hands and regaining composure. 'Her mom was a secretary or something like that. I don't think they had money. They might have been living in Glenndale.' He was referring to Grenville's only apartment complex. 'For thirty-four years I've carried that around. What was wrong with me? Why didn't I help that girl? Why didn't any of us?'

'What stopped you?' Lil had to ask.

'Fear. And thinking about it now . . . how pathetic. But that's what it was. Those three ran the school. People knew to not get in their way. It's like this fire is God's way of finally setting things right. Wally's dead, Dennis's father – dead, Jim Warren in some kind of big trouble, if not for arson for fraud. That just leaves Dennis, and of the three of them let me tell you, he is one scary bastard.'

She was about to press for a definition of '*one scary bastard*' when Sam's pager beeped, and then his cell chimed in. 'Lil, I didn't want to tell you any of this . . . and now that it's out there . . . I know you think I was trying to cover something up. At least with the fire I still think it was an accident . . . but I can be wrong.' He slid out of the booth.

As he did, dozens of questions queued in Lil's head, and the one that made it to her lips: 'Why didn't you say something about the typo on the Nillewaug license?'

His shoulders sagged. 'My dad's in that place.'

She nodded. 'And Jim Warren cut you a deal.'

'Yeah, I know I have to resign, Lil, but if you could keep that piece out of your story . . . at least for a little.'

'Sure,' she said, and she watched him leave the restaurant. Her head swam, and she thought of calling Fleming with what could potentially be not one, but two big stories. The fact that all of Nillewaug Village had been licensed as a nursing home added a layer to this whole fraud thing. She imagined it would also implicate someone – maybe more than one – in state government, much higher up than sad Sam King. Nursing homes get inspected annually, after ten years you'd think someone might have noticed that the seven hundred beds on the application bore little reality to the one hundred beds in Nillewaug's two nursing-home units. Someone had to have been paid off. But while big, it was the story of fifteen-year-old Victoria Binghamton that stuck. Sam's retelling, his obvious torment. Where was she now? Lil wondered. She nodded to the waitress, and asked for a check. There was no point in calling Fleming, he'd either tell her to give the information to a 'real reporter' or something equally dismissive.

As the waitress handed her the check, she gave a tentative smile. 'I couldn't help overhear that you're the reporter writing about the fire. My gran lived in that building. She's staying with my mom for the while. She lost everything she owned, not that she had a lot that was valuable. But all her stuff, her pictures, clothes. If someone set that fire . . . they need to pay.'

'What's your name?' Lil asked.

'Carrie . . . Carrie Ingraham. My gran is Mary Cody.'

Funny, Lil thought, *this is the story you're supposed to be doing*. But she couldn't stop thinking about Vicky Binghamton – *that poor girl, how terrified she must have been*. And Sam's words: '*This fire is God's way of finally setting things right.*' But what if God had nothing to do with this? It was a bizarre thought that took root. *What if* – leaving cash and a generous tip – *what if Vicky Binghamton, after all these years, had come back to take revenge against her rapists? Wally Doyle – dead;*

Dr Trask, the man whose house she was raped in – dead; his son, Dennis – being questioned by the cops; Jim Warren – federal investigation. It was far-fetched, but for Sam to break his silence after 34 years . . . *You're not the only one thinking this, Lil.* And regardless of what Edward Fleming did, or did not, want her to write she knew one thing. *I've got to find Vicky Binghamton.*

TWENTY-ONE

L il arrived home to chaos. As she turned into the cul-de-sac she spotted Kyle in blue scrubs and a lab coat following a leggy strawberry blonde – almost redhead – to a gleaming white two-door Mercedes SLK convertible with the top down. In the passenger's seat Alice looked out smiling. Her mouth was moving and Lil imagined what was coming out – 'Are we going home . . . Where's Johnny?' or the ever annoying: 'Which one's the boy?' Hanging back at the top of the hill were Ada and Aaron.

She pulled up behind the convertible as the blonde threw a small overnight bag into her tiny trunk and then opened the driver's door. 'Kyle, you've done enough. This is crazy, you're working yourself to death for people who don't give a shit.'

'Kelly!' His face flushed, his fists clenched at his sides. 'You don't have a clue. She's not a lap dog. You don't have a plan? How the hell do you think you're going to take care of her?'

Lil quickly pieced together the scene. This was obviously Kyle's sister, plenty of family resemblance, both tall and angular. But where his dark, hooded eyes gave him a haunted poetic look, Kelly was a bombshell. The kind of woman used to turning heads, from her riotous mass of curls, to her voluptuous curves in a beautifully draped cream suit with a mid-thigh slit that revealed long, toned legs that ended in a pair of stylish pumps. But it was her eyes that left Lil breathless, a pure cornflower blue, and in the late afternoon sun, dazzling. 'And these two,' Kelly said, casting Lil a dismissive glance, and then up at Ada. 'You leave Grandma with perfect strangers . . . and you're calling me the irresponsible one? Really?'

'Kelly, please. You have to think this through. Where will she stay? You're not prepared . . .'

'Sweetie, I love you more than life itself. But give it a rest.' She eased into the tan leather and swung her legs in a single graceful arc. She pulled out a pair of shades. 'Here,' she said, grabbing the seat belt and pulling it across Alice's shoulder and lap. 'There we are. Grandma, ready to go home?'

Alice was ecstatic. 'Yes, please!'

The engine roared and off they went. As they turned at the end of the road, Alice gave a backward glance. She seemed so happy, her dyed-red hair whipped in the breeze, her eyes fixed on Kyle. Restrained by the seat belt she gave an awkward wave.

Kyle stood motionless and defeated, his shoulders sagged. 'This is not going to work. Crap!'

Lil went to his side. 'Sorry,' she said, but she had more pressing things to attend to and started up the walk.

'She's right, you know,' he said, and Lil stopped. 'What's holding me here? I took this job so she could have a place to live, and now . . . But the funny thing is, I can't leave.'

'Of course not,' she said. 'Too many people need you right now. You're a good man, you did your best with Alice, and stuff happens. It's no one's fault.'

'I need to get back to Nillewaug. Kelly will figure it out, probably call me in a couple hours wanting to bring Alice back.'

'If she does,' Lil said, 'we'll take her back. Don't think twice about it.' But as the words left her mouth, she felt a guilty twinge. *For God's sake let his sister take care of Alice.* The poor man had enough on his plate, and Lil had been around enough to know what happens to good people . . . *They finish last.* 'Kyle, I think your grandma will be fine. And maybe if your sister doesn't have you to bail her out, she'll do what needs to be done. Sometimes people step up to the plate, but you have to give them the chance.' And, not knowing what else to say, she headed up the path.

'Lil.' Ada grabbed her hand at the top of the hill. 'Are you OK?'

She looked down at their entwined fingers. Aaron had headed back in. 'Where's your mother?'

'Cooking,' Ada said. 'She feels awful about letting Alice wander off.' She cracked a smile. 'Whenever my mother feels like she needs to apologize she'll never say it with words . . . but with pot roast.'

Still holding hands Lil inhaled. 'It smells delicious.'

'It will be,' she said. 'Think the paparazzi's watching? I mean really, *"Lesbians in their Midst."* They stole that from your column . . . Tchotchkes in the Mist.'

'That's what I thought. And I stole that from Dian Fossey. How are you holding up?'

Ada gave her a worried expression. 'The truth?'

'Yes.'

'Scared, and angry. How dare they?'

'I know, the first of those pieces about us appeared yesterday, and then one today.' She stood with Ada, feeling the warmth of her fingers. But something else, they were standing in front of their home, and someone, someone very close had been spying on them. 'We have got to find out who did this. I refuse to be frightened in my own home, and I can't stand that this happened to you.'

'Aaron's been on that blog trying to figure who it might have been, obviously someone who knows us, and knows enough about Pilgrim's Progress to find their way around.'

Lil glared across the walk. 'Bernice?'

'Or the bastard next to her,' Ada offered. 'But we'll figure it out. How did your interview with Sam King go?'

'You were right about that; he had quite the story to tell,' Lil said, turning away from the neighbors, convinced they were being watched. She stared deeply into Ada's eyes, their hands still connected. 'Have I told you how much I love you?'

'You have, and it's good to hear. You want to hear something cute that Aaron said?'

'I could use it.'

'He said we're in the Blue Lagoon phase of our relationship.'

In spite of everything Lil cracked a smile, feeling like she could lose herself in the warmth of Ada's gaze. 'He's right.'

'We have work to do, don't we?' Ada said.

'You don't have to . . .'

'Please, I'm not just talking about your story. But I'll be damned if some creepy imbecile is going to try and intimidate me and my girlfriend.'

'Really?' And, mimicking the recently departed Alice: 'Which one's the boy?'

Two hours later, and they'd not stopped. Lil had filled Ada in on Sam King's horrible story. Now, sitting next to each other – Lil on the desktop and Ada with her laptop – they were staring at two small mug shots of a tired-looking woman, her face bones and angles beneath pockmarked skin, and a limp mass of skunk-root blonde. Across her chest an identification number and her name – Victoria Binghamton. Only her china-blue eyes gave a trace of the beautiful child she'd once been. Next to Lil's keyboard was a small stack of Victoria Binghamton's electronic footprint, on the top was her obituary dated six years ago. She'd died at Bronx Memorial of an overdose. There was no mention of any family. Just her last address, age – 34, and date of birth – 4/23/62. Beneath that was a print out from the New York Department of Corrections website; it was her criminal record, mostly drug and small larcenies: sale of a controlled substance in various degrees, possession of stolen goods, two violations of parole. The list filled the computer screen and, when added up, it appeared that since her twenties, Victoria Binghamton had spent much of her life in prison.

Ada turned slightly, the Grenville high-school website open on the laptop. She flicked through 1976 and 1977, and in the latter found Victoria (Vicky) Binghamton's Sophomore portrait. 'It's the same girl. So now what? She's dead, and those three bastards just got away with it . . . you said Bradley treated her when she was a little girl. Any chance we still have the records?'

'Come on,' Lil said, scribbling down Victoria's date of birth.

They headed to their bedroom. 'I hate doing this,' Lil said. 'Bradley's got to be turning in his grave.'

'Yes, and . . . why do you hang on to them?'

'Touché. But it's not like I can just throw them out.'

'They have been helpful,' Ada added.

'But it's wrong.' Lil turned on the closet light and pulled back a rack of clothes to reveal two towers of neatly stacked archival boxes of patient records. These represented decades of his private practice. When he'd turned it over to a younger physician, he'd handed over all the records for active patients. But everyone who was dead, had moved away, or had not responded to the notice about his leaving the practice, he'd held on to their records; it was a sizeable number. 'I still don't know what to do with them.'

'OK,' Ada said, 'let's agree that this is the last time we do this.'

'You sound like an alcoholic trying to quit.'

'Fine,' Ada said, already tugging at one of the boxes labeled 'AA-CE'. Luckily it was near the top. Lil grabbed the other side, and they hauled it from the closet and dropped it on the bed.

'Hold on,' Ada said, as she pulled the drapes closed. She stared intently through an opening in the fabric, trying to imagine someone taking pictures. 'It had to have been someone who knows about photography.'

Lil, who was ripping the tape off the box, responded, 'How so?'

'They got the shot of us in bed. It was obviously at night. If they'd used a flash there would have been glare in the glass. So either they had an incredibly steady hand or had a tripod.'

Following her train Lil added, 'More likely they just rested it on the table,' referring to the iron patio set. 'But you're right.' She instantly thought of Sam King who'd shot all those wonderful pictures of the Ravens. She lifted the cover off the box and her fingers walked down the tabs. 'This brings back memories; it even smells like Bradley's office. And all this color-coding was my handiwork – state of the art at the time.'

'Very pretty,' Ada said. 'I'm thinking pink for girls and blue for boys.'

'Are you making fun of me . . .? There she is!' Lil checked the date of birth on the outer flap. 4/23/62. No need to delve further – she pulled out Victoria Binghamton's file. 'I can almost feel him watching us.'

'Bradley?'

'Yeah, he would not approve of this.'

'Let me.' Ada took the chart and opened it. On the inside flap was the birth information, born in Brattlebury Hospital by Caesarean to Mary Binghamton, and no father's name listed. Which, in 1962, in a town like Grenville, would have been noteworthy. Then came the page of vaccinations and Well-Baby visits. The back-to-school physicals, a tonsil-lectomy/adenoidectomy at eight. Nothing out of the ordinary, until the end.

'That!' Lil said, reading over Ada's shoulder. 'That's never a good sign.' She pulled out an unbound page of blue-lined progress note paper. Holding it into the light she knew some things without reading a word. 'Bradley would only do this if he was either stressed or hurried, and if it was the latter he'd leave it for me to file properly the next day.'

'Which leaves stressed,' Ada said, as she looked at the note.

'See how he timed and dated it, both at the beginning and at the end. He'd only do that when he thought a note might turn into evidence.' She read aloud:

'November 8, 1977. 3:15 a.m. I received a call from Mary Binghamton asking that I evaluate her daughter, immediately. I told Ms Binghamton that she should take her daughter to the emergency room at Brattlebury Hospital, which she was unwilling to do. Ms Binghamton arrived, with Victoria who had clearly been assaulted. I was able to do a very limited examination, and reiterated my grave concerns to Ms Binghamton that Victoria would need to be seen in an emer-gency room. While there were no apparent fractures, there were extensive contusions to the face, neck and shoulders. She had two ecchymotic orbits and was in obvious pain. Her vital signs were stable, and her mental status showed signs

of acute shock. She was barely verbal and answered most questions with a simple yes or no. When asked what happened to her, she either would not, or could not, answer. It was clear she needed more thorough evaluation, including a rape examination, and crisis counseling. As Victoria is a minor I informed her mother that the assault would have to be reported and Victoria would need to be seen in an emergency room. Ms Binghamton requested I not do that. I informed her that as a mandated reporter for the State of Connecticut I had no choice.

'She asked if Victoria had any broken bones. I told her that without X-rays I couldn't say with certainty, but on examination there were no acute fractures. At which point Ms Binghamton instructed her daughter to get dressed. I attempted to reason with her, and offered to call an ambulance, but she adamantly refused further treatment. When I reiterated that the assault would be reported, she replied, 'And you think that will hurt the animals that did this to my daughter? The only one it will hurt is her.'

I immediately contacted the Grenville police and spoke directly with Chief Henry Morgan at 4:10 a.m. He informed me that he would follow up immediately with the Binghamtons. I then left a phone message with the Department of Children and Families, reporting the assault, and will contact them during business hours.'

Lil looked at Ada, who was clearly distraught.

'That poor girl. Bastards!'

'There's more,' Lil said, seeing a quickly scrawled line from later that morning, where Bradley documented submitting a formal report to DCF and talking to a case worker who'd said there would be an investigation. And then the doorbell rang, and the phone, and Lil's cell.

Then, a knock at the front door, and a second and a third.

'What now?' Ada said.

The knock turned into a loud banging. 'Mrs Campbell, federal agents. Open the door.'

TWENTY-TWO

Dennis Trask's thoughts had laser-sharp clarity as his gloved hands found easy purchase on the familiar slope of Grassy Mountain. Since leaving the police station yesterday afternoon, he was certain of things he'd previously suspected. These were the facts as he saw them: Jim Warren killed Delia Preston. His good friend Jim Warren killed his father, and his lifelong pal Jim Warren was taking him for a fool. It was that last realization that had robbed him of sleep. *He actually thought he could pull this over on me?* Wally, if he was somehow caught up in Jim's machinations, couldn't be blamed; he was an idiot who needed to be told to wipe his nose . . . *You put it in her, you moron!* But Jim . . . the motive clear; he was in trouble for the scams he and Delia were running at Nillewaug. Couldn't leave well enough alone . . . and his response when caught . . . burn it down and eliminate anyone who could rat him out. *You killed my father!* As he scrambled up the wooded face of Grassy Mountain, he thought through his plan, looking for holes and not finding any. Pulling out a piece of dull tan fabric he scraped it against a tree trunk letting it snag and rip. The coat he'd torn it from, along with the Browning under-over shotgun slung across his back and the Timberland boots he was wearing had all been lifted earlier that evening from the unlocked workshop of Gary Grasso. And what a pain his mother, Betty Grasso, had been; his first-grade teacher, and one of the Nillewaug victims. Gary, whose wife had left years ago on account of his drinking, lived alone. He'd have no alibi, a pair of muddy boots, a torn coat, the gun that fired the bullet that ended Jim Warren's life and a whopping motive. The only tricky bit was avoiding the pair of Feds parked at the entrance to Jim's cul-de-sac. But they were concerned with Jim trying to make another stab at freedom. They would not be expecting this. And by the time they figured where the shot had come from, he'd be long gone. 'Nope, time to get what's coming, Jim.' And, clearing the crest, he stared at the Warren Manse, perched on the best lot of Eagle's Cairn, and moved into firing range. 'Ostentatious bastard.' The only lights were from a TV up in his son's room, a glance at his pretty little daughter's window let him know she was out for the night.

He pressed the only pre-programmed number in his disposable cell, and wedged the Bluetooth earpiece in place. He raised the shotgun as the phone rang, once, twice.

'Hello?' Jim's voice, although he sounded like he had a cold.

'Hell of a day, Jimbo. We need to talk.'

'Where are you?'

Dennis smiled as he stared down the barrel. 'Look out your back window.'

'You shouldn't be here.'

'I know. No one saw me. We have to talk.'

There was movement in the family room and then a curtain pulled back and the shadow of a head. 'Works for me,' Dennis muttered. And with steady aim, he squeezed off a single shot.

The window shattered, and as Dennis turned to flee, a blinding spot hit him in the face, and two others from either side. And Hank Morgan's voice: 'Put down the gun, Dennis. Do it now! Get on the ground! Now! Do it now!'

Dennis blinked, his agile mind processing the information, his pulse barely quickened as he saw and heard more than a dozen law-enforcement agents advance towards him. He thought through the options, including running for it, or even hurling himself off the side of Grassy Mountain. That last possibility brought a faint smile – *probably sprain an ankle.* What finally won out, as he lowered the shotgun to the ground, was curiosity. He looked up, blinded by the light. 'Hank?'

'Yes, Dennis.'

'How did you know?'

There was a pause, and Hank Morgan's words came slow; he sounded exhausted. 'I've known you a long time, Dennis. The moment you thought Jim had something to do with your dad's death, I knew you'd come after him. Couldn't stop yourself if you'd tried. Now turn around slowly, put your hands up where I can see them.'

He was about to comply, but squinting into the light. 'So did I get the bastard?'

'He's not even here. But if it makes you feel better, he's in a federal prison right now facing a few hundred charges of criminal fraud, and that's just the tip. You're not the only one who thinks Mr Warren set that fire.'

Dennis nodded, a thoughtful expression on his face. 'They're going to want my cooperation with that . . . I've got a lot to tell.'

'Good to know, Dennis . . . now turn around.'

TWENTY-THREE

*T*his isn't happening, Lil thought, as dark-suited federal agents, including the pair she'd met at the scene of Wally Doyle's suicide, carted out Bradley's records. She stood in the living room watching them like a stream of ants going out with a box or two, coming back empty, going out with another. In her hand were a subpoena and a search warrant.

Ada was by her side, having told Aaron to stay with Rose in her condo. She whispered. 'This can't be legal.'

Lil was struggling with what the agent who'd presented the warrant had said. 'They think Bradley had something to do with Nillewaug.'

'But he was their medical director for only a very brief time ten years ago,' she replied.

'They must know that.' Lil felt frightened, and it wasn't just this intrusion.

'Is that all of them, Mrs Campbell?' the square-jawed one whose ID said Fitzhugh asked.

She walked into the bedroom, and Ada followed. Where the boxes had been was now bare carpet, a lighter shade of tan than the surround. 'They've been there since we moved in.

That's all of them. But why?' she asked, struggling to make sense of this. 'Why now?'

Fitzhugh looked at Lil, and then at Ada. 'We received information that your husband was aware of fraudulent billing activities at Nillewaug.'

'But . . .' Trying to make sense of this intrusion. 'He wouldn't have any Nillewaug patient records here.'

'Probably true,' Fitzhugh answered. 'What we're banking on is his having had prior relationships with Nillewaug residents before they were . . . Nillewaug residents. We believe his records will help to establish a pattern.'

Lil nodded, following his logic to a degree. But the piece that was turning like a knife in her belly – *We received information.*' First the pieces on that damn website, then someone pointing a finger at Bradley. And then it came to her: 'Lesbians in their Midst.'

'Excuse me?' Fitzhugh asked.

She looked at Ada. 'Whoever posted those pieces about us had to have read my column before it appeared. It had to have been someone at the paper.'

'Not necessarily,' Ada said. 'Just someone who saw it before it ran. And who at the paper would be that interested in us? I mean, really. I think it's closer than that Lil. And you're right, whether intentional or not, they were influenced by your article. It was on your office computer, and then your flash drive and then the computer in the dining room. Usually you print one out for me to read, but you were in a hurry. I didn't see it until it came out, so someone had to have gotten on to either computer, or taken your flash drive.'

Fitzhugh was following their discussion. 'What are you two talking about?'

She looked at the agent. 'You said someone gave you information about my husband's records. Who?'

'It came through the tip line,' he said. 'Why?'

'And that's how you found out about Nillewaug in the first place. Someone called in anonymously.'

'Yes.'

'OK,' Lil said. 'Now in everything I've learned about

health-care fraud, if you whistle blow, and there's evidence that fraud was committed, aren't you entitled to a reward?'

'Also true,' he said.

'How big?' Ada asked.

'In the case of Nillewaug,' he said, 'big. Possibly a million-dollar payout, or more.'

'But if it's anonymous . . .' Lil felt something crucial just out of reach. 'If they don't take credit for it, they can't get a reward, then money's not the motive. This is personal, everything that's been happening is personal . . . I need to check something, excuse me.' With Ada and Agent Fitzhugh trailing behind she headed back to the dining-room table and the computer she used for the Internet. Clicking on to her web browser she checked the history. She'd set up her system so that the history and cache files got dumped every two days. As she scrolled down, she hit a block of sites she didn't recognize, and one that ran on for several lines – Grenville4Grenvillians.com. Behind her, she felt Fitzhugh and Ada watching. Lil looked back at Fitzhugh. 'What do those suffixes mean?' she asked, hovering the cursor over several lines on the history that all started with Grenville4Grenvillians.

'They're attachments,' he said. 'And that letter there lets you know they were from a peripheral like a camera, cell phone, maybe a flash drive. Someone uploaded files from this computer to that website. And if you move across . . . may I?'

She relinquished the chair and Fitzhugh switched screen views and came up with an expanded history that included a time log. Someone had been on Lil's computer in the early a.m. of Monday and then later that same afternoon.

'Lil.' Ada sounded scared. 'If this wasn't you and I know it wasn't me, that leaves Aaron and my mother, and I know it wasn't either one of them. My mom can barely turn on a computer let alone do something like this. And Aaron would never. Although Kyle was here . . . but he was long gone when this got posted.'

'We're forgetting someone,' Lil said, and little bits of data came to mind – like the way Alice could barely string a sentence together, but had little difficulty dressing or bathing.

Sure, she made a show of not knowing how to use her cutlery, but by the time her own mother was forgetting names, she'd also forgotten how to clean herself after going to the bathroom . . . but not . . . 'It was Alice . . . Oh my God. How did we miss this? The whole thing was an act.' As the words left her mouth, they sounded too implausible, and completely correct. 'She's not demented, Ada, not in the least.'

'And her first name's not Alice,' Ada said.

'What?'

'When we were cleaning out her place, all her papers have Mary A. Sullivan. Kyle said she didn't like the name Mary.'

'Show me.' She was jogging toward the front door.

Outside, Fitzhugh's partner, Connor, was waiting for him, the other two agents having already left. 'What's going on?' he asked.

'Not certain, but interesting,' Fitzhugh said, as he trailed behind Lil into Ada's condo. Where they found Aaron, who'd obviously been trying to listen through the adjoining wall. He started to ask questions. 'What's . . .'

Lil shook her head no and made a beeline for the room where Alice had been staying. Along one wall were opened black garbage bags, and she was barraged by incongruous bits of information. The woman had a hell of a lot of lingerie, but that's not what drew her interest. It was a framed photo of Alice with Kelly and Kyle on her lap when they couldn't have been more than two. A pair of chubby-cheeked toddlers, he in a sailor's outfit, his brown eyes looking back, and Kelly, who could easily have been a child model with her reddish-gold ringlets and luminous china-blue eyes, her mouth a perfect cupid's bow as though blowing a kiss to the camera . . . and right then Lil knew the truth. She'd seen those eyes before . . . her mother's eyes. She did the math, Kyle and Kelly had to be in their early thirties – were they the product of rape? Kelly's red hair – like Dennis Trask's. 'Oh my God!' Her knees felt week; she was trembling.

'What is it?' Ada asked.

Lil couldn't take her eyes off the picture. The two beautiful children, twins, but not identical. 'I know who phoned in your tip. And I know why.' With all eyes on her, she shared the story of Victoria Binghamton's rape. 'Mary A. Sullivan was her mother. Alice is Victoria's mother. She raised her children, adopted them, and thirty-four years after the fact she's come back to Grenville.'

'Interesting coincidence . . .' Fitzhugh took the picture from her. 'That's Kyle Sullivan . . . the nurse at Nillewaug.'

'Yes,' Lil said, 'and that's his sister, Kelly . . . who came and took her away this afternoon.'

'Where to?' Fitzhugh asked.

'New York . . . Manhattan. Kyle said Kelly has a loft in Soho.'

Lil stared at the photo, and thought of dotty Alice – *all an act*. And the two beautiful toddlers now fully grown. *Why did you wait so long to return to Grenville,* she wondered. They say revenge is best eaten cold, but thirty-plus years . . .

As though reading her thoughts Ada gave the answer: 'It had to have been Victoria's death. It was six years ago, and a year later she comes to Nillewaug.'

'Yes.' And Lil looked back at Agent Fitzhugh, now on his cell tracking down an address for Kelly Sullivan. She had so many questions, but something else, too. A horrible knot of emotion that was impossible to untangle. Everything from dread at having them find something wrong in Bradley's records, to a twisted admiration for Alice, to a sadness for what had happened to Vicky Binghamton.

Fitzhugh got off the phone and said something to his partner.

'You're going after them?' Lil asked.

He smiled. 'You ladies do good work. This was very productive.' And they headed out the door.

TWENTY-FOUR

'So, are you finally going to tell me?' Kelly asked, the wind whipping her coppery locks as she sped down I-684 toward Manhattan, top down on her gleaming Mercedes, but windows up, so she and Grandma Alice could finally have 'the talk'.

'Are you certain, dear?' Alice asked, relishing the cool open air and the warmth of the heated seats. 'You know enough, any more and you're an accomplice . . . probably already are.' A worried expression on her face . . . 'You know I would never harm you or Kyle?'

'Please,' Kelly said, glancing at Alice from behind dark glasses. 'You . . . and my brother, are the only people in this world I can count on. But I have to know.'

'Of course,' Alice said, taking stock of Kelly. It was always a shock to see those blue eyes – like Vicky's – but her personality . . . wild and fiercely self-centered. *A narcissist*, Alice mused, wondering if that personality trait could be inherited, and if so, it came from her father – Dennis Trask – and his father. 'When they question you,' she said, 'you know nothing. Your grandma, who loves you more than life itself, has Alzheimer's. How could she possibly have done these things?'

'Of course, but they'll make the connection, between you and . . . so Norman Trask was my grandfather?'

'Yes, and many years ago was my boss. Nowadays, I could have sued him for what he did. But then, I needed the job, and he was the only one who'd hire me. I was a single mother . . . and an idiot. I wanted your mother to have a good school system and Grenville had the best in the state. The best of a lot of things. I didn't want to sleep with him. I liked his wife, and for the eight years I was his receptionist, I was convinced she knew . . . how could she not? And you know I wasn't the only one he was screwing. Twice a year – at least – he'd go to orthopedics conventions in either Vegas or Hawaii. The way he described them they were nothing more than medically sanctioned ruses for a week's debauchery. He was obsessed with sex . . . and clocks. Every time his wife came to his office, so polite, so sweet. Always asking how Vicky was doing. But something not right about that woman. She had this little girl voice, very breathy. I thought she was a fool, but always nice to me. He treated her like shit and she never knew it, or more likely, refused to see it . . . I hate to say it, but your brother's a bit like her. And it was clear from the beginning. If I wanted that job . . . which to me was far more than a paycheck . . . it was either put out or get out. It's not like I was a virgin, and it's not like screwing him made my job easier. Norman was a bastard through and through, his only mistake was never being able to see beyond the end of his nose. The world stopped and started with him and his precious Dennis. It made all of this so much easier.'

'He never suspected why you'd returned?'

'Honestly, and let me say that your grandma is a fine actress, he took one look at me, and I swear he thought I was the Christmas Bunny.'

'Easter Bunny?'

'No, keep with mine, like an unexpected sex toy, who just happens to be so demented that you can do whatever you want and she'll never remember. Christmas and Playboy Bunny all in one.'

Kelly scrunched her face. 'Too much! How horrible for you.'

'Not really.' Alice let the sun find her face. 'To be fair, he was a self-centered bastard who deserved what he got . . . but not awful in the sack.'

'Again, ich. Don't want these details. But he did know it was you?'

'Oh yes, and that's what made it so easy. I think a lifetime of buying off people led him to the conclusion that he owned them. To him, there was something natural in my showing up. Like of course I'd be there, and we'd get together once or twice a week. The bit that was shocking . . . his apartment. It's one of the few times I felt I'd let something slip. The place was a death trap, and he'd go on for hours about those stupid clocks, and I'd smile, and listen and learn how important it was to dispose of the oily rags . . . wouldn't want them to start a fire.'

'No,' Kelly said, as they approached the Whitestone Bridge. 'You know they have cameras as we pass through.'

Alice said nothing, just tilted her head back and stared blankly at the sky, a dull open-mouthed grin on her face.

Kelly slowed so the scanner could catch the tag on her windshield, the gate clicked up and she accelerated down the Henry Hudson Parkway.

Like flipping a switch, Alice resumed. 'Did you know that

almost to the minute a turpentine-soaked rag will self-combust in four hours?'

'I didn't,' Kelly admitted.

'A bit quicker if you add denatured alcohol. He taught me so much, never once thinking I was soaking it all in. To be honest, when I came back to Grenville I knew that Norman, his son, and those other two animals needed to pay. I had some idea of what they were up to, but not the details. It's strange,' she said, a thoughtful look on her face, as she stared toward the right at the sweeping expanse of the Hudson River below. 'I never doubted things would work out. They had to pay for what they did to Vicky, and that entire town colluded. If everyone in that building had died in the fire . . . I would have been OK with that. But even better, as the fraud investigation rolls out over the coming years, all those greedy families will have their actions held up to the light of day. There's going to be a lot of ugliness in that town for years to come. And all I can think – they had it coming.' Alice shuddered, not wanting to remember that horrible night thirty-four years ago. Everything she'd worked for, to give her beautiful daughter a better life, destroyed. Vicky brutally battered, barely able to speak. Alice getting the details as her daughter sobbed and begged to die. 'They all knew,' Alice said softly. 'Even the doctor I took her to – he didn't really want to help. He kept saying he had to report the assault.'

'You didn't want that?'

'Are you crazy? Do you know what happens to fifteen-year-old rape victims? And in a town like that? They'd all say she'd been willing. Those boys owned that town – big football heroes. I had no choice but to get her out of there.' Alice gave a mirthless laugh. 'It's like God's playing a joke, but I wind up being taken in by the wife of the doctor who saw Vicky. And here's the kicker . . . she's a lesbian now. Go figure, and thanks to me, the whole town knows. Yup, something for everyone.'

Traffic slowed as the first lights of 12th Avenue came into sight. Waiting for the red to change Kelly pressed for details. 'Back up. So you knew Norman Trask had moved to Nillewaug, and between the two of us we maneuvered Kyle into taking that position. And that's where they could nail me as an accomplice . . . they'll try to go after him too.'

'Not at all, dear.' Alice patted Kelly's leg. 'You knew I had fond memories of Grenville and when the opportunity presented itself, it just made sense . . . don't stray from that. The less detail you give, the better. You saw the ad in *The Times*, showed it to Kyle . . .'

'You're a little scary,' Kelly said, as the car inched toward the next red light.

'I wasn't always. It comes down to this. Leopards do not change their spots. If they were a pack of sadistic animals thirty years ago, and no one had stopped them, it would only be worse. That was my only assumption and I wasn't wrong. Eight years with Norman Trask I knew about his business practices. He liked cash transactions, and kept crazy amounts on hand. I'd often thought of reporting him to the IRS, but what would that have done? And more importantly, I needed his money when Vicky and I left Grenville. He assumed the pennies he gave were buying himself and Dennis out of trouble. There's over four hundred thousand in cash and another three hundred grand in bearer bonds in my bag in your trunk. All of it was just stuffed into boxes in his apartment. I'm sure there's a lot I missed.'

'OK, then . . .' Kelly shook her head. 'So you started the fire and then . . .'

'Back up, if you want the details. It starts before then, and as you're the only person who'll ever hear this . . . I feel kind of proud of what I did. But if you don't want to hear it, just tell me.'

'Hell no. How *did* it start?'

'With a phone call,' Alice said, holding up her hand, examining the chipped pink polish that a hack beautician at Nillewaug had applied. 'Once I saw those Medicaid treatment plans in Norman's apartment things began to click. I spent years working for doctors, so while at first I didn't know the specifics of what he was up to, it was clear that someone was running a Medicaid mill and paying Trask to sign off on the billing. So not only was Norman committing fraud, but in Jim

Warren and Wally Doyle's facility – three birds with one stone. And if they were involved, I knew Dennis couldn't be far off. So I called the fraud-abuse hotline, and gave them enough specifics – patient names, ID numbers . . . that kind of stuff.' Alice chuckled. 'I should have been in the movies, you never met the director of that place, but trust me, I do a damn good impersonation.' And modulating her voice, and sounding frightened, and a lot like Delia Preston: 'Hi, I'm so sorry, but I think a crime has been committed at Nillewaug Village. They're billing nursing-home services for people who aren't in a nursing home and who shouldn't even be eligible for Medicaid. I'm so sorry . . .'

They'd hit another red light, and Kelly turned. 'I love you, Grandma. But you are one scary chick.'

Alice gave a thoughtful smile. 'If I'd been able to save your mother this would have gone differently. Maybe even found a way to forgive and move on. I think a lot about that saying, "that which doesn't kill us makes us stronger". With Vicky, not only did they kill her, they crushed out every bit of light. Her life after that night was unbearable suffering, and nothing I did could change that. And I tried . . . the only piece of this I have any regret, and it's a small regret, is that Delia woman. Even though I knew she was in deep.' As if sensing Kelly's next question, she added, 'She was signing all those treatment plans as the nurse. I'm sure she was raking it in. But I knew she had a kid; I hope he's OK.'

'How did you know . . .?'

Alice stopped her. 'A demented old lady can learn lots of useful things. Like Delia was having an affair with Jim Warren. Dotty Alice was forever getting lost and winding up in her office suite at all the oddest times. It appeared that Saturday night was their regular "get together". So last Saturday I popped some Xanax into Norman's drink and left him passed out in bed, a big pile of rags all set to combust and waited outside Delia's office. Like I knew he would be, Jim Warren was there. And they were fighting, and screwing on her couch. It was clear something had spooked him, he was threatening Delia, I couldn't get all the details, but he knew the Feds were starting an investigation. I waited for him to leave and then Alice

wandered in, and conked Delia on the head.' She glanced
down at her ankle bracelet . . . 'I'm going to need that taken
off.'

'You killed her?' Kelly's tone subdued.

'I did,' Alice said with a stony expression. 'This couldn't
just be about fraud, with fines paid and slap-on-the-wrist jail
sentences in some cushy white-collar country club. Your
mother was gang raped and brutalized. What they did to her
left her destroyed and in the end killed her. This was justice.
Arson and homicide – when connected – can send a man to
the chair, or at the very least, life in prison.'

'You think Jim Warren will be charged with Delia's murder?'

'I do.'

'And Doyle shot himself, which leaves Dennis Trask, who
from what I know is the worst of the bunch . . . and my
biological father. You have no idea how much I want to meet
him.'

Alice startled. 'Seriously?'

'Of course, he's my father. I at least want to see him once
face to face.'

'He has no redeeming qualities,' Alice stated. 'He's as
close to pure evil as a person can be.'

'Said my saintly grandma who killed a woman and set fire
to a nursing home.'

'Assisted care, dear. And remember, I had a front row seat
of the young Dennis Trask's life. He was a vicious boy who
enjoyed inflicting pain, and knew his father would protect him
from the consequences. He didn't just rape Vicky . . .' Her
expression twisted. 'He tortured her. He's a man who derives
pleasure from making others suffer.'

'But it seems like he's the only one who gets off,' Kelly
said, 'or am I missing something?'

'You're not. I got two out of three Ravens, and Norman.
I'm certain Dennis will be implicated in the fraud, and I'm
banking on human nature . . . his nature, to follow my trail
of bread crumbs. I could be mistaken, but I don't think I am.
Once he believes Jim Warren was responsible for his father's
death, he'll go after him. He'll either kill him, or get caught
trying. Either way is fine by me.'

Kelly took a left on Houston, her expression thoughtful as she eased into the parking garage. 'He'll think Warren killed Preston and his father to cover up the fraud?'

Aware they were now in a public space, Alice smiled, and looked at the attendant as he came for Kelly's key. 'Are we going home? I want to go home.' There was so much more Alice wanted to say, but it would have to wait. For now, she slipped back into the role of demented Alice, smiling and rambling, and to all the world . . . invisible.

TWENTY-FIVE

T he following morning Alice let the strong hands of Henri, the Algerian shampoo specialist at Chez Philippe on Lexington just north of Grammercy Park, cradle her head and neck as he eased her back to the sink.

'Not too hot, dear?' he asked, as his strong fingers made contact with her scalp.

She smiled and cooed in a little-girl voice, feeling every muscle in her neck and back dissolve with the shivering goodness of warm water, lilac shampoo and Henri's firm digits washing away the thick stripper, and with it that horrible trailer-trash red. It had been years since she'd felt anything so wonderful – *no*, she reminded herself, *decades*. Yes, the last five years the most difficult, playing a part, feeling as though her brain was divided in two. One half showing the world demented Alice, while the other clicking away at a million miles an hour.

'What's it look like under there?' Kelly asked Henri.

'Silver,' he said, as his fingers found a rhythm that sent shivers of pleasure from Alice's scalp to her toes. 'Lovely silver. Almost a shame to color it.'

'Agreed,' Kelly said.

Alice cracked open her eyes, saw Kelly standing in front of her in an exquisite black suit cinched at the waist that set off her pale complexion and fiery hair to perfection.

'You sure you don't want some color?' Henri asked Alice.

'Where's Johnny?'

He turned to Kelly. 'No color?' he asked, a hint of disappointment in his voice.

'No,' she said, knowing that Alice wanted to change her appearance as radically as possible before disappearing into a beautiful retirement community with ocean views in Boca Raton.

'I could,' Henri offered, 'use a creme developer. It brings out the shine. Yes?' He looked briefly at Alice and then back to Kelly.

'Fine,' Kelly said, her eyes fixed on her grandmother's contended smile.

'What about a mask while we leave it in? Excellent for the pores, like a mini face lift without the surgery, yes?'

'Lovely,' Kelly said, 'I'm certain she'd like that.'

Henri looked at Kelly. 'And for you, as well?'

Kelly laughed, her tone throaty and rich. 'Not today, Henri.' Her gaze never leaving Alice, whose face was now being covered in green mud.

When Henri completed the mask he gently took Alice by the hand and, with Kelly following, led her to a comfortable salon chair, turned on the warming lamp, and promised, 'I will return in twenty minutes, and you will look ten years younger.'

Alice sighed and gazed at her beautiful granddaughter. 'I feel light,' she whispered. 'After so many years . . . everything is calm. All the anger . . . it's gone, Kelly. Such a strange feeling.'

'Do you think she'd be happy?' Kelly whispered.

Alice's brow furrowed, making dark indents in the clay mask. Traces of the old fury returned, of what those sick bastards had done to Vicky . . . but no. One dead and the other two would rot in prison . . . or kill each other. And Norman dead in his bed. 'Yes, I think she'd be happy. I think she can rest. There's no undoing the past, but they didn't get away with it, none of them. And you and Kyle turned out so well. And Kelly, he must never know about any of this . . . Correct?'

'Of course,' Kelly agreed. 'It would destroy him. My sainted brother, the things he doesn't know . . .'

Alice turned at the sound of a commotion; there were

flashing lights through the shop's windows. Her eyes widened, and she stared at Kelly. 'Something's wrong!'

Kelly ripped off the apron and pulled Alice from the chair. 'There's got to be a back way out. Hurry!'

Double-parked in front of Chez Philippe, Mattie Perez and Jamie Plank listened in with FBI Agents Fitzhugh and Connor. As Connecticut state police they had no jurisdiction in Manhattan, but when Connor and Fitzhugh had made the offer to be present for the sting, it had been a no-brainer.

Fitzhugh spoke into his cell: 'Go time.' And armed agents in black Kevlar vests emerged from the cars behind them.

Startled Manhattanites stepped back, as dozens of cell phones emerged to video the scene.

Fitzhugh looked at his partner as they exited the vehicle. 'So much for the humdrum world of fraud investigation.' And, lagging behind the tactical team, they entered the posh salon.

Mary Alice Sullivan felt her pulse quicken as Kelly urged her toward the back exit. Her attention pulled to a commotion. *Something's wrong.* It was such a blur, still feeling the soothing tingle from the black man's fingers, and now the pretty redhead pulling her by the arm. *Why's her hair red? It should be blonde.* And she pictured bouncy soft curls, like silk on her fingers.

'Grandma, hurry! We need to get out of here!'

Such pretty eyes, Alice thought. 'Vicky!' *No.* She shook her head. But who else could it be? 'Vicky!' But it was hard to see, like curtains falling at the edges of her vision, and rainbow lights. So when she looked straight at the woman with the pretty blue eyes, it was harder to see her. 'Vicky!'

And then men came dressed in black. Alice's eyes saw them, like bogey men from a dream, yet when she tried to look directly at them, they vanished, but she could hear their angry voices. She twisted her head from side to side, and saw mouths moving, and heard harsh words, like dogs barking. 'Mary Alice Sullivan, you're under arrest for the murder of Norman Trask.'

Vicky . . . no, not Vicky. 'What's your name?' she said, trying to focus on the redhead who should have been blonde, so hard to see. 'What's your name?'

A man's angry voice as rough hands grabbed her: 'Nice try, Alice.' They bound her wrists.

Vicky was screaming, 'You're hurting her. Leave her alone!'

'Kelly Sullivan you're under arrest for . . .'

That's her name, Alice remembered, her body limp as rough hands seized her. *It's Kelly, who's Kelly?* A rhythmic pounding in her head behind her right temple. Like waves rushing back and forth. Someone pulled her bound wrists, and was trying to move her across the floor. *Where are my feet?* She stumbled, and tried to scream out. But the words refused to form and strange syllables dribbled from her lips. 'Ah cannnnut felll mah.' Fear welled. 'Ah cannnnut fett mah fell.' And then her vision faded entirely from her left eye. She could still hear the men in black and the woman who might have been someone named Vicky, but none of it registered, as the right side of her body went limp, and if it hadn't been for the man holding her wrists she would have fallen hard. Instead, he eased her to the floor.

'You have got to be kidding.' The agent stared at the silver-haired woman with bits of clay mask still clinging to her face. 'Does she really think . . .' He stopped himself. This old biddy was one good actress, but why was the entire left side of her face different from the right. 'Shit . . . look at her eye.' He pulled out his cell and dialed 911. His partner grabbed a flashlight from her belt and shone it into Mary Alice Sullivan's eyes. First into the right and then the left.

Kelly Sullivan was screaming, 'You're killing her!' She broke free of the agent who was trying to restrain her wrists in nylon flexi-cuffs. Kelly dropped to the floor and cradled her grandmother's head. At first she felt a surge of hope – *she's faking it.* Thinking Alice was trying to pull a fast one, a desperate stab for her freedom. That wish died as she stared into Alice's eyes, the pupil on the left fully dilated and not moving when the agent shone the bright light directly into it. The one on the right small as the head of a pin. *She's not faking it.* 'What did you do to her?' Kelly screamed. 'Get an ambulance!' As drool trickled from the corner of Alice's mouth and nonsensical syllables blabbered out.

'Ah wanna ga ham. Ah wanna ga ham.'

TWENTY-SIX

'He's a bigot. That's why he didn't want you reporting for the paper; nothing to do with the actual content of your articles. It's obvious,' Aaron said as he slathered herb butter on to his fourth steaming popover.

'Impossible to prove,' Lil said, looking around the dining room of The Greenery, where they sat at their usual table overlooking Town Plot for Sunday brunch. She felt on edge, exposed and borderline paranoid, and had all morning. Sitting in the pew at St Luke's Episcopal with Ada on her right and Aaron next to her. He'd joined them for their first community outing after their . . . Internet outing. And there was no getting around it; they were being scrutinized. Lil caught the eye of one of the local antique dealers she'd featured in a recent column. She gave Lil a quick nod, a nervous smile and then gave full attention to a piece of toast, as though suddenly entranced by it.

'The proof of the pudding is in the tasting,' Ada added, as she grabbed the last of the popovers, one of the few things The Greenery made well. Although, to be fair, their brunch wasn't nearly as bad as their dinner offerings, which disguised bone-dry meat loaf, and overcooked roasts and canned vegetables boiled to the consistency of toothpaste as 'Colonial Fare'. 'It was your story; he should never have pulled you from it.'

Unlike her table companions Lil had little appetite. Her stomach in knots, the last few days since the arrest of Kelly Sullivan and Alice's near-fatal stroke a blur of frenetic activity. 'If that was all it was,' she said, finding words for her simmering rage, 'but the way he did it. And I . . . believed him. I suppose that's my fault.' There was more too, a feeling of being trapped. She desperately wanted to write – and not just her weekly columns, but real news. *The Brattlebury Register*, which owned several of the smaller local papers, was pretty much the only show in town. The competition – *The*

Brattlebury Reporter, a weekly free paper with far more liberal politics – had a fraction of the readership.

'How could it be your fault?' Ada said. 'You're new to this. He's the expert. Of course you'd believe him.'

'It does make you wonder,' Aaron added, 'about the supposed objectivity of the news media. Aren't you guys supposed to be a non-biased source of information?'

'In an ideal world,' Lil said, tearing a piece of warm popover, as two women in floral dresses she recognized from church but didn't know by name approached their table.

'Mrs Campbell?' The younger looking of the two with short brown hair in a purple and turquoise floral print dress gave Lil a nervous smile.

'Yes?' Wondering what these strangers could possibly want from her.

'I just wanted to thank you for your amazing coverage of the fire.'

'Thank you,' Lil said, realizing she had more to add.

'My mother lives in Nillewaug. They say she'll be able to return in a few weeks. It makes me nervous.'

'I think it'll be OK,' Lil offered, realizing she was in fact something of an expert at this point. The piece she'd written for the Sunday edition – the bit that Mr Fleming thought he'd leave her as a table scrap – covered the saga of three displaced Nillewaug residents. And, despite his directives to leave it alone, she gave succinct who, what, where, when, and whys about the fraud perpetrated by Jim Warren, Wally Doyle, Delia Preston and even sad Dr Trask. And while she knew it galled him, it had run with minimal changes. 'The state is going to manage the facility until everything gets sorted. Once the Fire Marshall signs off on the individual apartments it should be fine.'

'That's good to hear.' She glanced back at her partner, and then to Lil. 'I should have known something was wrong with that place.'

Lil nodded, having by now heard similar confessions from more than a dozen families. 'They were very convincing,' she said. 'A lot of people got taken in.'

'We should have known better.' She impulsively bent over and kissed Lil's cheek. 'Thank you.' And off she went.

'Hmmm,' Ada commented with a raised eyebrow. 'Fans already.'

'Please.' Then she spotted Hank by the hostesses table. He was scanning the dining room and spotted them.

Heads turned as he made his way to their table, and the conversation level dropped to where the kitchen clatter and his footsteps were the only noise. 'Lil . . .' He nodded at Ada and then Aaron. He squatted by her side, holding the edge of the table to steady himself.

'Hank, grab a chair.'

'No . . . thanks. I was going to leave a message but figured you'd be here.' He looked around, making eye contact with several of the diners. 'I've got a story for you, and you alone,' he said softly. 'It's going to break fast, and I'd rather you get it.'

'About the murders?'

'Yes.'

'And Vicky Binghamton and what happened to her thirty-four years ago?'

'Yes . . . I know you talked to Sam. He called me to say he's handing in his resignation tomorrow. But I need to explain what happened . . . at least my part of things. I need to. And then . . .' He shook his head. 'But not here. I'll give you the exclusive, but it has to be soon. Today if possible. There's a lot of details you don't know . . . no one knows. And it's all yours as long as you at least hear my side of things.'

'Of course.' She looked at her brunch companions. And then out at the diners, most of whom she knew by name. Several were openly watching them, while others feigned interest in their meals.

'Go,' Ada said, and added with a wicked grin. 'It'll just kill Fleming if you get the exclusive.'

Hank looked at Ada. 'He won't be the only one,' he said, his expression serious. 'This town said nothing; I played a part in that. And for what? A winning football team?'

Lil pulled her napkin off her lap, and hoisted her bag from the back of the chair. 'Thirty-four years is a long time for something to fester,' she said, wondering how many in that restaurant had been at the party where Vicky had been brutalized. She met Hank's gaze as he stood, and realized that when this story was told in full he'd be out of a job, and he knew it. 'It reminds me of something Bradley used to say,' she said, looking at Ada. 'Pus under pressure must be lanced.'

'Gross!' Aaron snorted.

'But true.' And feeling every eye in that dining room on her, she leaned over to Ada and kissed her full on the lips. It was a very good kiss. 'Love you. I'll call you when I'm done.'

Ada smiled, and her eyes twinkled wickedly. 'Love you, too.'